COWBOY COMMAND

Cowboy Justice Association

Book One

BY OLIVIA JAYMES

www.OliviaJaymes.com

COWBOY COMMAND

Copyright © 2013 by Olivia Jaymes

E-Book ISBN: 978-0-9899833-0-3

Print Book ISN: 978-0-9899833-1-0

Cover art by Sloan Winters

DEDICATION

To Jean and Danielle

CHAPTER ONE

Lunch with her sister was never easy, but today seemed extra difficult. Katie Johnson pushed her salmon around on her plate and tried to listen patiently. She hadn't done anything her sister approved of since two thousand five. It was a record anyone would be proud to have.

Not.

"All I'm saying is," Nora Shefflin said, pointing her fork at Katie, "sleeping with your boss is stupid. What were you thinking? I didn't get you that job so you could coast on your looks."

And there it is.

Katie hadn't had a conversation with her older sister where physical beauty wasn't brought up since they were kids. Nora was obsessed with it. She'd had her chin done only six months ago. Nora wasn't beautiful by most standards but she was impeccably groomed with her dark brown hair in a sleek bob, her face perfectly made up, and her nails always chip free. She was what many people would call a 'handsome woman.'

"I didn't plan it. He's a nice man and part of my duties as his assistant was to host parties and go with him to social functions. It just sort of happened."

Katie shifted uncomfortably in her seat, not wanting other diners to overhear their conversation. The clientele at this restaurant was decidedly upscale, but then Nora wouldn't be seen in any old restaurant. Her world was about networking, connections, seeing people, and being seen.

"He'll dump you for a prettier face eventually," Nora said, disapproval written all over her face.

Katie gave up on the salmon. "Probably. I'm not in love with him. He treats me well. We have fun." That was all Presley was looking for. Love was the last thing on her mind.

Nora wrinkled up her nose. "Fun? How can you have fun with a man like Randall Simon? He's a billionaire businessman. He doesn't have fun. He has business deals."

"Well, we have fun. A few nights ago we went to a late movie and saw the Avengers."

The waiter approached their table. "Anything else I can get you?"

Nora dabbed her mouth with her napkin. "Nothing else, thank you. Just the check."

Katie raised her hand. "Lunch is on me. It's my turn."

"Lovely." She waved to the waiter. "Lunch is on my stepsister."

Katie felt the stab Nora had deliberately inflicted. Katie called Nora her sister. Nora called Katie her stepsister.

Nora stood, checked her phone and shook her head. "If you don't mind, I do have an appointment. Call me in a few weeks and we'll schedule another lunch."

"Of course, I'll just get the check and head home. I want to—"

Nora was gone in a cloud of Clive Christian perfume before Katie had finished her sentence. She dug in her handbag for her wallet, pushing aside the notebook she dragged with her everywhere, and handed her credit card to the waiter. While he ran her card, she checked the texts on her phone and laughed at a silly one from Randall. It might not be a good idea to get involved with her boss, but he was pleasant and non-demanding. She wasn't looking for love and commitment, simply someone to do things and go places with. Randall fit the bill perfectly.

The waiter returned with her credit card, and she signed the slip, adding a hefty tip for having to put up with Nora nit picking the cleanliness of the silverware and the preparation of the food. She shoved everything back in her handbag and headed to her car, the heat and humidity hitting her the minute she stepped outside. Florida in October wasn't supposed to be this warm but they were having an unusual heat wave. The tourists loved it, but longtime residents such as her were worn down from months of oppressive heat.

Katie unlocked the car and pulled open the door to her Civic, clawing through her purse for her phone so she could call her friend Mandy and let her know she was running a few minutes late. They planned to spend the afternoon cleaning out Mandy's closet and talking about her latest and greatest boyfriend. Katie squinted against the blinding sun and sighed, slipping on her sunglasses.

Dammit.

She must have left her phone at the table. Katie rushed back toward the restaurant hoping it would still be sitting there. She was halfway back when she heard and then felt a gigantic boom that knocked her off her feet and sent her sprawling on the pavement. Panic clawed up her sides. It was as if the earth had literally rolled and rocked under her shoes. Her head slammed against the unforgiving concrete, and her vision blurred. Stunned, she pressed her hand to her head. When she pulled her fingers away, red streaks covered her palm.

Holy shit.

Debris rained down from the sky and she wrapped her arms over the top of her head to protect herself. Her pulse skyrocketed as she hovered close to the ground. A strong ache shot through her body from her forehead down her spine.

I need to get out of here.

The heat was searing and she tried to push to her knees to crawl away from the flames but her body didn't seem to be taking commands from her brain. She gathered her strength and tried to push up again but a wave of dizziness took over and she fell back to the concrete. Her heart slammed against her ribs. She was going to die.

She must have been knocked out for a moment because when she came to, the sounds of sirens and screaming could be heard, although muffled by the ringing in her ears. She lay still on hard concrete, too dazed to move. Her nostrils were full of the acrid smell of smoke, gasoline, and burning tires. Her eyes burned and her head continued to throb. She could hear the pounding of feet on the pavement and she tried to lift her arm to wave for help. She'd fallen between two cars and feared no one would be able to see her. She opened her mouth to yell but nothing but a croak came out of her raw throat.

She pushed up on one elbow and turned her head back toward the jumping, orange flames, her horror growing. It was her car engulfed by the explosion.

Her car.

She rubbed her eyes again, her vision still blurred from smoke and tears. She had to be wrong. Why would her car explode? She'd never heard of a car spontaneously combusting before. There was a large cloud of smoke and fire in the parking lot and the sound of car alarms going off everywhere playing havoc with her hearing.

Grabbing hold of the bumper in front of her, she pushed to her feet. Out of nowhere, a set of hands were holding her down, and once more terror twisted her stomach.

"Try not to move, Ms. Johnson. We've got you."

Confused, she looked up with panic and then relief as two large men with kind faces came into view. They were lifting her up and gently setting her in the back of a vehicle. She wondered dazedly how they'd even managed to get their car so close to the blaze.

"Wait." Katie held up her hands. "Where are you taking me?" This wasn't an ambulance.

The two men exchanged a glance before the older male answered. "Somewhere we can get you care, where you'll be safe."

Katie relaxed back grateful to be out of the heat and smoke. There was a woman there who started dabbing at Katie's head wound with a handkerchief.

"Ouch! Shit, that hurts." The younger man slid behind the wheel, while the older man sat next to her, sandwiching her between him and the woman.

"Let's go. We need to get her out of here before they realize she's okay," said the older man to the driver.

She didn't like the sound of that statement. Her mind whirling frantically, she instinctively reached for the door handle, the car still going slow enough where she could jump from the vehicle. She was already beat up by the explosion. A few more bruises wouldn't make any difference. The thought she would have to jump over either the woman or the man made her hesitate briefly, her hand hovering a few inches from the lever.

The older man clasped her arm and guided her back into her seat. "Calm down, Ms. Johnson. I swear we're here to take care of you. Please just calm down."

The man's voice was deep and commanding but Katie was too frightened to heed the warning. She struggled against them but they firmly held her down. Her heart accelerated again in fear for her life. She was being abducted off the street not thirty seconds after her car blew up in a parking lot. She could see the smoke, fire and chaos as they exited the restaurant parking lot. No one would know she was gone. Their actions were lost in the confusion of the moment.

"Wait, dammit, I said wait!" Their hands finally lifted off her but the car had already shot into traffic. The SUV pulled into three lanes of streaming traffic going sixty miles an hour. Jumping from the vehicle now was not an option.

The older man held out his hand. "Ms. Johnson, please calm down. I promise you we're here to protect you."

It was starting to penetrate her fog they were calling her by her name.

"How do you know who I am? Shit, are you kidnapping me? I'm calling the police."

She was still clutching her purse, and she dug into it to find her phone, and then realized it was still in the restaurant. The man pulled his identification from his pocket.

"Ms. Johnson, Katie, we are the police. I'm Federal Marshal Evan Davis."

He held his badge out for her to see and she blindly reached for it, removing it from his hand and looking at it for a long time. She handed it back to him, the wind out of her sails.

"Please tell me I just hit my head really hard when I fell and all of you are a figment of my overactive imagination."

His expression was sympathetic and he shook his head. "I'm sorry, ma'am. Although we will get your head looked at." He shoved his identification back into his coat pocket. "You're a very lucky woman. What made you head back to the restaurant? Did you know about the bomb?"

She pressed the cloth to her head. "I forgot my phone on the table. I went back to get it." She slumped back on the seat. Talking made her head hurt even worse. "Shit, it's still there. I need to go back." She took a deep breath. "So it was a bomb?"

The Marshal nodded. "The bomb must have been on a time delay. When you opened your car door, it set off the mechanism. They wanted to give you time to get into the car and start it."

"Wait." Katie held up her hand. "What do you mean they? Who bombed my car? Why would someone bomb my car?"

Her voice had gone up hysterically and the female she'd barely noticed sitting next to her patted her on the shoulder. "Relax. You're alive. Cars can be replaced. You cannot."

The woman's voice was firm and no-nonsense and it was just what Katie needed at the moment. She looked between the woman and the man. "Why would someone try to blow me up? Why have Federal agents kidnapped me and shoved me into the back of a car? I'm just an administrative assistant. I've never even had a speeding ticket."

Katie thought she was holding herself together well. All she had to do was keep telling herself none of this was really happening and she'd be fine. This was some kind of fucked-up dream and she'd wake up any minute, late for work.

The Marshal nodded. "We know. You're Randall Simon's assistant. And I'm sorry if you were hurt further when we put you in the car. We tried to be as gentle as possible. I promise there will be a doctor to look over your injuries. We think Randall had that bomb planted in your car. We think he wanted you dead."

The words hung in the air between them and she let them stay there, like a banner in front of her eyes.

They were dead wrong. She winced at her wording. No, they were terribly wrong. That was it. "Why would Randall want me dead? I'm meeting him for dinner tonight. Is this some kind of governmental fuck up? I see stuff like that on television all the time."

The Marshal seemed to ignore her question as the vehicle zipped in and out of traffic. The driver hadn't even turned around but she could see he had dark-hair and was wearing a suit in this heat. Just like the man sitting next to her. "We've been watching you. You and Randall Simon, along with his lieutenants. He's a dangerous man, Ms. Johnson. I can tell from your reaction you didn't know that."

"Randall? He can't even kill a spider. I had to do it for him the other night. Are you sure we're talking about the same Randall Simon?"

Marshal Davis nodded. "The very same. Listen, we'll give you all the details but for now, know that your boss is involved in some illegal dealings. Dangerous and illegal."

A horrible thought occurred to her. Her hand flew to her throat. "You think I was doing something wrong? That I was in on it?"

"Shit, this isn't going the way we planned. We didn't know he was going to set a bomb. We'd hoped to have this conversation in a more businesslike setting. When your car exploded we had to change plans quickly. We didn't think he would make his move this early." Marshal Davis pulled at the knot on his tie. "No, we don't think you're a part of this. The chatter we've heard from Simon and his associates is you're an innocent pawn."

That almost pissed her off more than a car bomb. "A pawn? I'm just a fucking pawn? That's great. Fucking story of my life."

She pulled the handkerchief down from her forehead and saw the stain of blood. She must have really slammed her head into the cement to be imagining all of this.

The Marshal grimaced. "Early conversations seemed to point to you as their fall guy. Lately, that seems to have changed. Either way, we suspected Simon might need to get rid of you at one point. We've been following you for weeks."

The SUV drove into a parking garage and pulled into a spot near the elevator. The Marshal drew his gun from his shoulder holster with a grim smile. "Stay here while we check the perimeter."

Check the perimeter?

This was all too much like a spy novel. Her head pounded and her muscles protested when she turned to the woman sitting next to her, really seeing her for the first time. She was younger than she first thought, probably near Katie's own age of twenty-six. She tossed the handkerchief into her purse. "He's kidding, right?"

The woman shook her head. "No. You're in a great deal of danger. Actually, less danger now. They think you're dead. We want them to keep thinking it."

The door of the SUV opened and the Marshal beckoned to Katie. "It's clear. Let's get you inside. Quickly."

Before she could protest, a blanket was wrapped around her head and torso, and she climbed out of the SUV awkwardly. The world spun and the floor seemed way too close.

"Marshal Davis? I think I'm going to be sick."

The earth bucked underneath her and she pitched forward into a welcoming blackness where no one was blowing her up or making her a pawn. She heard voices calling her name in the distance but she shunned them and headed straight for the cool darkness of oblivion.

* * * * *

Katie was wrapped in a hotel robe, freshly showered, her forehead and knee rocking Spiderman Band-Aids from the doctor that had visited. He had looked her over, cleaned and bandaged her wounds, and decided she needed to be watched closely for the next twenty-four hours. The Marshal had nodded and said that was exactly what they planned to do.

She was a little embarrassed she'd passed out in the parking garage but considering what she'd been through since lunch she was contemplating passing out again just so she wouldn't have to hear any more words out of Marshal Davis's mouth. Every word seemed worse than the last.

She sipped the ginger ale. "So you think he's selling arms to terrorists?"

Marshal Davis nodded. They'd gone over this once, but dammit, they were going to do it again and again until she believed them.

"You think I might know something that could incriminate him?"

"You've worked for him the last six months. You may have seen or heard something you didn't realize was important at the time. We can help you put what you know into perspective. That's why we've been so open with you about what we suspect him of." He pushed three photos in front of her. "Are you familiar with any of these people?"

She leaned forward and pointed to the picture on the left. "That's Steve Tessler. He's a purchaser for the Federal government. I've seen him at parties." She tapped the photo in the middle. "That's Don Keigh. He works for a shipping firm that does big crating jobs for overseas. I met him my first day in the office." She gestured toward the last picture. "I don't know that person."

The Marshal picked up the last photo. "This is Tim Mordon. He works for another defense contractor. We think he's been selling out his boss and giving trade secrets to Randall." Marshal Davis picked up the second picture. "Don Keigh is an alias. He's actually a for-hire arms runner. I'm surprised you saw him at the office. Simon would have wanted to keep him away from there. What day was that? We can go back and look through our surveillance tape. We may have missed something."

"April the eighth. That was my first day of work."

Evan Davis scratched something in a notebook and then picked up the last picture. "Steve Tessler is more than a purchaser for the Federal government. He is also the go-between for arms dealer and small terrorist cells around the world."

"You mean like Al Qaeda?" This was starting to sound like a James Bond movie.

"Sometimes, although Tessler isn't fussy about his clients. He deals with the former Soviet Union, Al Qaeda, drug dealers in South America, and independent so-called patriot militias in the United States."

"American citizens," she gasped. "Like Timothy McVeigh?"

Evan Davis nodded grimly, his lips drawn flat. "Just like that. We think that's how Simon was drawn in to this. They appealed to his patriotism and talked about the evils of a government that had all the weapons and power. We think that's when he decided to arm rebels against the U.S. Government."

"'If guns are outlawed, only outlaws will have guns.'" Katie shook her head. It was all so unreal.

"Pardon?" The Marshal was frowning.

"It was something Randall said a lot. He talked about how citizens had a right to be armed and how the government was becoming too powerful. He talked about Big Brother knowing our every move and controlling us."

"That makes sense from what we know about Simon. From the transcripts I've heard, we believe he thinks he is doing the right thing for the country."

"Arming Al Qaeda is the right thing for the country?" Randall wasn't a stupid man.

"He may not even know that's where some of his weapons ended up. Tessler probably only told Simon what he wanted to hear."

"So where do I come in on all this?"

The Marshal gathered up the photos and tucked them in a folder. "You can place them together. You can help connect the dots between the men. Plus, you may have seen something in the office that seemed innocent at the time, but could mean something to our case."

"So he had me blown up?"

Marshal Davis nodded again. Damn, the man had patience, she'd give him that.

"Everyone thinks I'm dead?"

Marshal Davis walked over to the television and turned it on to the local twenty-four hour cable news network. Immediately, video of the burning wreckage of her car was playing before her eyes along with the words "Tampa woman dead in car explosion."

He didn't need to turn the sound on. The grisly pictures said it all. No one would believe she'd survived it. They'd bundled her in the car before the smoke cleared. He snapped the television off with a definitive click, bringing her out of her daze. Seeing it in this way had brought it home. She'd almost been blown up by a car bomb.

"I have to call my sister. I can't let her think I'm dead."

Nora must be losing her mind right about now, frantic at the news. Despite their chilly relationship through the years, they were all the family each other had.

Marshal Davis patted her hand. "Ms. Johnson, listen, can I call you Katie? You can call me Evan, okay?"

"Sure," she shrugged. "May I call Nora now?"

"You can't call your sister. No one can know you're not dead."

Katie jumped up from her seat and her head spun until she grabbed on to the back of the chair. "I have to call Nora. She's my only family. She'll be beside herself if she thinks I'm dead."

The enormity of the day started catching up to her and tears welled up in her eyes. She needed someone familiar, not these strangers who were trying to tell her what to do.

"Your sister is friends with Randall Simon."

"So? Nora got me the job. She won't tell him. I'll make her promise."

Evan stood and scraped a hand down his face. "I can't keep you safe on a promise, Katie. That's my number one job, keeping you alive. Nothing else matters to me. To do that I have to make sure everyone thinks you're dead and to remove you from where people might recognize you."

"Remove me? What does that mean exactly, I ask with deep fear of your answer?" Katie's fingers squeezed the chair, her knuckles white. She was being sarcastic and bitchy but she'd had a hell of day.

"Put you into protective custody. Civilians call it Witness Protection. We'll give you a new identity."

She dropped down into the chair, her knees giving out. The right one still ached from her fall on the pavement. She was pretty fond of her current identity.

"For how long?"

"Perhaps until we bring Simon to trial, definitely until you're able to testify for the Grand Jury."

She buried her face in her hands, tears starting to leak from her eyes. "This gets better and better every moment. So, I'm going to be stuck in this hotel room until then? I'll go crazy."

Evan shook his head and started pacing the room. "No, we won't keep you here."

Katie scrubbed at her wet cheeks. Crying wasn't going to solve this. "Then where?"

"Montana."

"Montana?"

"Harper, Montana to be exact. I have an old Army buddy there who is now the sheriff. He said he'd take you in, watch over you. I've already talked to him. He's a good man. You'll be okay there."

She shook her head. "No, thank you."

His face went slack and his eyes widened. She'd managed to shock the Marshal. Good, it was time someone else was surprised in this little scene. "What do you mean, 'no thank you?'"

"Just that. No, thank you. I appreciate what you're trying to do but I think I'll pass." She shook her head when Evan started to protest. "You're telling me Randall wants me dead. Listen, Randall can be an ass sometimes, but he's no killer."

A muscle worked in Evan's jaw. "Then explain your car being blown up."

She licked her dry lips. "I can't. I just know I can't let you hide me in the wilds of Montana until you figure this out. I can't do it. I don't want Nora to believe I'm dead. Hell, I don't want my friends to think I'm dead. You can release a statement saying that I miraculously survived or something. They can say they assumed I was dead but then they didn't find a body. See? That makes sense."

"We've already fixed it with local first responders. The body was blown into tiny bits and then burned beyond recognition. Trust me when I tell you we've dotted every *i* and crossed every *t*." Evan rubbed the back of his neck. Katie assumed she was the cause of the pain located there. "So you think this is all a mistake and we should let you waltz out of here?"

He was starting to understand. "Yes. I'm a nice person. I volunteer at the animal shelter. I let people with one item go in front of me at the grocery store. I brake for squirrels crossing the road. Nice people don't get blown up by would-be terrorists." Too late, she realized how stupid her statement sounded. "What I mean is, yes, sometimes nice people get blown up but this was some kind of a mistake. I want to go home."

He couldn't possibly realize how much she wanted to go back to her own house and her own bed and curl up for a week. She craved something, anything, familiar.

Evan closed his eyes, his expression a mask of frustration. "Katie, I can't let you go home. You'll end up dead."

"Isn't it my choice? Don't I get a say in this? If I don't want protection, can't I refuse?"

"Do you have some kind of death wish?" Evan's eyes snapped open and he practically yelled the question. "Do you want to die? Because you will. You'll be dead within days."

Katie bit her lip. "I don't want to die," she said in a small voice. "I just want to go home." She tugged at the robe she was wearing. "I don't even have a change of clothes."

"I sent Marisa to your home to pack you a bag."

She planted her hands on her hips. "Did you take my keys?" These federal agents were high-handed and pushy.

"Let's just say there was no need." Evan smiled.

She threw up her hands and whirled around at the sound of the hotel room door. The other agent, who must be named Marisa, was striding in with a grim, pale expression. Katie searched for a suitcase or even a duffle bag but saw nothing. Her hopes of a fresh change of clothes sank like a stone.

"We need to talk, Evan." Marisa looked at Katie.

"Did you get my clothes?"

Marisa pressed her lips together. "Unfortunately, no. Have you been watching the news?"

Evan turned back to the forgotten television. "Earlier. What's going on?"

"They got there first, Evan. The place was a disaster, fire and smoke. The fire department was already there. We high-tailed it back here to make sure this location was still secure. I left Donovan back there so he could search the remains for any laptops or electronic devices. Assuming they didn't get them before they torched the place. We also tried to retrieve the cell phone she left behind at the restaurant. It's gone. They must have got there first."

"Shit," Evan muttered under his breath. "Is there anything left?"

Marisa shook her head. "Nothing." She turned to Katie. "I'm sorry about your house."

Katie desperately wanted to wake up from this nightmare. "My house was on fire? It's destroyed?"

Evan put his hand on her shoulder as she fell back into the cushions of the chair. "I'm sorry, Katie. They probably thought you might have paperwork or any sort of evidence at your house. They wanted to destroy anything that might incriminate them."

"I didn't have anything work related at home." Tears stung the back of her eyes. "My stepfather left me that house when he died."

She felt a welcome numbness spread through her body. It was a relief from the pain and confusion she'd been feeling since she'd met these people. It was better to not feel anything. She couldn't deal with reality at the moment. She swallowed hard and looked up at Evan. His eyes were sad but his expression was determined.

"I need to see it," Katie said. She wasn't sure she could trust these people to tell her the truth. They'd say anything to get her to go into hiding.

"You need to see it?" Marisa looked at Katie like she had two heads.

"I'm not sure I can believe you. I need to see it with my own two eyes."

Evan crossed his arms over his chest, his eyes narrowing. "If I arrange for you to see your home, and it is in fact burned to the ground, will you go to Montana? Will you go into protection?"

She swallowed hard, her throat still raw from the smoke. "We'll see."

Evan shook his head. "Not good enough, Katie. I'll be taking a huge risk letting you go back to your home. I need some assurances that it's worth it."

She might be beaten and battered, but she wouldn't be bullied. "You'll have to take the chance because if I don't get to see my house, I'm definitely not going. Let's say if I saw my house burned to the ground, I might be in more of a frame of mind to cooperate with you."

Evan swore and shook his head. "Fine. After dark we'll take you to see your house." He pointed to her, his jaw set and firm. "But you will not get out of the car no matter what. You will stay in the vehicle, see your house, then come right back here." He nodded to Marisa. "We'll take you about ten o'clock tonight."

They suggested she take a nap, but she was too wired to sleep. Instead, she paced back and forth and watched the local cable news as they covered the car bombing. By the time ten o'clock rolled around, she was as nervous as a cat. She was also starting to feel sick to her stomach as the inevitability of what she was going to see started to creep into her consciousness.

If they were willing to let her see her house then she figured it had, indeed, been on fire. The only question was the extent of the damage. She prayed there might be something she could salvage, something familiar.

When the car pulled onto her street and she saw the smoke rising from the pile of rubble, she clapped her hand over her mouth, determined not to be sick. Marisa didn't pull up in front of the house, which was surrounded by yellow tape, but she did park close enough that Katie could see there really was nothing left. Tears leaked from her eyes and ran down her cheeks unheeded.

"I don't know what I did to deserve this," Katie said quietly.

Evan patted her shoulder. "You didn't do anything, Katie. You're an innocent pawn in all of this. These are ruthless people,

people who value money over life. That's why I'm determined to get you somewhere safe."

Evan let her stare at the charred remains of her home for quite a while before signaling to Marisa they should go.

"We can't stay here, Katie. People will get suspicious about a car parked here for a long time. We need to move."

She nodded, the numbness back. She welcomed it. The pain was too acute to bear. It was better to feel nothing until she could feel everything. She dashed the tears away with her fingers, making her decision silently. She really didn't have any choice. Someone wanted her dead and she wanted to live more than anything.

"What part of Montana am I going to?"

CHAPTER TWO

Evan carefully watched the woman sitting in front of him instead of looking out the window of the airplane. Katie Johnson had been through hell and back in the last twenty-four hours and, other than fainting and being incredibly stubborn, she'd been remarkably resilient. After his partner had delivered the news yesterday that her home had been destroyed, the life seemed to have leaked from her and she'd been quiet, stoic, and compliant with their requests.

It all added up to someone who could fall apart at any minute. He wouldn't blame her if she did. She probably deserved a good cry and a couple of drinks, although he'd deliberately kept her away from alcohol. She was currently sipping a root beer as he reviewed her new identity and life.

"How long do I have to stay here?" she asked finally, peering out the window at the mountainous terrain. She'd told him she'd never traveled to the west so this would be strange and new to her.

"Until the Grand Jury testimony, at least. Afterward, if it's still not safe, well, maybe we can find you another new place. A new identity." He flipped open a file folder and pushed it toward her. "I think you'll like Harper. It's a nice little town with friendly people. I served in the Army with the sheriff there. Seth Reilly is a good man who'll protect you."

She gave him a quivering smile. "Let's hope he doesn't have to."

Evan admired her bravery. She wasn't a whiner, which was a point in her favor. Seth wasn't the most patient of men.

"Let's go over your new identity again. What's your name?"

"Presley Abigail Lawson. I'm twenty-six and I grew up in Wheaton, Illinois, which is just outside of Chicago. I root for the Cubs and the Bears and I like deep dish pizza."

He nodded. She was also a damn quick study. She'd barely glanced at the file and she'd been spouting facts to him the entire flight.

"That's great. From now on, we never mention Katie again. You have to start thinking of yourself as Presley. No one else knows your former identity. What else can you remember? It's all the details that make this believable, Presley."

"Can I ask you first where you get these personas? Is this someone's job to make up people and build them a life?"

"Actually, yes, it's someone's job. Now what else can you remember?"

To his amazement, she reeled off the entire file in practically one breath. He sat back in his chair, dumbfounded. If she'd memorized a third of the file they would have been thrilled.

"How did you do that? You only looked at the file for a short time."

Presley shifted in her chair and shrugged. "I have a good memory."

"You have a terrific memory. That's amazing. I've never seen anyone remember the entire file before."

Presley took a drink of her root beer before answering. "As I said, I have a really good memory."

She didn't want to talk about it. Fine. "We can move on then. Harper, Montana has about ten thousand people. Small enough to keep an eye on you, but large enough that you can blend in. And make no mistake, Presley, we want you to blend in. That's what the clothes are all about."

Presley lifted a foot in the air and regarded the cowboy boots solemnly. "I didn't think the clothes Marisa bought me were about my taste, I assure you. I've never worn a pair of cowboy boots in my life."

"We filled your wardrobe with jeans, sweaters, and boots because that's what the residents of the town wear. You need to blend in. Look like one of them. That's why we changed your hair, too."

Katie Johnson had been a stunning blonde. Presley Lawson was a sultry brunette. Marisa had suggested cutting Presley's hair short as well, but when he'd seen the tears well up in her eyes he just couldn't make her do it. He had talked her into wearing her hair pulled back in a French braid instead of wild around her shoulders.

It hadn't made one bit of difference to how beautiful this woman really was. She was someone who was going to get attention wherever she went, which was why Evan had chosen Harper. If she'd been plain or even ugly, he would have hid her in a big city. He didn't know why those particular combinations worked for witness protection, but they did.

Presley laughed this time. "Actually, all you did was change my hair to its natural color."

Evan smiled. "That's why it looks so good on you then." He pushed a plastic bag across the table. "This is your new driver's license, social security card, credit card, and check book. All the things you'll need to start fresh. There's money in the checking account and a decent credit limit on the card based on what Seth's going to pay you to be his secretary. Don't worry, you'll earn every penny of it."

"I'm sure I will. Is he okay with my being his assistant?"

Evan cleared his throat. She might as well know what she was getting into. So far, she'd had a strong backbone on her. "About that, well, Seth can be tough to work for. He's gone through quite a few secretaries. He's a little impatient, but don't worry, you'll be fine. He knows you're coming and is glad to have someone take the job."

"You mean assistant."

Evan frowned. "Pardon?"

"You called it a secretarial job. Those don't exist anymore. The modern term is administrative assistant."

"You may find some things in Harper haven't changed," he laughed. "You'll get plenty of respect, don't worry, but they may refer to you as a secretary. They don't mean anything bad by it."

She shrugged. "I guess it doesn't matter what they call me. I won't be there very long."

Evan sighed. The only thing this woman wanted was her life back. "Ka—, Presley, it could be months before we convene a Grand Jury, maybe years before he comes to trial. He's got a phalanx of lawyers that will delay as long as they can until witnesses have hazy memories or—" He broke off abruptly.

She rolled her eyes. "Or disappear? Or end up dead? That's what he's counting on, right?"

"We're not going to let him get to you. You'll be safe in Harper with Seth. All you have to do is sit tight while we build a case against him. Once he's behind bars and all his assets seized he won't have any power to hurt you. No one will do his dirty work for him if he can't pay them."

"That's the truth," she snorted. "He employed a bunch of vultures who were only out for themselves. His friends weren't much different." She turned and looked out the window. "Is my sister okay? I feel badly that she has a funeral to arrange for a body that doesn't really exist. I still wish you'd let me call her."

That was the last thing Evan was going to allow. His investigation had found Presley's sister, Nora, to be one cold-hearted bitch, living off her dead father's and ex-husband's money. A rather plain woman, she didn't appear to be as fond of Presley as Presley was of her, although she was putting on a good show of grief for her society friends.

"Your sister is fine. I'm going out on a limb here and guessing your sister is always fine."

She turned back, her mouth drooping. "Yes, Nora's that kind of person. Always fine. She'll move on without me pretty quickly."

It appeared she already had but this wasn't the time for telling Presley that. The plane was starting to descend and the Fasten Seat Belt light came on. They would be landing in a few minutes.

He leaned forward and patted her hand, knowing she wouldn't believe what he was about to say. "We're almost there. Time for your new life. Just think, a brand new start. Lots of people would love to trade places with you."

* * * * *

Evan was only doing his job, but she had to resist the urge to kick him in the shin. He'd been so nice to her this far that she didn't have the heart to tell him he was full of shit. She'd happily change places with anyone who wanted a brand new start. She'd loved her old life.

Okay, maybe loved was a strong word, but she'd liked it. She might not have made all the best decisions but she'd done her best. She'd had a good job.

Scratch that. My boss is a criminal.

She'd had friends and family.

Her sister had been a little cold, but she did have a few good friends. They would probably be sad when they learned she was dead. Her neighbor would probably be sad, too. She picked up the mail for her elderly neighbor, Mrs. Sanborn, every day. Mrs. Sanborn was eighty-five and her children never visited her. She couldn't get around well so Katie, no, Presley, tried to help out when she could. She needed to start thinking of herself as Presley, not Katie.

The plane landed with a few bumps and then smoothly taxied down a deserted landing strip. Presley peered out the window and saw nothing but darkness. Not one building, or other planes to break up the blackness outside.

The door to the aircraft opened and a bone-chilling blast of cold blew into the cabin.

"Holy shit, that's cold! It's fucking October!" She grabbed the jacket they'd purchased for her, but it wasn't much protection from the biting wind.

Evan chuckled. "October is winter in Montana. That's why we bought you warm clothes. As warm as we could find in Florida, anyway. I warned Seth you'd need a few things. Hopefully he brought you a real winter coat."

As they descended the stairs, Evan led her toward an oversized truck with big tires. Presley dragged her feet. As crappy as the last twenty-four hours had been, at least she'd been in Tampa, her hometown. Now she was in a strange place with a strange man who was supposed to protect her.

Evan guided her towards the man standing by the truck. She didn't know much about cars and trucks, but it looked powerful, its tires massive. The wind easily penetrated her thin jacket so by the time they reached him, Presley was blue from the cold, her teeth chattering.

Evan grinned and shook the man's hand. "Good to see you, Seth. Thanks for doing this. This young woman is Presley. Presley, this is Sheriff Seth Reilly. He's going to take over from here, okay?"

He phrased it as a question but it wasn't really a question. He wasn't asking permission. Evan was going to get back on the plane and it was going to turn around and head back to Florida, or maybe someplace else. He was dumping her here. Evan was the only familiar person in her life now and she didn't want to see him go.

He patted her shoulder. "We'll be checking on you." Evan leaned forward to look into her eyes. "You're going to be okay, Presley. I promise."

She nodded mutely. She didn't know what to say. If she spoke, she'd beg him not to leave her here, but she knew she couldn't do that.

The Sheriff held up a long coat he'd had draped over his arm. "It looks like you need this."

"Thank you," she croaked, reaching gratefully for its warmth. "I'm freezing."

She didn't even bother to take off the thin jacket she was wearing. She simply pulled the long wool coat over it buttoning it up with relief. She shoved her hands in the pockets and found leather gloves, which she quickly pulled on her cold fingers.

Evan nodded in approval. "Glad you didn't forget. Presley's from a southern state."

The sheriff's eyes appraised her head to toe, not giving away his thoughts, before turning back to Evan. "I'll take it from here. Next time you come, stay for awhile and I'll buy the first round."

Evan slapped him on the back. "I'll hold you to that." He turned to Presley and handed her the carry-on. "Take care. Do what Seth says and you'll be safe."

She didn't even have time to answer before he was hurrying back to the plane, pulling his phone out of his pocket as he left.

She was alone in the middle of Montana with a man she didn't know. And it was freezing.

"I'll get your bags." He strode toward the large suitcase the flight crew had placed on the runway. He lifted it effortlessly, despite the fact she'd shoved her entire new wardrobe in that bag. He came back and stopped in front of her.

He didn't say anything else, just reached for the shoulder strap of her carry-on and slid it off her arm, turning toward the vehicle. She followed reluctantly, maneuvering around him to the passenger seat, but he was quicker and opened the door for her, offering a hand up. She murmured her thanks as he stowed her bags in the back seat, then swung into the driver's side of the truck.

"Thank you for getting my luggage. It's cold out there."

He started the truck and they pulled away smoothly heading down a dark, deserted road. She studied his profile as slyly as she could, admiring the square jaw and classical bone structure.

"Your welcome. This valley gets some bitter winds in the winter," he said.

She couldn't really see anything out of the windows. It was too dark but at least the cab of the truck was toasty warm. She was almost lulled into relaxing when something darted in front of the headlights and he had to slam on the brakes and swerve to miss it. His arm flung out in front of her despite the fact she was wearing a seatbelt.

"Fuck! Shit! Are you okay? That was a coyote that ran in front of us."

"I'm okay. Is the coyote all right?"

"He's fine. We didn't hit him." He grimaced. "Shit, I didn't mean to say fuck. I mean, I didn't mean to say shit. Aw hell, my daddy's going to kick my ass if he finds out I swore in front of a lady I just met."

That made her smile. It also made him more human. "Your secret is safe with me. I think my virgin ears can stand a few cuss words. I might use a few of my own every now and then."

"Virgin ears?" Seth laughed. "I haven't been with a virgin since high school."

"You're not with one now," she retorted. "That honor has come and gone. I was a freshman in high school. Billy Sanders, was the grandson of my church pastor."

"That's young. I mean, for a girl that seems young."

"How old were you?"

"Sixteen." Seth's grin spread a mile wide. He must be imagining that night. "Sixteen, in the back of my old man's Chevy four by four. Damn, those were the days. I have sweet memories of that night. That night and Sheryl Albright."

"I have fond memories, too. Billy eventually went into the clergy himself."

Seth glanced at her with a frown before turning his eyes back to the road.

"I've heard a girl's first time isn't usually very good."

She shrugged. "It wasn't bad. I thought it was exciting."

Seth smiled again. "Damn, girl. You got me talking about sex and we just met. How did you do that?"

She laughed and looked out the window, the scenery passing in a gray and black blur. "My mother once said I could have a meaningful conversation with a place mat. Total strangers tell me their life stories in line at the grocery store. It's a curse, I guess."

"Seems to me it would come in handy. We went from barely speaking to each other to talking like friends in nothing flat."

She looked back at him. "It's a curse. Trust me on this one."

The start of all her problems was being someone anyone could talk to. That's what Randall had said. He could talk to her about anything. This trip to Montana was the culmination of one bad decision after another, starting with Randall Simon.

"Evan asked me to get you a place to live and I've fixed up the apartment above the sheriff station. The apartment is in the center of town so you won't need a car. It's small but you can always move elsewhere later if you like, as long as I think the new location is safe." He slid her a sidelong glance. "I was hoping you could start work the day after tomorrow, but we can wait a few more days if you like. I'm between secretaries at the moment."

Fatigue and depression were starting to creep over Presley. She shrugged.

"I can start in the morning, if you want."

He looked surprised. "Are you sure? Don't you want to unpack and rest? How long have you been traveling? You're probably tired."

She hadn't slept more than thirty minutes at a stretch in the last twenty-four hours. "We left about ten last night, while it was dark. I haven't exactly been sleeping very well since this all blew up, so to speak. I might as well be productive."

"I imagine it's been tough." He never took his eyes off the road.

"Tough? I'm looking at tough in the rear view mirror. My car was blown up, and my house was set on fire, destroying everything I own." Her voice cracked. "A few hours ago I had a different name. I've been given a new driver's license, check book, credit cards, and past. They actually went to the trouble to create a past for me. I grew up in Wheaton, Illinois. I've never fucking been to Wheaton, Illinois. I had to practice talking about myself on the flight here."

Her eyes started to brim with tears and she fought to keep them from falling. She'd always hated women who cried and whined. Crying and whining wasn't going to change any of this.

Seth pulled the truck over on the shoulder and handed her a handkerchief.

"It's going to be okay. You'll like Harper. Nice people, nice town. I'll try not to be an ogre of a boss."

He gave her a lopsided smile. He really was a handsome man. Even in the dim light, she could see he had a square jaw and a nice smile. She swiped at her wet cheeks, sniffling.

"I'm sure you'll be a good boss. You're a nice man. You must come from good parents."

"You'll meet them eventually. You'll meet everyone in Harper. You won't be able to help it."

"Please don't take this wrong, but I just want to go home. I just want to testify and get my life back." She didn't want him to take it personally. Wanting to go home had nothing to do with him. "None of this is your problem," she said briskly, handing him his handkerchief back. "It's my problem and I need to deal with it. I don't have any choice."

He started the truck and pulled it back onto the road. "That's where you're wrong. My job is to make sure you stay safe. I can't help you get back to wherever it is that you come from, but I can protect you while you're here."

"Florida."

"Huh?"

"I'm from Florida."

Seth burst into laughter. "That explains why you didn't have a coat and they couldn't find you one. I thought that was strange. By the way, it's okay if you tell me about your past, but don't mention it to anyone else. I'm sure Evan told you secrets are a good thing in this situation."

"He did. I won't say anything." She sighed. "It was eighty-five degrees yesterday."

Seth grinned with delight. "It got into the fifties yesterday, and down below freezing last night."

Presley shivered. "Yeah, I felt it when I got off the airplane. How do you stand it?"

"You'll see in the morning. The beauty of this area will take your breath away. You look at something that amazing and you don't care what the temperature is."

She wasn't sure she would ever be able to ignore the temperature but decided to keep her thoughts to herself. He sounded like he really believed what he said.

"Are we almost there?"

She needed to get out of this truck and find a place to curl up in the fetal position for a few hours. She shifted uncomfortably in her seat enjoying his warm scent, a mixture of something woodsy and something warm, reminding her of a roaring fire and a soft, flannel blanket. She wanted to curl up on his lap and draw comfort from that warmth and his innate strength. She mentally slapped herself. Men couldn't be trusted to provide comfort and care, only sex and heartache. If she hadn't known it before Randall, and she should have, she knew it now.

"About another forty-five minutes. We chose an out of the way airstrip that's rarely used. You can close your eyes if you like, maybe catch a nap."

She wouldn't sleep but closed her eyes, slumping against the window. She wouldn't need to talk to him if she pretended to be asleep. She didn't want to talk about things any more. It only made her depressed and she wasn't the type to be depressed.

No matter how depressing reality actually was. She would keep thinking about going home. Keeping the thought would get her through this.

She wanted her life back. She only needed to figure out how to make it happen.

CHAPTER THREE

"Pass the butter, son." George Reilly, Seth's father, and the patriarch of the Reilly family, held out his hand. Seth passed the dish and looked back down at his plate. He didn't really want to talk about his upcoming day, as was the norm at breakfast time. The fact was he didn't really know how he felt about the woman he had vowed to protect.

She was more beautiful than he'd expected, and definitely younger. Evan hadn't described her at all, but for some reason he'd pictured her differently. Perhaps older and more cynical. She'd worked for a billionaire financier for the last six months, after all. Seth had been shocked to find her quite young and astonishingly pretty, with her long wavy brown hair and her golden brown eyes. Her complexion was clear and creamy with a touch of gold, probably from the Florida sun. He hadn't been able to discern if her figure was as attractive as her face in the large coat she wore, but from what he could see she looked tiny and delicate.

Or maybe she looked delicate because he could remember how sad she'd looked with tears running down her face, making a mess of her mascara.

He'd also been surprised by how easy she was to talk to. He'd always had trouble making casual conversation with strangers, but she had him talking right out of the gate.

"You're quiet this morning. Rough day ahead? Setting up a speed trap or something?" Seth's brother, Jason, grinned at his own joke and shoveled more pancakes into his mouth. His pretty wife,

Sarah, elbowed him in frustration. "Will you please chew your food? You know you get indigestion if you eat too fast."

Jason paused to give his wife a loving look. Seth came from a long line of love. His grandparents, now retired in Arizona, had been married more than sixty years. His parents had been married for over forty years. Jason was married to his high school sweetheart, Sarah, with a baby on the way. His older brother, Sam, was married to Cindy, the girl from the ranch down the road. When Cindy had shown up at the local watering hole with another cowboy, Sam had quickly dispatched the other man and closed the deal. Two months later they were married and seven months later they had a beautiful baby girl, Amie. Sam had recently built a new house on the family ranch so he and Cindy didn't always come to eat at the 'big house.' Seth and his brother also had their own homes, but Seth found it easier to eat with his parents. It wasn't worth it to cook for only one person.

Seth was thirty-five years old and he'd never been in love. Not really. He'd felt lust and even care, but never love. He was pretty sure no one had ever been in love with him either, which made him wonder whether he was lovable at all. Maybe he lacked something his brothers, and other people, had. His girlfriend, Eliza, often told him he could be remote and controlling. He knew she was right but he also knew without control and order there was nothing but chaos. No one knew better than he what tragedy it could bring.

"Nothing special today," Seth answered. He might as well tell them. They'd find out eventually. There weren't many secrets in a small town. "I hired a new secretary."

Jason laughed. "Are we taking bets on how long she'll last?"

Seth's mother, Marion, poked her fork in Jason's arm. "Stop teasing your brother. He's had a run of bad luck with secretaries that's all. I'm sure everything will work out fine this time."

"I'd hardly call over a dozen secretaries a *run of bad luck*," Jason smirked. "I'd say that my hard ass, control freak brother is a jerk to work for. There isn't a woman in town who will work for him."

Seth couldn't argue with Jason on that point. He probably wasn't the easiest man in the world when it came to his work. "Maybe. Hopefully she'll do fine." He really didn't have a choice. He needed to keep an eye on her to keep her safe. "She's from out of town."

His statement grabbed everyone's attention. New people in town were always a hot topic of conversation.

His mother smiled with enthusiasm. "Where is she from? Is she married? Does she have kids? Where is she living? You should invite her to dinner tonight."

His mother fired off her questions with lightning speed. His father patted her hand. "Take a breath, darlin'. Give the boy time to answer one question before asking another."

His mother blushed. "Sorry, Seth. It's just exciting when new people come to town."

Seth wiped his mouth with his napkin and avoided his mother's first question. "She's not married, and no kids. She's going to live in the apartment above the station, at least for now. I cleaned it up and it looks pretty good. I promise I'll bring her to dinner one night soon. I'm letting her get settled in. She got in late last night."

"How did you find her?" Sarah asked.

"She was a friend of an old friend. She was looking to make some changes." Seth had already practiced this part of the story.

"You can grill her with questions when I bring her here. Let her tell you about herself. I only know her professional story."

His mother wasn't done. "She's not married? Is she pretty?"

Seth sighed in exasperation. His mother was desperate to get him married off and seemed to think he was avoiding the institution just to frustrate her.

"She is pretty. And young, Mom. Too young. Besides, I have a girlfriend."

Marion Reilly pursed her lips in disapproval. "There's no passion between you and Eliza. No spark. You act more like buddies. You need fire and desire, Seth."

Seth wanted to crawl under the table. He didn't want to talk about desire and fire with his mother, for chrissake.

"Nothing's wrong with a younger woman." George Reilly waved his fork. "Your mother is younger than I am. Priscilla was younger than Elvis."

Seth's father loved Elvis Presley. It probably wasn't the moment to remind him that Elvis and Priscilla divorced.

"Her name is Presley," Seth admitted reluctantly. It wasn't her real name but his parents would never find that out.

"It's a sign," his mother crowed.

"It's not a sign, Mom."

"It's a sign that she's the one," his mother insisted, her eyes alight.

"It's only a coincidence."

"A weird one," Sarah conceded. "Is she nice? Maybe I should invite her to lunch or something since she's new to town."

Seth remembered Presley's tears in his truck. His heart had twisted at her heartbroken expression. "I don't know her well enough to say whether she's nice or not. She didn't seem not nice. She has a good work ethic. She offered to start working today."

"I'll come by sometime in the next few days and ask her to lunch." Sarah set her napkin on the table. "It's got to be tough moving to a town where she doesn't know anyone."

That was the whole damn point, but Seth couldn't say anything. He wasn't sure Presley was really looking to start a new life here. She seemed pretty focused on getting back to the old one.

"Give her some space to get settled in. A new town and a new job would be overwhelming for anyone." Seth stood up from the table, wanting the conversation to be over. "Excuse me, but I have an early morning. I need to get Presley started in her new job."

Luckily, his family seemed to accept the excuse. He carried his plate into the kitchen then headed out the back door to his truck. Today he'd show Presley the job and hope she wouldn't be too much trouble. He didn't expect much from her, actually. She'd made it clear she was only marking time until she could go back home. He didn't blame her for that. Hell, she was only a kid, really. She probably wasn't any more than twenty or twenty-one.

He slapped his hat on his head and gunned the engine, heading for town. He had a new secretary to train.

God help them both.

* * * * *

The office was cold. Presley rubbed her arms and flexed her fingers, stiff from the temperature. She'd been warm in the apartment upstairs for the few hours she'd slept. She'd been shocked she'd fallen asleep but by the time he'd dropped her off, showed her the thermostat and a few food items he'd put in the kitchen, she'd been exhausted.

She walked over to the ancient coffee pot in the corner of the large room and growled. She was a real caffeine addict. Her local Starbuck's knew-her-by-her-first-name-and-regular-order type of caffeine addict. She'd barely seen the town when they'd drove in the wee hours of the morning, but she was sure she hadn't seen the familiar green and white mermaid logo.

She dug into a box of filters and started making a pot of coffee. She hadn't been sure what time the workday started but she'd woken up after a few hours and figured there was no time like the present to start her new life.

Her new life. She needed to woman up and stop whining about things. She'd cried in front of Seth last night. He probably thought she was a real wimp. Yes, she wanted to go home but that didn't mean she had to bitch and moan about it. She was here and she needed to make the best of her situation. As Evan had pointed out, she could be here a really damn long time.

By the time she'd finished her second cup of really crappy coffee, found several interesting notes from previous admins, and thoroughly explored the filing system, she had a list of things she wanted to work on or update. Number one was that coffee pot. Technology had made great strides in the preparation of coffee since nineteen seventy-five.

She was engrossed in list making when Seth pushed open the door, letting in a blast of cold air with him. He looked surprised to see her as he shrugged off his coat and hung it on the tree next to the door.

She got up and poured him a cup of coffee. "How do you take it?"

His eyes widened even further. Maybe he didn't like coffee.

"You're getting me coffee? My last secretary told me she wasn't a waitress and to get my own damn coffee."

Presley shrugged. "You looked cold. I thought I'd be helpful."

"Thank you. A dollop of cream and one sugar."

She fixed his coffee and followed him to his desk on the opposite side of the room. He grimaced at the file folders stacked in a teetering pile.

"I didn't expect you in so early. You have to be worn out from traveling all night."

"I've been in about an hour or so. I'd rather be busy, honestly."

He took the mug from her gratefully. "That suits me. I'm not sure where to start. There's so much that needs to be done around here."

She held up her notes. "I've been nosing around a little bit. Maybe if I go over what I've seen so far we can decide what I should tackle first?"

He nodded and settled into his chair, indicating she should sit across from him. "Sounds as good as any plan. Shoot."

Thirty minutes and another cup of swill later, Seth was wearing a dubious expression.

"I can see you aren't convinced."

Seth tapped his chin. "I like everything to be orderly. That's why I set up the filing system the way it is. You want to change it and then I won't be able to find anything."

She held up a piece of paper. "I found this shoved in a desk drawer. I'm guessing it's from a former secretary? 'To the next poor woman who has to deal with the Sheriff, he never puts the files back in the right place. Then he yells. Just stack all the current cases on his desk.'" Presley eyed all the files stacked up. "'Then if he can't find anything, he can just yell at himself.'"

Seth flushed a dark red and ran a finger around the back of his collar. Apparently she'd hit a nerve.

"Some people have found me hard to work with, I gather. I admit I can be difficult…and controlling. At times."

Presley hid her smile. Seth was clearly a man's man but she'd had bosses who were much worse. She had a particular memory of one who liked to throw office supplies when things didn't go his way. Another had punched several holes into the drywall. They never in a million years would have said they were difficult to work with.

"Admitting you have a problem is the first step. Give me one week to reorganize things. If you don't like it, I'll put everything back. I promise."

"I haven't even gone over the daily duties with you. How do you know how to reorganize?"

Seth seemed exasperated so Presley held on to her cool, calm demeanor.

"There were copious notes in the desk from the last several people. I think I've got the schedule pieced together."

Seth blanched. "There were more notes?"

"Oh yes," she answered sweetly. "Very illuminating. You certainly inspire a certain passionate response in your employees."

He stood up, probably trying to intimidate her. She wasn't one to be easily intimidated. "Look, I know you mean well, and I'm very impressed by your go-getter attitude today. Really. But I like things the way I like them. Change isn't always good."

If she laughed at his petulant expression, he'd be really pissed. Seth Reilly might not be afraid of the people trying to kill her, but he was clearly afraid of a few changes around here.

"I guess I'm asking you to trust me. I've screwed up many things in my life, but I know how to organize."

"What have you screwed up?" Seth scowled. "That doesn't bode well."

"Hello? I'm in a small town in the middle of nowhere working for a sheriff who thinks I'm crazy, all because of my choice of employer. Shit, I was just trying to make a living."

Seth pulled up to his full height and squared his shoulders. "I think we need to keep things the same. I expect your full cooperation."

Presley smiled. "You're the boss."

"I'm glad to see we agree on one thing." Seth's voice was gruff.

He was cute when he was frustrated. Last night she'd been struck by how handsome he was, but today with his golden hair rumpled by the wind and his overall air of fatigue, he looked like a little boy just out of bed. If she'd been looking—no, she wasn't looking for anything. She was simply trying to survive.

Another blast of cold air made her shiver and Seth strode past her. He rummaged in a closet and pulled out a small space heater before greeting the person who had let in the cold air.

"You can use this. It should keep you warmer."

She took it gratefully, pondering her new boss. Seth Reilly was a strange man. Strong and stoic one minute, an old-fashioned gentleman the next. She'd even seen a glimpse of the controlling asshole and it hadn't been too bad. Seth was shaking hands with an older man and ushering him to his desk.

"Trask, what can I do for you today?"

The man took off his cowboy hat and sat heavily in one of the wooden chairs.

"It's about my Millie. She's been gone for a few days and I'm worried about her."

"When did you last see her?"

The man stroked his chin. "I guess it would be Friday night, late. We were in the barn checking on the horses. Haven't seen her since. Not like her to be gone this long."

"Maybe she just got a turkey or something."

Until Seth's statement, Presley had assumed they were talking about a human. Clearly, Millie wasn't this man's wife or daughter.

Presley cleared her throat. "Can I get you some coffee, Mr. Trask?"

The older man turned to her and his eyes lit up. "You must be the new secretary. What's your name, darlin'?"

She smiled and poured the man a cup of coffee. "Presley. Presley Lawson. Cream and sugar?"

"No, take it black." He held out his hands with a grin. "Presley, huh? Seth, does your old man know this pretty little girl's name?"

Seth looked anything but happy. "I told him this morning. It doesn't mean anything."

Trask chuckled. "Maybe yes, maybe no. Damn, this hot coffee hit the spot. Winter's comin' early this year."

This was not welcome news to Presley. She'd been hoping for a reprieve.

"So you want me to take a look around for her?" Seth asked, clearly trying to move the subject back to business.

The men stood up and drained his cup. "If you don't mind. I don't get around like I used to."

"I'll try and find her, Trask. I'll call you."

Trask slapped Seth on the back and tipped his hat at her. "Nice meeting you, miss. This old boy gives you any problems, you just call old Trask, you hear?"

She liked this man. He was funny and polite. "Thank you, but I think I can handle him," she said with a smile.

The man nodded and headed out the door. "I just betcha you can."

When Trask was gone she turned to Seth. "Millie isn't a person, is she?"

Seth shook his head. "No, she's a dog. She's getting up there in age and I fear something has happened to her. She doesn't see well any more. Trask has several dogs, but Millie is his favorite."

Seth reached for his coat. Suddenly, she felt the walls start to close in on her. She'd been inside pretty much twenty-four seven since her car exploded. She needed some fresh air and new scenery. "Do you want me to come with you? I can help look for her."

Seth looked like he wanted to refuse, but then thought better of it. "Actually, yes, if you don't mind. Another set of eyes will be helpful."

She grabbed her coat. "Do we have an answering service or something?"

Seth held up his cell. "If we don't answer here, it's routed directly to my phone."

Presley blinked in surprise. "Shit, you must not get much sleep."

Seth chuckled and locked the door to the Sheriff's office. "I can route the calls to any phone. If I need time off, I'll route it to one of my deputies. You'll meet them eventually. Hank is working a couple of calls from last night still. Tom is off duty."

"Is it just the three of you?"

He opened the car door and gave her a hand up. "We have others, but Hank and Tom are my right hands."

They headed off and this time Presley was able to get a better look at the town. It looked small and a little rundown, with some buildings needing a new coat of paint while others looked brand new. She saw a sign for a diner, a doctor, and a hardware store on one side of the street. On the other she could see a bar and a small grocery store.

"Is there a coffee shop in town?"

In the blink of an eye they were out of Harper and on to the open road. Seth picked up the radio and called his deputy Hank, letting him know they were out of the office.

"Are you almost done there?" Seth asked.

"Almost. Perry is still pissed so I'm trying to calm him down."

"Let me know if you need me. Ten-four."

Seth finally turned to her and grinned. "There's no coffee shop in town. I guess you could say we're self-sufficient that way. We don't need a yuppie shop selling flavored coffees and muffins."

"That's what I was afraid of. For the record, I like those flavored coffees and muffins. A lot. What does Millie look like, by the way? I'm supposed to be looking, too."

"We won't see her this close to town. Trask's place is out a ways, but she's a black lab."

They were quiet as they drove, the only sound the rush of air from the heater. His masculine scent wafted around her and she had to admit he smelled damn good despite the fact he didn't talk much. She was starting to get impatient when he slowed the SUV and rolled his window down, blowing on a soundless whistle.

"Dog whistle?"

He nodded but never turned back to her, blowing the whistle every quarter of a mile or so. She kept a look out of her side of the car but there didn't appear to be a living soul for miles. He pulled onto a dirt side road and parked the car.

"I think we need to go on foot from here."

She pushed open her door and zipped up her coat as high as she could and pulled her gloves back on. She wasn't going to complain about the cold. She'd watched the news this morning on the television in her small apartment and the people in Harper apparently didn't consider fifty degrees cold. They thought it was downright warm, in fact. She didn't agree but she wasn't going to make a big deal out of it.

She walked with him a little ways until Seth pointed to the other side of the gravel road. "Check that side and I'll check this one."

They walked for a while until she saw something black from the corner of her eye, way in the distance. She plunged into the brush, wading through it until she was close enough to see the large black outline of an animal. She swallowed hard and forced herself to keep walking toward it, not wanting to see what she knew was there. When she came up on it, she had to put her hand over her mouth not to vomit as bile rose in her throat. Tears welled up in her eyes and she whirled around to yell at Seth, who was still looking.

She shouted and waved her arms until she had his attention, motioning for him to come. He ran quickly but stopped abruptly when he saw what was at her feet. His skin paled and he closed his eyes for a minute.

"Fuck. I'd hoped I was wrong. Shit." Seth looked heavenward then looked at her.

"Good job finding her. Why don't you get the blanket out of the back of the truck and we'll wrap her up. Trask will want to give her a proper burial."

She nodded, her throat tight, dashing the tears away with the back of her hand. Presley retrieved the blanket, handing it to Seth, and then hung back, unsure what to do. He laid the blanket flat and lifted the cold body onto it, then wrapped it up gently. His hands moved quickly but surely and she was impressed that he didn't try to hide how this affected him. His expression was grim and his eyes bright with unshed tears.

He patted the blanket. "That's a good girl. We're going to take you home now."

She stood back as he easily lifted the canine into his arms and hiked back to the truck, carefully placing his burden into the back. He leaned against the bumper and took a deep breath. "This is going to break Trask's heart. Man, he loved that dog."

"Was she hit by a car?" Presley sniffled. She'd never seen anything like this and she wasn't good with blood.

"Yeah," Seth sighed heavily. "It looks like she got hit and then wandered away from the main road to die. Dammit, I hate this shit."

She patted his arm. "You did a good thing, wrapping her up. I'm not sure I could do that."

He shook his head. "I bet you could. You found her and got me here. I know it wasn't a pretty sight. Are you okay?"

The fresh air was working on her nausea and she felt surprisingly fine. She'd been of more use this morning than she had in the last six months. Doing right by Millie was a buttload more important than organizing a cocktail party or reserving a charter flight.

"I'm okay. Let's take her to Mr. Trask."

Seth nodded. "Let's go." He touched her sleeve. "Thanks again. I don't know if I would have found her without you."

"You would have, but it would have just taken you longer, that's all."

Seth turned the car around and headed back to the main road.

"Hell of a first day for you. You must be really missing Florida right about now."

Funny thing was, she hadn't thought about Florida for the last hour.

* * * * *

"They have good food here. I hope you're hungry," Seth said, opening his menu. Presley was surprised to find she was starving. Maybe it was the fresh cold air, but she had an appetite for the first time in days.

She and Seth hadn't had the most pleasant of mornings. When they'd pulled up to Trask's place, the old man had known the truth just by their expressions. He'd been sad but determined to give Millie what he called a "Christian burial." Seth had insisted on digging the grave and they'd laid the dog to rest with its favorite toy and pillow.

It had been a simple gesture but spoke volumes of how deeply this old man felt for the dog. Presley had tried to comfort him but he had shaken his head with a sad smile.

"No need, darlin'. Life can be hard here in these mountains. Millie lived a good, happy life with not a worry in the world. We should all live like that."

Presley had agreed wholeheartedly. Worry-free living was looking pretty good these days. She perused the menu, but felt the heat of eyes everywhere. She peered over the plastic menu. "Is it my imagination or are there people staring at us?"

Seth shook his head. "No one is staring at us. They're staring at you."

She felt heat creep into her cheeks. "Because I'm new in town?"

Seth nodded, still studying the menu. "That and you're not bad to look at."

"Thanks," she said dryly. "When I was a little girl my dream in life was to be not bad to look at."

She felt a warmth in her stomach at his words, despite her sarcastic response. She'd seen an attractive side to him this morning in addition to his physical charms, which were more than abundant.

He chuckled. "You sure are different than I expected."

He had her attention. "What did you expect?"

He shrugged. "I don't know, just something different. Evan told me you worked for some billionaire. I was expecting...I don't know. A glamorous blonde or something."

Was he disappointed? Had he secretly hoped for a blonde he could have a fling with? "Would it make you feel better if I told you I was a blonde yesterday?"

He tilted his head, studying her closely. "I can't imagine you with blonde hair. The brown looks so natural."

"That's because it is. This is the color I was born with. The blonde was just for fun."

"Fun? I hear blondes have more fun. Did you?"

No, she hadn't. Not really.

She held up her menu, not liking where her thoughts were going about her boss. She changed the subject. "What do you recommend?"

"I'm having the meatloaf. Do you eat meat? If you don't, I wouldn't recommend saying it too loud. This is Montana."

Presley smiled. "I do eat meat, but I'm not fond of meatloaf. How are the burgers?"

"Good. The fries are—"

Seth broke off as the waitress came to take their order. He ordered the meatloaf special and she ordered the bacon cheeseburger with home fries. They didn't talk much as they waited for their food, so it was almost a relief when an attractive young woman with short dark hair came into the diner, heading straight for Seth.

"Seth, I was hoping I'd run into you here."

Seth stood up, his chair scraping the floor in his haste. "Eliza. I didn't expect to see you today. I'd like you to meet my new secretary, Presley Lawson. Presley, this is Eliza Denton. She's the librarian in Harper."

Presley shook hands and the woman's smile widened. "Do you like to read? It would be wonderful if you could join our ladies' book club. We meet once a week. Six o'clock on Wednesdays at the library. End of the street next to the school. Please say you'll come."

Presley remembered Evan's words about being here awhile and blending in. She smiled back. "I do like to read. What kind of books does your group read?"

The woman waved her hand. "Oh, this and that. A little of everything."

"I'd be pleased to join you and see what it's all about then. Thank you."

Eliza turned back to Seth. "I saw your mother at the library this morning. She invited me to dinner tonight and wanted me to remind you to invite your new secretary." Eliza smiled at Presley. "I'm so glad I ran in to you. His mother is a fantastic cook. You don't want to miss her fried chicken."

Seth looked distinctly uncomfortable and Presley wasn't sure if it was because he didn't want her to come to dinner, or he didn't want her talking to Eliza. She decided she wanted to do both.

"I'd love to come to dinner. I love fried chicken."

Eliza's eyes lit up. "Great. I'll call Marion."

Presley waited for Seth to be polite, but when he didn't Presley nodded toward a chair.

"Please join us for lunch. There's plenty of room."

Eliza laughed and sat down next to Seth. "I am hungry. Have you ordered yet?"

"We did, but not that long ago."

Seth still hadn't said anything, which Presley thought was strange. When his phone rang, he excused himself from the table. Eliza leaned forward, her eyes twinkling.

"You lasted the morning. That's more than can be said for his last secretary. Did he tell you there isn't a woman in town who'll work for him?"

"He didn't, but I got the gist from the notes that were left in the desk. It appears that someone started a diary a few years back and each secretary kept notes on him. They made him sound like Attila the Hun."

Eliza slapped a hand over her mouth. "He's actually a very nice man, but he's tough to work for. He can be difficult."

"I can deal with difficult, so we should get along well. How do you know Seth? Are you family?"

Eliza leaned forward even further, her mouth in a wide grin. "I'm afraid it's worse than that. I'm his girlfriend."

Presley felt a shock run through her body. For some stupid reason, she'd thought Seth was single, which was absurd. He was a very handsome man and probably had many women after him.

"Seth seems like a nice man," Presley said awkwardly. "You make a cute couple."

Seth came back to the table with a frown. "I'm needed out at Perry's place. Can you find your way back to the station?"

Presley nodded. "Of course. Is everything all right? Isn't that where Deputy Hank is?"

Seth's brows came together. "It is. Perry is screaming about some of his cattle being missing and some dead. It's a big mess." He pulled a key off his key ring and handed it to her. "Here's the office key. I'll call in a little while."

The waitress came and put their plates down on the table. Seth sighed. "I was hungry, too."

Eliza grinned and picked up a fork. "Don't worry, I'll eat it. It won't go to waste."

Seth grumbled as he left the diner and Presley tucked into her cheeseburger. It was really good and before she knew it, it was gone from her plate. She'd been hungrier than she'd thought. It felt good to be pleasantly full again.

Eliza was making similar progress on the meatloaf and soon they had two empty plates.

"So have you lived in Harper your whole life?"

Eliza nodded. "I have, except for when I went away to college. I like small town life, I guess."

"Have you been dating Seth a long time?" Presley wanted to smack herself upside the head. She really didn't want the details, but she couldn't stop herself.

Eliza rested her chin on her hand. "About six months or so. If you live here long enough, you eventually date everybody."

"Everybody?" Presley pictured some sort of square dance where the people changed partners.

"Everybody. It was only a matter of time before either Seth and I married someone or started dating each other." Eliza flushed. "We're not what you would call 'in love.' We like each other. We have a date for family functions and Saturday night. He's a good man, but..."

Eliza's voice trailed off and Presley could see there was more to the story.

"There's a man."

Eliza sighed. "Isn't there always?" She shook her head. "It doesn't matter. It would never work. He wouldn't be interested in a boring librarian."

Presley straightened in her chair. "You're not boring."

"You just met me."

"I can tell," Presley argued. "You're not boring."

"I am. That's why Seth likes me. He likes everything to be calm and controlled."

"Seth sounds like he's got a big stick up his butt. What's the other guy like?" If Seth liked calm, he wasn't going to be interested in Presley. Her life was anything but calm.

Eliza giggled. "I can't wait for the day you tell Seth Reilly to pull the stick out of his ass. Please tell me so I can be there."

"You can be there. Now tell me about the other guy."

Eliza's face went dreamy. "He has long dark hair that pulls back into a ponytail. He drives around on his Harley in tight blue jeans and a black leather jacket. He's muscular and his face is carved from granite. And he has the most beautiful green eyes. He's sex personified."

"Holy crap, he sounds hot. All women love a bad boy. What does he do?"

Eliza scrunched up her face. "He's the town blacksmith."

Presley's eyes went wide. "They still have those? I had no idea."

"They do. You should see him stripped to the waist, with his leather apron and blue jeans, black boots." Eliza shuddered delicately. "Oh man, he's like a god."

Presley's eyebrows shot up. Eliza looked decidedly smitten. "You should go for it. You're pretty. I bet he would love it if you came on to him. Men love that shit."

Eliza shook her head. "I could never do it. I wouldn't know what to do, what to wear."

Presley glanced down at the woman's clothes. She was wearing the usual City of Harper uniform of jeans, boots, and a sweater.

"How about you and I go shopping? I can help you pick out some clothes."

Eliza grinned. "Would you do that? I never know what to wear."

"I'd love to. Are there stores near here?"

"We can go into the city on Saturday. I can drive."

"Sounds like a plan. Now how do we get you two together? Hmmm…" Presley tapped her chin in thought. "If only we could get you in the same place together at the same time."

Eliza's face lit up. "The barn dance. There's an autumn barn dance this weekend."

"Perfect. We'll shop for clothes early in the day and do this dance thing in the evening. What's this guy's name?"

"Alex. Alex Peterson."

Eliza was beaming, but then her face fell. "There's only one problem."

"What?" Presley thought they had a good plan.

"Seth." Eliza slumped in her chair. "Seth. How can I do this to him?"

Presley sighed. "Oh, yeah. I don't want Seth to be hurt."

Eliza shook her head. "He won't be hurt. We don't have those kinds of feelings for one another, but it isn't truthful. I can't try and lure in another man if I'm dating Seth."

Presley nodded. "You're right. So you just go the dance and have a good time. With Seth. I'll still help you shop, though, if you want."

"I'd love that." Eliza looked at her watch and signaled for the check. "I better get back to the library. I'll see you at dinner tonight." Eliza reached out and hugged Presley. She hadn't been expecting it but she really liked this woman right off the bat, and returned her hug. Presley tossed a few bills on the table alongside Eliza's. Prices were very reasonable in Harper compared to Tampa.

"It will all work out. I'll see you tonight."

Presley walked slowly back down Main Street to the sheriff's station. It was nice to make new friends in town but she wasn't sure how wise it was for the friend to be the girlfriend of her new boss.

A girl who wanted another man.

And Presley was attracted physically to her boss.

Shit. This was so fucked up, on so many levels.

CHAPTER FOUR

Seth had to hand it to Presley. She really was a charming woman. His entire family was hanging on her every word, smile, and gesture. Or maybe it was just him. He'd driven her out to the ranch after work and her sweet scent had about driven him over the edge the entire way. She smelled like flowers and vanilla and he'd had a tough time not pressing his nose to her neck to take a deep breath.

Besides, he had a girlfriend. He and Eliza might not have a great passion but they had friendship and respect. Eliza was quiet and shy. She never made a scene or tried to piss him off just for fun. She was the kind of woman he never had to worry about.

Presley was a woman who would keep him up at night. She was talking to his mom and dad, gesturing with her hands while she told a story about one of her friends. Her face was lit up and she looked so animated. So damn beautiful. Almost as beautiful as she had looked this morning when she'd found Millie. She was soft-hearted and she'd tried hard to make both him and Trask feel better, when it was clear her own heart was breaking for the animal.

Presley looked around the room appreciatively. "You have a beautiful home. The fire makes the room cozy."

Seth sat down on the couch and stretched out his long legs. "Presley has been suffering from the cold since she got here."

His mother looked puzzled. "I thought you came from Illinois? It must be cold there as well?"

Fuck. Shit. He needed to remember her new identity. It was a good thing Evan had never told him Presley's real name. He'd blow it for sure. This woman had his brains scrambled like his morning eggs.

Presley smiled, cool as you please. "I did, but the wind here is much sharper than I'm used to, that's all. Seth worries too much."

His mother laughed. "Yes, Seth is our worrier. Would you like to see the Elvis room?"

Seth wanted to hide in the cushions of the sofa but he wouldn't fit. He'd hoped they'd be able to get through the meal without the eccentricities of his family coming to light, but it wasn't to be.

If Presley was surprised by the request, she didn't betray it with even a flicker of an eyelash.

"I'd love to see it. Are you fans of Elvis?"

His dad grinned, eager to show off his Elvis collection. "We are. You can imagine our excitement when Seth told us he'd hired a woman named Presley. Are your parents also fans of The King?"

Presley shook her head. "I'm afraid not. They just liked the sound of the name."

"It's a lovely name. Let me show you the room." His mother and father led her down the hall and Seth relaxed, drinking his beer. His new secretary was too disturbing. He hadn't expected to like her so much. There was something eminently nice about her, almost innocent and fresh. She'd said people opened up to her and talked about their personal lives, and Seth could see why. She had an open, trusting face. Luckily, he wasn't the chatty type or she would have known all his secrets by now.

He heard the squeak of the screen door and Eliza walked in, shaking the wet snow from her short hair. He felt a twist of guilt in his gut. He liked Eliza and she was his girlfriend. He shouldn't be thinking about another woman. That was not the kind of man he was. He'd always prided himself on his loyalty and fidelity.

He took her coat and hung it in the closet. "Beer? Wine?"

Eliza nodded. "A glass of wine would be good. Where's Presley?"

"Seeing the Elvis room with my parents." Seth poured her a glass of wine. "Did you have a good day?"

Their conversations were like this. Nothing too deep or personal. Nothing like when Presley got him talking about losing his virginity within five minutes of meeting her. This was better, nothing out of control or crazy. Eliza was soothing to him after a long day.

She sipped at her wine. "I did. Listen, Seth. There's been something on my mind for awhile and well, after talking to Presley today I think you and I need to talk."

The words came out all in a rush and Seth sucked in a breath. It appeared Eliza wanted to have a personal conversation. One he wasn't prepared for.

Because she'd talked to Presley.

"Of course we can talk. What do you want to talk about?"

"Us, Seth. I think it's time we talked about us."

* * * * *

Seth looked pissed. Presley wasn't sure about what, but in the last twenty-four hours she'd started to recognize his moods and this one looked dangerous. He was scowling at her, his eyebrows drawn down. It was apparent everyone at the table had noticed as his parents kept cajoling him out of his black mood, and Eliza kept looking down at her plate then looking at Presley with an apologetic expression. When dinner was over, she pulled Eliza aside.

"You've been giving me looks all evening. What's going on? Does it have anything to do with Seth looking like someone peed all over his pot roast?"

Eliza nibbled on her lower lip. "I kind of broke it off with him before dinner."

Presley leaned back against the wall in the hallway. "You did what? Are you serious?"

"It wasn't fair to lead him on," Eliza whispered. "I have feelings for another man. Seth isn't hurt, he's just mad because I've messed with his well-ordered life."

Presley blew out a breath slowly. "Are you sure? He looked pretty upset. Maybe he's really in love with you."

It bothered her to say it, but it had to be said.

Eliza shook her head. "He isn't. He once told me he'd never loved anyone and no one had ever loved him. I thought it was sad."

It was sad. And puzzling. Seth seemed like the kind of man a woman would fall in love with. Any woman but her, of course. She knew what men were really like. She'd seen enough of their handiwork.

"Then why is he mad?"

Eliza covered her face, then peeked through her fingers. "I think it might be because I mentioned you and I talked at lunch today."

Presley groaned. "Outstanding. He thinks I'm the reason you broke it off. That's great."

Eliza shook her head. "I told him it didn't have anything to do with you but he looked pretty steamed." She straightened up. "Don't let him bully you. He will if he can get away with it."

Great. Just awesome.

"I'll deal with it. I don't intimidate easily."

As soon as they walked back into the living room, Seth jumped up from the sofa.

"Are you ready to go, Presley? It's getting late."

His mother and father protested, but she could see the determined glint in his eyes. They were about to have it out in the truck.

Good. She'd been blown up, set on fire, foisted on this man in a small, backwater town, and pulled in to the middle of his so-called relationship. And all of it in the last forty-eight hours. She was spoiling for a good fight.

Head held high, she marched out to the SUV, hopping into the passenger seat without his help. He got in, started the truck, and headed back toward town. The tension was so thick between them it was palpable. He was waiting for her to say something, but she decided to let him stew. This was his issue, not hers. She hadn't done anything wrong.

Finally, he turned to her, a white line around his compressed lips. "I guess Eliza told you she ended things with me tonight. I'm told I have you to thank for that."

"I'd like to take credit for it, but I think my part in this has been misunderstood."

"All I know," he said, his hands tightening on the steering wheel, "is that when I left the diner today everything was fine, and tonight it wasn't. The only thing different was you."

"That's where you're wrong. Things weren't fine between you two. Listen, I told you how things were with me. But did you listen? Hell, no. I told you complete strangers tell me their life story. Eliza told me she's in lust with another guy. She thinks she couldn't get his attention and I told her she could. That's it."

"There's another guy?" Seth asked incredulously. "She didn't say anything about another guy. She simply said she didn't think our relationship was going anywhere and we shouldn't see each other anymore. Fuck, there's another guy?"

This whole day had gone from bad to fucking worse. One thing was clear. Seth wasn't hurt. He didn't act like a man who had been wounded. This was clearly his pride talking.

"Was your relationship going anywhere? Were you going to ask her to marry you?"

Dead silence. She heard Seth sigh. "I don't know. Probably not. We had fun though."

"What fun things did you do?"

More silence. "Shit, why are you asking me all these questions?"

"Eliza said you're pissed because she messed up your well-ordered life. Is she right?"

"Maybe. I don't have to apologize for liking things the way I like them."

"No, you don't, and no one is asking you to. I just suspect that your outrage about being dumped has more to do with your gigantic ego than any real feelings between you two."

"Gigantic ego?" He sounded pissed again and she grinned in the darkness. This pompous ass needed to be taken down a peg or two. "I don't have a gigantic ego, darlin'."

"When you get mad, you start talking with a twang. Did anyone ever tell you that?"

Seth let go a string of expletives that would have made a sailor blush beet red. Luckily, Presley had heard and said every one of them. "You make me crazy, do you know that? You waltz into my town and my life and proceed to turn it upside down in one day." He pointed at her. "I will not allow you to do this, do you understand? I'll protect you with my life, but I will not turn over my life to you. Got it?"

"Got it," she retorted. "Don't flatter yourself into thinking I want any part of your life. I got pulled into this, not the other way around. If anything, you should be apologizing to me."

Seth sputtered and fumed, much to her amusement, as they entered town and parked outside the station. "I'll come up with you to make sure everything is okay."

"You don't have—"

"Stop." He raised his hand. "I do have to. I may be pissed as all hell, but it's still my job to protect you."

She didn't bother to answer. She led the way upstairs and let him check the tiny apartment for intruders. He turned to leave, apparently satisfied she wouldn't be murdered in her sleep.

"Good night, Seth. I am sorry about you and Eliza."

He stopped right outside the door, but didn't turn around.

"It's okay. Eliza was right. It wasn't going anywhere. Good night, Presley."

The sound of his boots on the stairs trailed away and Presley tossed her coat on a chair and went into the kitchen to make some tea. It was going to be another long night of no sleep. Too much had happened today and she needed time to process it. Mostly she needed time to figure out what she was going to do about her attraction to Seth Reilly.

She pulled her notebook from her handbag. It was the only thing she had left from her former life, and began to write. It was the one thing she knew would make her feel better. It would make her feel sane.

CHAPTER FIVE

It looked like the entire town had come out for the barn dance. Presley hadn't known what to wear to a barn dance but between herself and Eliza, they'd managed to find perfect outfits. Eliza was wearing a plum jersey long-sleeved dress that fell to the tops of her cowboy boots. It skimmed every curve without being obvious and Presley had assured Eliza it would have the desired effect on one Mr. Alex Peterson.

Presley chose a crimson ribbed sweater-dress paired with knee-high taupe suede boots. She'd let her long hair dry naturally and left it loose around her shoulders. A touch of makeup completed her outfit and gave her a boost of confidence to meet so many new people. Eliza had warned Presley she'd be much in demand tonight. New people in town were few and far between.

Presley scanned the crowd of bodies for Seth. All week her awareness of him had increased until by the end of Friday her libido was screaming. It wasn't fair for one man to be that sexy. And maddening. He could teach a mule a thing or two.

"That's him." Eliza grabbed Presley's arm.

"Seth?" Presley sucked in her breath.

"No! Alex. Right over there." Eliza pointed to a man who exactly matched the description she'd given. He was long, lean, and oozed a sexual vibe. No wonder the librarian was intimidated.

"Holy smokes, he is hot." Presley watched as Alex Peterson strode into the party with a few of his friends. "Do all cowboys look this good?"

Eliza pointed to a few men in the corner. "No, not all. But they do all seem to have hearts of gold."

"It looks like he doesn't have a date," Presley stated. "Go get him."

Eliza's eyes were wide and her complexion had paled considerably. "I can't just walk up to him. What would I say?"

"How about hi? You know him, right?"

"I know everyone in this town. I'm the librarian."

"Well, there you go." Presley patted Eliza on the back. "Does he come into the library at all?"

"No," Eliza shook her head. "He never has before that I can remember."

Presley looked down at her root beer. It looked like she would have to take one for the team. She tipped up the plastic cup and slugged the entire thing down.

"Okay, follow my lead." Presley headed toward Alex and his friends, with Eliza right behind her. When Presley was right beside them, she held up her empty cup with a forlorn sigh, and faced her new friend. "I think I'm turned around, Eliza. Weren't the refreshments over here?"

Alex tipped his hat. "Excuse me, ma'am? The drinks are on the other side of that wall. We'd be happy to get you and Eliza something."

"There's no nee—" Eliza began but Presley elbowed her hard.

"That's very sweet of you. I'm Presley Lawson, by the way."

Alex took off his cowboy hat. "I'm Alex Peterson, and these two are Sully Fairfield and Buddy Jacks. Pleased to meet you. You're new in town."

"I am, I'm afraid. I'm lucky to have Eliza here taking good care of me."

Presley stepped back to put Eliza front and center. Eliza opened her mouth and then closed it, clearly not sure what to say. Alex was a smooth talker though, so Presley needn't have worried. One look at the bad boy's expression told her he had a thing for Eliza. And he wanted to show it to her.

The biker and the librarian. Very hot and naughty. Eliza was a lucky girl.

"I'm sure Eliza is doing a wonderful job." Alex's voice was soft and sultry and Eliza's face flushed in response.

"I'm really not all that thirsty after all. You should ask Eliza to dance."

It was apparent these two didn't need foreplay or a bunch of conversation. Alex only needed the slightest bit of encouragement, which it appeared he'd never received before this moment, and he was off to the races. Or the bedroom, whichever came first.

"I would like to dance. Eliza, would you honor me?" Eliza nodded wordlessly, never looking at Presley, and they headed for the dance floor.

My work here is done.

"Ma'am? Can I interest you in a dance?" One of the other men, either Sully or Buddy, she didn't remember which, asked her and she agreed. She wanted to have fun tonight and not think about her handsome and sexy boss. She'd spent the entire week in close proximity and it was making her crazy. He looked good, he smelled good, and he was kind to animals. His only negative quality was he was a pain in her ass about the office.

Every time she tried to improve something he would get argumentative. She'd then explain what she was doing and after giving her the silent treatment for a few hours, he would admit it was a better way to do things. This had happened numerous times this week and she was mentally exhausted from playing these fencing games with him. Why couldn't he be a typical male and not care where something was filed?

Sully or Buddy's hand moved a little lower, down to her ass, and pulled her body closer to his. She didn't know this guy well enough to be held this tight. She could feel his belt buckle against her belly and she gently pushed back from him, trying to hike his arm up at the same time.

His eyes crinkled at the corners. "Relax, darlin'."

Presley usually wasn't very relaxed when a man had his palm on her ass cheek. She pulled away further as they negotiated a turn. It was a relief when Sully or Buddy's shoulder got a tap from someone wanting to cut in.

"Do you mind?" Seth's deep voice sent shivers through her body. Damn it, she'd only wanted one day not thinking about him but it looked like she wasn't going to get it.

"No problem, Seth." Sully or Buddy scurried off and found another partner immediately. She moved into Seth's arms just as the band started playing a super-slow romantic ballad.

Well, shit.

They danced in silence for a few minutes before Seth finally spoke. "I saw what you did earlier. That was nice of you."

"What did I do?" Presley frowned.

"The whole thing with Alex and Eliza. She was too shy, but you got them together."

Presley lifted an eyebrow. "You seem awfully happy about that, considering you blamed me for ending things between you. I hesitate to call it a break up when there were no broken feelings, from what I've seen."

Seth chuckled and she could feel the vibration from his chest. "I guess I should apologize for being a dick, huh? Eliza's right. I don't like change very much. She and I were south of casual, if the truth be known. We were pretty much dating so people would leave us alone and stop matchmaking. I'm happy for her and Alex. Hope it works out. Despite his biker appearance, he's a hardworking guy."

She leaned back to look up into his light blue eyes. "Well, well, well, you can apologize. And thank you, I accept. I think they make a cute couple."

Seth nodded toward the duo, their heads close as they swayed to the music. "Did you two go shopping this morning in the city? You both look nice. That dress on you is very, um, red. If you were trying to blend in, you failed. Although you would have been the center of attention no matter what you wore tonight."

"My favorite color is red." Presley laughed. "Yes, we did. I really like Eliza. She's sweet and we had a lot of fun. Thank you for not making a big deal about me going."

Seth shrugged. "I talked to Evan and he didn't see any reason you shouldn't go. No one seems to have any idea you're here."

"Since they think I'm dead," Presley drawled.

"There's that."

They danced until the song ended and she pulled away regretfully. She'd liked being in his arms more than she wanted to admit. His body had been warm and strong, his scent tantalizing. It made her want to press her face to his muscular chest, run her hands over his wide shoulders, and breathe deeply.

"How about some air?" Seth pointed to some partially open barn doors. She nodded in agreement, letting him lead her to several stacked hay bales with blankets thrown over them. They sat and his thigh was close to hers. If she moved they would brush against one another, so she stayed as still as possible. In less than a week, this man had her tied into knots. Usually she could take or leave a man. This one she wanted to take.

The evening was chilly but there were portable heaters positioned all around the barn to keep the dancers warm. Presley looked up into the sky, mesmerized by the amount of stars twinkling overhead.

"I can't get over how many stars I can see out here. You can't see this many at home."

"We're away from the lights of the city. You can't see stars because of the lights."

"How do you know I'm from the city? I could be from a rural part of Florida."

She heard his soft laugh. "No, Presley. You're not a country girl."

She elbowed him. "Are you saying I don't blend in? That I'm all citified?"

His fingers captured her chin and turned her so she could look into his eyes. "I don't think you could blend in anywhere. You'd stand out no matter where you went or what you did."

"Maybe." She reached up and captured his hand with her own. "You've been pretty mad at me this week. Is all forgiven now?"

"I've been a jerk this week." Seth shook his head. "You've done a great job organizing the office. You've revolutionized the place.

You're easily the best secretary I've ever had. And the thing about Eliza, well…"

"Well?" Presley prompted.

"I was embarrassed," Seth admitted. "I got dumped while you were watching. I didn't want you to think less of me."

"You didn't get dumped." She squeezed his hand. "I don't think less of you. Actually, I really kind of like you. You're a nice man." She giggled. "Kind of a pain, but a genuinely nice man."

It struck her at that moment how few nice men she'd ever known. She scoured her memory banks but couldn't come up with a name quickly. She could only think of him at this moment. He seemed to take up all the physical space around her and all the real estate in her mind as well.

"Next thing you'll tell me that we can be friends or that I'm like a brother to you."

"I never had a brother before," Presley teased. "That might be nice. Unfortunately, my feelings aren't the least bit sisterly."

He leaned closer, their lips only a few inches from each other. "I can work with that. I like you, Presley. You make me mad and you make me happy, but dammit, you make me feel something. What do you feel about me?"

She shook her head. "Damn, are all cowboys so upfront with their feelings? I'm used to men playing it cool and hard to get."

Seth tipped the brim of his cowboy hat up. "Never liked games between men and women much. That's why I like you. Seems like it just wastes time better spent kissing and touching."

Heat swept through her body at his bold words. He was absolutely correct. There were much better ways to spend their time.

She simply needed to make one thing clear. She placed a hand on his chest, his heart beating underneath her palm.

"I think a kiss would be a good idea. There's one thing we need to get straight before any lips touch, though. I don't know how long I'll be here in Harper. It could be weeks, months, maybe years. But when this is over, my plan is to go back to Florida to my family and friends. My life is there."

"Fair enough." He nodded. "I appreciate the honesty. Let me be honest right back. I want you. This past week has only built the attraction I felt for you the first night. If I promise right here and now, under these stars, to never ask you to stay in Harper, will you explore this thing between us? I think we could have something good. While you're here, that is."

"You'd really promise that? What if we fell in love?"

"I've never been in love." Seth shrugged. "Maybe I'm not the type. But, yes, I'll promise. When the time comes, love or no love, the decision will be up to you. I won't ask you to stay."

It was what she needed to hear although somehow the words managed to hurt her heart a tiny bit. He'd made the promise easily enough and she should be grateful. He understood where she came from and where she was going. This time in Harper could be a pleasant interlude for both of them.

She slid her hands up his chest and around his neck, pulling him down for their first kiss. Her palms were sweating and her heart was galloping as arousal flew through her veins and fizzed in her abdomen. She'd been fantasizing about this moment for days and it was here.

Nothing prepared her for the first touch of his lips. She felt the heat crackle between them, his mouth pressed to hers. His tongue demanded entry and she opened to his exploration eagerly, consumed by sensation. Seth's kiss wasn't tentative in the least. The kiss was like Seth himself, confident and controlled. Her fingers gripped his shoulders and she lost herself in the taste of him. He was a mixture of coffee and something spicy and she couldn't get enough, instantly addicted to his flavor.

She was so immersed in the kiss she was dumbfounded when he threw her to the ground, covering her body with his and pushing the breath from her body. He was heavy and she struggled to breathe, but he held her down easily, his strength far superior.

"Stay still," he commanded.

"What in the hell," she hissed but then heard loud popping noises not far away. She immediately froze, holding her breath until the sounds stopped. He lifted himself up slowly, pressing her shoulder down with his hand and looking around cautiously.

He held a finger up to his lips and shook his head. She nodded in understanding. She'd stay quiet while he investigated. He crawled on his hands and knees a few feet away so he could see beyond the hay bales. When he came back, he helped her sit up.

"Let's get you in the barn where there are more people." He kept his voice soft but the thread of steel was instantly recognizable. Suddenly, it became clear as to why Evan had trusted Seth to protect her. His eyes were narrow and hard, his expression cold and calculating, and every muscle in his body on alert. He was in warrior mode. Just that quickly, her passionate lover had turned into a soldier.

He lifted her to her feet and quickly hustled her into the barn area. He was looking side to side, his arm still around her, holding her close to him. She leaned into his strength, happy to allow him to be in charge at this moment.

"I'm going to check out the noise we heard." He looked over her head and then nodded, turning her around and navigating her through the crowd until they were next to Alex and Eliza. "Stay here for a few minutes while I take a look around. Don't move, understand?"

He was gone in a second. Eliza and Alex were looking at her with their mouths hanging open. It must have sounded strange to hear Seth talking to her in that way, but it couldn't be helped. She certainly couldn't tell them he was only trying to protect her because someone wanted her dead. She tried to joke it away.

"He's so protective, you'd think I didn't have a lick of sense." She laughed and their expressions relaxed slightly.

Alex frowned. "Where is he going?"

Presley licked her dry lips, tasting a trace of Seth still lingering there. "We heard noises that sounded like gunfire. Seth went to check it out."

Alex rolled his eyes. "Probably a bunch of cowboys who had too much to drink tonight. Seth will be rounding them up to sleep it off in the county jail."

Presley hoped it was exactly as Alex described. She didn't want to think she'd been found.

"Can I get you something to drink?" Alex asked.

Presley dragged her gaze away from where Seth had disappeared and nodded. "Thank you, that would be great. A root beer?"

Alex headed to fetch her drink, but Eliza had a shrewd expression on her face. "What's going on? I've never seen Seth so riled up about gunfire before. Heck, every home in this county owns at least one gun. Something is going on."

Presley tried to appear relaxed. "The gunfire was too close. Someone could have been hurt, or even killed. You know how Seth is about the safety of his town."

"I guess," Eliza conceded. "He seemed very worried about you. His face went pale. I've never seen him like that before." Eliza's face lit up. "Oh! I'm such an idiot. You and Seth. It's perfect."

With her lips still swollen from his kiss, it would be stupid to deny it. She didn't like lying anyway. "Are you really okay with it?" Presley chewed her lip. "I didn't plan this, it's just..."

Eliza waggled her eyebrows. "It's just there's sexual chemistry between you. If I had been paying attention I would have seen it at the diner that first day. I'm fine with it. You're just what Seth needs, someone to jerk him out of his comfortable routine."

She didn't have time to respond before Alex returned with her root beer. They were all chatting when Seth strode back into the room with an angry expression.

"It was a bunch of drunk as skunk cowboys from the Perry ranch blowing off steam way too close to the barn. They could have killed somebody. I've got Hank rounding them up but I need to help him." Seth blew out a breath. "I was planning to drive you home, but I need to do this. Can you get a ride home with Eliza?"

Alex raised a hand. "We'll see that she gets home. Don't worry."

Seth nodded. "I appreciate it." He turned to Presley. "I'll call you tomorrow, okay?"

"Okay, be safe." She was talking to his retreating back.

"Is it always this exciting at a barn dance?" Presley asked, trying to lighten the atmosphere.

Alex grinned. "This may be the most exciting thing to happen all year in Harper."

She could only hope and pray it was true.

CHAPTER SIX

Seth turned up the volume on his truck radio and relaxed back in the warm leather seat, listening to Blake Shelton. He loved this drive through nowhere. It was the time he needed to get his thoughts straight and his mind quieted down. Last night had been scary as hell for a few moments when he thought Presley was being shot at.

It had turned out to be drunken cowboys, but it brought home the reality of getting involved with a woman people wanted dead. Hopefully everyone would keep thinking she was dead and they would be left in peace. In the meantime, he needed to tighten the security around her. He'd been far too lax in the last week. Letting her go to the city with only Eliza had been a huge mistake, no matter what Evan said. Evan wasn't here, but Seth was. He was the only thing standing between Presley and an assassin.

The weather was holding nicely for the hundred-mile drive and he was almost regretful when he pulled into a parking spot at the roadhouse off 90 and headed inside. The building was closed on a Sunday at ten in the morning but it still smelled like the night before. Stale beer, cigarettes and sweat permeated the air. Seth was glad the lighting sucked as he sure as fuck didn't want to see what made his shoes stick to the floor as he found the rest of the guys seated around a couple of tables pushed together.

"You're late." Tanner Marks grinned, pushing a can of soda his way. The other men chuckled in agreement. Seth flipped Tanner the bird before shedding his heavy coat and sitting in the last empty seat.

"I'm right on time." Seth tapped his watch. "You're all early and a bunch of assholes. Call this meeting to order. I've got better things to do than hang out with a motley crew of lawmen on a Sunday. The Broncos are playing today."

Griffin Sawyer pounded the table twice with his fist. "I think you're the asshole but I'll call this meeting to order anyway." He grinned at the assembled men. "First up is old business. Logan, do you have an update on the suspected drug traffic through your town?"

Logan leaned back in his chair and stretched out his long legs. "From what I've been able to find out, they're using our back roads to traffic drugs from Miami up to Canada. Unfortunately they've decided to make a stop along the way. Drug related arrests have tripled in my town in the last six months. We've even had two drug related fatalities." Logan leaned forward, his expression intent. "It's like chasing shadows, for fuck's sake. Just when I think I have a lead, it's gone."

Reed Mitchell nodded in understanding. "Although we're over a hundred miles away from you, we're also feeling the effects. Drug related crime has gone up a hundred and fifty percent in my town. As soon as I round 'em up, another set comes in and takes up where they left off. It's getting so I can't tell the good guys from the bad guys."

Jared Monroe pursed his lips in thought. "I have a buddy at the DEA I can call in if it's that bad. He might be able to put someone in undercover. From what he says, that's usually the only way they can be brought down. From within."

Seth took notes as the discussions continued. This group of sheriffs had been meeting once a month for the last four years and the information sharing was invaluable. Logan had played football against Seth in high school. Somehow Logan knew Jared, but Seth didn't remember how. Jared knew Reed, who knew Griffin or Tanner, or some shit like that. No matter. When they'd decided to team up and share information, their ability to fight crime and keep the peace had grown exponentially. They always had each other's backs and Seth could truthfully say these were five men he trusted with his life.

When there was a break in the discussion Seth asked, "Are you guys still seeing the work of the vigilantes? Has anyone in your jurisdictions been killed? Harper's been quiet this last month."

Tanner shook his head. "Fuck, yeah. I arrested a man for domestic abuse. Never made it to trial. He ended up with a blunt object to the back of the skull. Wasn't his wife. She's still in the hospital where he put her after the assault. This is the third one in the last three months. I don't like people taking the law into their own hands."

Logan shrugged. "Seems to me your taxpayers were saved some money. I wouldn't complain, personally."

Griffin straightened in his chair. "Shit, Logan. What if the guy was innocent?"

Logan raised his eyebrows. "Was he, Tan? Was the guy a choir boy?"

Tanner swore. "No, we caught him doing it. Neighbors called it in. It took two of my men to pull him off her. The guy had a list of priors as long as my arm. But, fuck it, he still deserves his day in court."

"And he would have been out in less than six months beating the shit out of her again. Or worse, he would have killed her the next time. It sounds like the karma bus pulled up in front of his house, that's all."

"Man, you are stone cold, Logan," Seth said. "I don't want vigilantes interfering in my town. I'm the fucking law."

"I'm the fucking law in my town, too, Seth," Logan argued. "But, shit, I'm fucking tired of perps waltzing out of jail on some technicality or because of prison overcrowding. They come back and wreak havoc and people get hurt. I'm tired of trying to keep the peace with one arm tied behind my back. If someone wants to help me, well, I'll take the help. Doesn't mean I won't arrest them, if I catch them. It just means I don't think they're the most evil things we face every day."

Jared held up his hand. "Enough. These fucking vigilantes got us fighting with each other. That's just what they want. We have to stay together on this." He turned to Seth. "We haven't heard any updates from you, Seth. Anything to report?"

Seth shook his head. As much as he wanted to talk about protecting Presley with these men, he couldn't. He'd promised Evan and Seth never broke a promise.

"Nothing really. Perry had some cattle stolen and a few mutilated last week but it's getting that time of year when the crazies come out and sacrifice a fucking cow for harvest festival or some shit like that."

Reed groaned. "Shit, we had a group of, I don't know, tree hugging, hippie types come through and I'll be damned if they didn't picket all the ranches. Apparently they're worried about the souls of cows. I couldn't eat meat for a week I felt so guilty."

The idea of any Montana cowboy feeling guilty about eating meat made Seth laugh. Tanner slapped Reed on the back. "Did you get over it or are you a vegan now?"

Reed snorted. "Shit, I don't even know what a vegan eats. This is cattle country, for fuck's sake."

"Did you run them out of town?" Griffin asked.

Reed shook his head. "Naw, we let them picket and when we didn't give them any attention they moved on." Reed shook his finger at the group. "Your town could be next," he laughed.

The ribbing continued until Tanner looked at his watch and grimaced. "Shit, I need to get back to town. I'm on duty tonight. Same time next month, gentlemen? And I use that term loosely."

The men nodded and Seth headed for his truck. He needed to see Presley and make sure she was safe. It was an irrational need because he was sure she was fine, but he needed to see her for himself.

Besides, they never got to finish the kiss.

* * * * *

Presley lounged back onto the couch, her feet propped on the arm. It was Sunday, which to her usually meant brunch with the girls, but here in Harper there really wasn't a restaurant to go to for brunch. The diner was closed on Sundays, although the Chinese take-out place was open. There was a barbecue joint that opened at noon so she could put some shoes on and head there, but eating by herself really didn't appeal to her. She was going to sit here, watch television, and feel a little sorry for herself.

She missed her friends. They were probably sad she was dead. Would they raise a glass to her passing today? Would they shed a tear or simply move on with their lives? She didn't want anyone to mourn for her, but she didn't want to think her life hadn't touched anyone else's either. The pounding on her door broke her out of her reverie. That authoritative, impatient knock could only belong to one person. She swung her legs down from the couch.

"I'll be right there, Seth! Hold your horses."

She flung open the door, as Seth was ready to pound the wood again. He scowled. "How did you know it was me? I could have been someone here to hurt you."

She opened the door wider to let him pass. "Criminals rarely knock. Besides, I don't know that many people in town and you do have a certain something that made me think the battering my poor door was taking was from your fist. I thought you were going to call me."

Seth tossed his cowboy hat onto the kitchen counter. "How do you know what criminals do? Have you been around quite a few? And I was going to call you. I decided to skip that and just stop by."

She gestured toward the couch and he sat down. "As far as I know, I've only known one. My homicidal boss. Of course, he did knock so I could be completely wrong."

She headed over to the refrigerator and grabbed a couple of sodas. "Soda?" He nodded and she settled next to him. Not too close, but still close enough to smell his aftershave and feel the warmth from his body. She felt a pang of regret their kiss had been interrupted the night before.

He popped open the can and contemplated it for a moment. "You know, I really don't know anything about you other than your life is in danger."

"You told me not to talk about myself, remember?" She leaned back into the cushions.

"To others, not to me. I was just wondering about your life, that's all. For example, how old are you?"

She giggled. "Are you worried you kissed jail bait last night? I can assure you I'm of age. I'm twenty-six. In my family, that's an old maid."

He didn't look any more comfortable or happy. "I'm older than that. I'm thirty-six. Well, almost."

Presley shrugged. "Okay. Am I supposed to be horrified? That doesn't seem all that old. I had a psychic tell me once that I was an old soul. So there, I guess that makes me older than you."

He finally smiled. "You look like a teenager today in your sweats and T-shirt."

She took a sip from her soda. "I haven't been a teenager for several years. So what else do you want to know? My life, what there is of it, is an open book. Do I get to ask you questions as well?" He looked unsure and she had to laugh. "If I'm going to talk about me, you have to talk about you."

He shifted on the sofa. "I'm not very interesting. I was born here, I grew up here, and I'll probably, God willing, die here."

"Your parents really like Elvis Presley. That's pretty interesting."

His cheeks went red. "That's them, not me."

"You don't like Elvis?"

"I like Elvis fine, but I've never felt compelled to build a shrine to him in a spare room. Dad's convinced Elvis is still alive." Seth rubbed his chin, frustration written in his expression. Seeing Seth with his mom and dad, it was clear he loved them dearly. But love didn't preclude being embarrassed now and then. She decided to have some fun with Seth. Her eyes went wide and her voice as sweet as sugar.

"Elvis is still alive." Presley smiled. "He's in the Witness Protection Program just like me. It's one of the secrets they tell you when you're in the club."

Seth's lips twitched. "In the club, huh? Is there a secret handshake too?"

She nodded solemnly. "There is, but I can't show it to you. It's a secret."

"What about Bigfoot? Did they tell you about Bigfoot?"

She liked this silly side to Seth. She bet he showed it rarely, always in sheriff mode. "They did. He's real. He's also in Witness Protection. He stopped shaving to disguise himself."

Seth slapped his thigh with a smile of triumph. "I knew it. I knew Bigfoot was real. Wait until I tell Dad."

She giggled and rested her head on his shoulder, wanting to be closer to him. He wrapped his arm around her shoulders, pulling her closer still. She lay there for a few minutes absorbing his strength and command. Seth Reilly was in control at all times.

"I have a sister," she said, tracing invisible patterns with her finger on the fabric of her sweats.

His hand pressed over hers. "She thinks you're dead." He didn't phrase it like a question. She nodded.

"Yes. They said I couldn't tell her. That she might tell my boss. She got me the job with him."

"The guy who wants you dead?" Seth's voice was soft and close to her ear.

"Yes, although it doesn't sound like him. He's kind of a nerd, if the truth be known. He doesn't seem like a guy who orders people dead. He's no Tony in Scarface. He's more like Sheldon in Big Bang Theory."

"Can I ask what they think he's done?"

"They think he's selling arms to terrorists."

Saying it out loud sounded pretty awful. Seth must have thought so too, as she was promptly hauled up on his lap.

"Arms to terrorists? What does Sheldon do?" She didn't correct Seth about Randall's name.

"He's a weapons manufacturer. I was his administrative assistant for the last six months."

Seth whistled. "And your sister got you the job?"

She nodded, her chin rubbing against the cotton of his shirt. "I'd been out of work for awhile. The economy isn't great in Florida and although I inherited a house from my stepfather, my sister's father, I still needed to be able to pay bills." She played with a button on his shirt. "I kind of quit college and haven't gone back. Yes, I know I should." She nibbled on her lips as she tried to explain something even she often thought was inexplicable. "I quit between my junior and senior year. I'd been dating my professor. I found out he was married with a couple of kids. I was pretty broken up so I decided to take a semester off. The semester sort of dragged on."

There was no pity in Seth's expression, only understanding. "He broke your heart?"

"He was the first man I ever loved." She shrugged, trying not to remember the days, weeks, and months of pain she'd felt over Oliver's betrayal. "But I understand now."

Seth frowned. "Understand what?"

"That men are driven by their hormones. They're driven to cheat. Once I understood that, I knew I had to keep things casual in my relationships. I can't handle someone I love cheating on me."

* * * * *

Seth reeled at Presley's matter of fact tone. She was speaking as if she was talking about a scientific discovery instead of some asshole's weak, cowardly arguments for sticking his dick where it didn't belong. A man who was unfaithful or who lied wasn't a man at all. Integrity was the measure of a man. His father had taught him that by the time Seth was five.

"Presley," he began, "that's just an excuse men use. We can control ourselves. We are not slaves to our hormones. There's no good reason for a man to rape or cheat. It's not written in our DNA, honey."

She looked doubtful. "I've seen a lot of men cheat. My stepfather cheated on my mother. I really loved him, too, but we weren't enough for him. He needed to sleep with another woman on the side. He had another woman and baby."

It sounded like Presley hadn't known many good men. "Men can be faithful. I'm sorry your stepfather and professor were assholes but not all men are like that."

"A lot are."

He didn't argue. He'd seen his share of jerks in his line of work. "That's true. I won't make excuses for other men. I'll just tell you that while we're together, I won't be seeing anyone else. I'm a man of my word."

She nodded. "I believe you. I don't know why I believe you but I do." She flattened her hand against his chest as if to feel his heartbeat. It was important to Seth that she see he was trustworthy but he knew this was something he would have to prove to her over time. Words weren't going to do it.

He looked deeply into her eyes. "I have another question. It's a very important one and the future of our relationship relies on your answer."

She smiled. "Shoot, Sheriff."

He tucked a silky strand of hair behind her ear. "How do you feel about football? Specifically the Broncos?"

She leaned down and kissed his lips softly. No tongue, just a sweet, soft pressure he had to fight himself not to deepen. "I like football just fine. I'm not a fan of any particular team so if you want me to root for the Broncos, I'm good with that. Do you want me to turn on the pre-game shows?"

He chugged some of the soda and grinned. "Sounds good. I'm hungry, too. I can go pick us up something to eat."

She pressed the Power button on the remote. "I went to the grocery store yesterday. I don't like to cook for only me, but I don't mind cooking for two. Do you like spaghetti?"

"I love spaghetti. Are you a good cook?"

"I— I—" the color had drained from her face and she looked stricken. She was staring at the television as if she'd never seen it before. She pointed and seemed to be trying to speak, but the words weren't flowing. He turned to see what she was watching but couldn't understand what she was so upset about. He wrapped his arms tighter around her, tipping her chin up so he could look into her stricken eyes.

"Presley, what's wrong? You look like you've seen a ghost."

She swallowed. "I have. That's Randall, my boss, on the news." She pointed again to the network cable channel she must have been watching when she'd last turned off the television. "It's his annual fundraiser for the city's homeless. He supports a shelter in town."

Seth watched as a non-descript middle aged man in a tuxedo was interviewed by the reporter. He grabbed the remote and zoomed the volume up in time to hear the reporter say that Randall Simon, a billionaire businessman, had raised over two million dollars for the local charity. They made him sound like a really good-hearted philanthropist, always thinking of others before himself. A quick look back at Presley's expression told him she wasn't in love with this bozo, but she still looked distressed.

"It appears they haven't arrested him yet. Did they tell you when they're going to do that?" Seth asked.

Presley rubbed her forehead. "I never actually asked. They said they needed to keep me safe while they finished building their case against him. Honestly, I kept thinking this was all going to go away. That they were wrong about Randall and that I would get to go home, and never have to testify. Shit, I am such an idiot. My car and house are destroyed. Of course, this isn't all just a mistake. I'm so fucking stupid."

Seth shook his head, trying to make sense of everything. "You mentioned this before. What exactly happened?"

Presley tilted her head. "Evan didn't tell you? Randall hid a bomb in my car. He set it to go off when I was in it but I forgot my phone so I was heading back into the restaurant when the bomb went off. It's pure dumb luck I'm alive." She scrubbed at the tears that were trickling down her cheeks. "They set my house on fire. Burned it to the ground. I wasn't all that fond of the house since my liar of a stepfather left it to me, but it was paid off and it was mine. It's gone now. Randall took everything."

Holy fuck, this guy really wanted her dead. Seth pulled her close, her head lolling on his shoulder. "Evan didn't give me any details. He only said he had a woman who was in danger and needed to be hidden." He wiped her tears away, her skin soft underneath his fingertips. "And you're not stupid. Shit, you're the best secretary I've ever had."

"Administrative assistant." Presley's voice was muffled against his damp shirt.

"Huh?"

"You don't call anyone a secretary any more. They're administrative assistants."

He stroked her back, trying to get her to relax. She was like a coiled spring in his arms. "Honey, I'll call you whatever you want as long as you don't leave me to manage the office by myself. Hell, you can even be the boss if you want." He felt her muscles start to soften under his hands. "You say you have to testify. Did you suspect what he was doing?"

Presley straightened and moved off his lap. He immediately felt the loss of her warmth and wanted to reach out and pull her back but it appeared she needed the distance to be able to talk about this. "No, which makes me look stupid, I guess. Looking back, we did socialize with many people from foreign countries with varying feelings about the United States. I didn't think he was doing business with them. I thought it was more of a networking thing."

Seth didn't like the sound of the word 'socialize'. "You spent a lot of time with this guy? You went to parties and things like that?"

Her face dropped down and into her bent knees. "I was dating Randall. He was nice and undemanding. I knew there was no danger of any love growing between us."

Seth didn't like the pang of jealousy he felt hearing about it. He wasn't a jealous man by nature but there was something about this tiny, ferocious woman who brought out instincts he never knew he had. He wanted to protect her and keep her all to himself, which wasn't like him at all. In fact, when he was with Presley, he felt like a different man. He could joke and relax and just be himself. He rarely felt that way with other people. He tipped her chin up so she was forced to look him in the eye. "It's no big deal. I bet he was charming and probably spent a lot of money on you."

She started laughing and he scowled. He hadn't said anything funny. He was trying to be understanding, dammit.

"Randall was far from charming. I told you he was a big geek. He was easy to be with, though, because he didn't have any expectations about how people should act and talk. As for spending money on me, I drew the line there. I wasn't with him for his money and I think he liked that. We went to movies and ate at dives. He liked to slum with me. I only got dressed up fancy every now and then. Mostly for business."

Now Seth was truly confused. "If you go for a geek like that, what do you see in me? I assume you're attracted to me since you let me kiss you."

She was smiling at him now. "Kind of. You're different. Randall had no expectations and you have tons. But you have two very important things Randall lacked. Empathy and passion. He didn't have a speck of either. You have both in spades. You can feel for other people and the passion you have for your job, your family, your town, well, it really shows through." She shrugged. "You look good in your uniform too."

That set him on his heels. "He sounds strange."

"He is strange," Presley said. "A strange billionaire genius. Like Tony Stark without the cleverness, sexiness, and social skills."

Seth tapped out a rhythm on his thigh. "I'm not wearing my uniform today."

Her hand cupped his jaw and her eyes were shining with mischief. "True. You don't look too bad in those jeans either."

He leaned forward and let his lips leisurely explore hers, his tongue dipping inside her warm mouth. He didn't hurry the kiss, but pulled her into his arms so he could not only taste her, but feel the softness of her skin and smell the scent of her silky hair. Her hands were exploring his body, her palms gliding over his arms and chest. His cock, ignored for too long, instantly jumped to attention, hardening against his fly. He had to shift to relieve the pressure or it would have left dents in his flesh.

When he finally lifted his head, his heart thudded in time with hers. He pressed his hand to her chest so he could feel it underneath his fingers. "I want to make love to you, Presley. I want to lay you on the bed and strip all your clothes from you. I want to kiss and lick every inch of your soft skin before burying myself so fucking deep inside you we'll both scream from the pleasure. Do you want that? Me?"

He waited as her eyes widened and her pupils dilated. She was as aroused as he but it didn't mean she was ready to say yes. He swallowed the lump that had formed in his throat, disturbed by how important her answer was to him. He not only wanted her, fuck it, he needed her. Every cell in his body cried out for this one woman. No one else would do at this moment.

Her fingers traced his lips, sending tingles straight to his cock. She smiled. It was a woman's smile. The kind that said she had a secret and she was about to share it with him. He held his breath in anticipation and fear.

"You're poetic for a cowboy. I like it. Yes, I want to make love with you. I only have one request."

He would have promised her the world right then. "Anything. What do you want?"

"Can I strip your clothes from your body, too? It sounds like fun."

CHAPTER SEVEN

Seth had a wicked grin on his face. It made him even sexier and she wrapped her arms around his neck to pull him down to her. She yelped in surprise when he scooped her up in his arms to carry her the seven feet to the bed, located behind a flimsy room divider. The apartment was small but it had everything she needed. She certainly wasn't going to complain about how quickly they made it to the bed. In seconds, he had her lying on her back, his hard muscled body above hers. She gave in to the temptation to explore those muscles more thoroughly, plucking at the buttons on his shirt. Seth was so strong, easily carrying her in his arms. She was dying to see what his shirt covered and trace patterns on his skin with her tongue.

She had opened the last button and was pushing his shirt off his shoulders when his pocket started to vibrate. He slumped back on the bed and sighed, glancing at the screen in resignation.

"I need to take this. I'm sorry, honey." His lips were pressed together as he swiped the screen. "Seth," he barked. His facial expression changed rapidly from slightly pissed off to angry and frustrated. She didn't know who he was talking to but his answers were brief, almost monosyllabic. It wasn't a happy conversation.

"Don't worry, Trask. They've done this before. I'll go out and put a stop to it."

Seth stuck his phone back in his pocket and started to re-button his shirt. She stilled his movements with her hands but knew from the hard line of his jaw it was only temporary. He was a man on a mission and at the moment it wasn't to make her scream.

He sighed. "Honey, that was Trask. There are some kids out on the road near his place raising hell and trying to get themselves killed. I need to make sure that doesn't happen."

"Who's on duty? Can't they go?" It was a waste of time to argue with him in this mood but she couldn't stop herself. Her body was humming and she wanted him to stay with her.

Seth shook his head. "This is something I have to do."

He didn't elaborate as to why and she was afraid to ask. His face had turned to carved granite, almost forbidding in its coldness. She marveled at how easily he moved between passion and duty. He finished tucking in his shirt and started to turn toward the front door, but she captured his arm before he could get away.

"Why don't I come with you?" She didn't want to lose this connection between them. She could feel him pulling away mentally as well as physically. "Afterward, you can take me to eat. Like a real date, Sheriff."

A dozen or more emotions flitted across his face, and she was sure he was going to shoot her down so she was surprised when he nodded. "That's a good idea. This won't take long. I'm not going to arrest these kids, just scare them a little."

She didn't have a chance to ask where they were headed as he bundled her into the car. He drove like a bat out of hell until they were flying down a dirt road in the middle of nothing. There was no one around, and in the distance she could see two pickup trucks coming toward them, side by side on the two-lane road.

Seth suddenly turned the wheel of his SUV, veering the truck so it was perpendicular to the road and crossing both lanes. He opened the door and strode over to her side and stood in the middle of the road, arms akimbo. It was as if he was daring them to come any closer. It was only as the two pickup trucks drew closer that she saw why they were there.

A person, who looked like a boy, was straddling the rolled down windows of each truck, Footloose-style. The drivers must have been practiced at this as the vehicles stayed side by side, one never moving ahead of the other. The person had one foot on the door of each truck and was waving his arms in the air triumphantly. Presley marveled at the balance and grace he or she displayed, but it didn't stop the acceleration of her heart. She imagined the worst, fear forming a pit in her stomach. One misstep on the rider's or driver's part and they would be caught between the two cars, crushed under the wheels. It was a grisly thought.

The trucks started to slow down, the dust trailing behind as their vehicles died down and the rider dove into one of the open truck windows. Both vehicles came to a stop and Seth simply stood there, waiting for the people to get out of the trucks. Seeing them, Presley was struck by their youth. She blew out a breath in relief, her heart resuming a more normal rhythm.

They were just kids. Probably about sixteen or seventeen, the boys had acne and that gangly look they'd eventually grow out of. The girls were giggly and wore too much makeup and not enough clothes, not even jackets for the cold October weather. One was wearing a short jean skirt with cowboy boots, while another clearly had forgotten her bra that morning. They made Presley feel about a hundred years old. She'd forgotten what it was like to be that young until this brought it back. She'd felt invincible then. Apparently, these kids felt the same. She'd like to pull them aside and tell them how life could turn out, but it wasn't the time.

One of the boys ambled up to Seth cautiously. "Hey, Sheriff. Thought you'd be watchin' the Broncos today."

"That's what I was planning to do until I got a call from Trask. You scared the shit out of him. He's too old for your stunts, and you're too young to realize how stupid you're being."

From her angle, she couldn't see Seth's expression but she heard the exasperation in his voice with a touch of hard-ass anger. The boy's expression paled slightly and he took a step back, clearly out of his depth with a pissed off Seth Reilly. One of the girls, however, had no qualms about stepping forward with a petulant look on her face. She stuck out a painted lower lip, her hand on her hip, a tragic expression on her face. Presley guessed that expression worked wonders with the girl's parents. It didn't appear to be having any effect on Seth.

"We were just having fun, Sheriff." The girl took another step forward. "It's not going to end up like Trent Bauer."

Seth sucked in a breath and muttered a low curse word. The girl must have seen immediately she had played her cards wrong, and took several steps back, bumping into the hood of the truck. Presley hopped out of the SUV to stand next to Seth, who looked ready to explode. For a moment, she feared he might hurt them, but then she remembered this was Seth. He was always firmly in control, even if he did look madder than she'd ever seen him.

He got right into the four kids' faces, his eyes dark with anger. "Do you think this is a joke?" His voice was quiet but deadly cold, which only served to send a shiver up her spine. "Do you think your parents will think it's funny when I have to tell them that you were killed under the tires of a three-ton vehicle?" He turned to the young woman, now cowering and close to tears. "Think your parents will laugh when I show them your ripped-apart corpse after what happened to your brother when he was drinking and driving? You don't appear to have any more sense." Seth straightened up. "What happened to my friend Trent could happen to any of you. There was nothing special about that day. He's dead because we did something stupid. We'd been told not to do it, but we did. Now I'm here, and he's not."

One of the girls rolled her eyes and Presley could feel Seth stiffen beside her. The girl looked at the other kids to back her up. "We weren't doing anything. We didn't hurt anyone. We were just having fun."

The girl had Seth's undivided attention, which was probably not a good thing at the moment. His gaze focused on the young girl, his expression hard. "You almost scared Trask into a heart attack. His reflexes aren't what they used to be. What if he couldn't veer off or stop in time and ended up hurting one of you? Or himself, for that matter? Are you okay causing the death of another person? Is that acceptable as long as you're having *fun*?"

Seth's emphasis seemed to shake the girl's confidence and she wisely stayed silent. He hooked his thumbs into his pockets and surveyed the youths. "I've a mind to call your parents. I could also write both of you boys a ticket for reckless driving. That would drive up your insurance rates and your parents wouldn't be too damn happy about that either." He crossed his arms over his chest, giving them a stare that turned their faces white and their eyes wide with fear. "What do you think I should do with you?"

The four kids glanced at each other and the first young man finally spoke up. "Give us a warning?"

Seth smiled, but it wasn't a happy or loving smile. His lips were curved but his eyes glittered like stones. "I did that last time. This time I think I won't tell your parents, though." All four kids simultaneously sagged with relief, but Seth continued. "You will tell your parents. I'll check and make sure you do. If you think you've done nothing wrong," Seth gave the young girl a hard stare, "it shouldn't be a big deal. I'll give you one week to do it."

All four kids started talking at once, clearly dismayed by Seth's edict. The voices grew so loud Seth finally held up his hand. "Hush. If you don't want to tell them, I will. Your choice."

Realizing they were beat, the kids nodded and drifted back to their vehicles, their shoulders hunched. She and Seth watched as the kids reversed direction and headed off, blowing up dirt and dust in their wake. It was a small bit of rebellion on their part, but Seth didn't bat an eye. He turned on his heel and opened the passenger door of his SUV.

"Let's get something to eat."

Presley nodded and slid up onto the seat. She didn't say anything, giving Seth time to calm down and let his anger drain away. The drive to the barbecue place was silent and filled with tension. Luckily, the restaurant had several wide screen televisions so they settled in to watch the Broncos game and eat some of the best beef brisket she'd ever tasted. Seth slowly relaxed as the crowd cheered and booed at the game. It was halftime before either one of them said more than an occasional "Pass the salt" or "This is really good. Do you want to try a bite of mine?"

She took a casual sip of her iced tea. "So who's Trent Bauer?"

Pain flashed in Seth's eyes and then was gone. "You heard that?" He looked at a commercial playing on television then looked back at her. "He was my best friend growing up."

She didn't say anything else. Seth was a man who kept his own counsel. He didn't spill his emotions all over the place and sure as hell wasn't going to do it in front of a couple hundred people in a barbecue joint. She went back to watching television, letting his words echo in her brain over and over.

Trent was Seth's best friend, and obviously something bad had happened. It wasn't any of her business really. She wouldn't push him to talk about something that was clearly painful.

"He was straddling the two cars," Seth said suddenly. "Just like Adam was today." Seth's throat worked and she reached out to grab his hand. "I was driving one truck and Harley Madison was driving the other. We did it all the time. We were always trying to impress girls like that, doing crazy shit to get their attention." He shook his head. "We'd heard about it from our parents and the sheriff a million times. They told us we were going to end up breaking a leg or something."

Seth paused, his eyes far away. "Breaking a leg would have been a good thing compared to what really happened. It was a cold day. Colder than today. We were deep into November and it had snowed, but most of it had melted. There was a patch on the road that had frozen again and when my truck hit it, the wheels spun."

Presley listened in growing horror as Seth recounted that day in a tight voice, as if he were trying to keep a rein on his emotions. She didn't respond. She didn't know what to say to such tragedy. Seth took a long drink from his beer. "I got control of the truck quickly. Shit, I'd been driving in this weather since my dad put me behind the wheel at twelve. It only took a split second and suddenly Trent was gone. I couldn't seem him anymore so I hit my brakes. Harley had already done that but I didn't know why."

She squeezed Seth's hand but he didn't seem to notice, lost in the past. "When Trent fell, he went under Harley's tires. Harley ran over him. That's why he stopped. He'd run over Trent."

Seth's lips curved into a smile. "You had to know Trent. He was the nicest damn guy I've ever known. We laughed all the time. He was the quarterback on the football team and I was a receiver. He was smart and every girl in school wanted to date him." Seth's smile fell. "After I stopped the car, I ran back to where he'd fallen. He was dead. The doctor's said it was a blessing he didn't suffer."

The thought of what Seth had seen that awful day wrenched at Presley's heart. She'd been through some shit the last week or so, but her best friend hadn't died. No one she cared about had lost his life. It was clear why Seth took protecting her so seriously. Why he took the safety of his town so seriously. Fuck, why he took everything so seriously. Even where things were filed in the office.

"It wasn't your fault, Seth." She put every ounce of conviction she felt into her statement.

Seth gave her a sad smile and it broke her heart. "Honey, you're sweet to say that. But the truth is, it was my fault. I know it, and Trent knows it. Now you know it."

She shook her head, not wanting him to take the blame. "It's not. Kids do stupid shit."

"I didn't steal a rival school's mascot, Presley. I killed my best friend."

"It was an accident," she said desperately.

Seth took another long swallow of his beer, his face unutterably sad. "Yes, it was an accident. That doesn't make Trent any more alive, does it?"

It didn't, but that wasn't the saddest thing of all. Trent had gone on to a better place. Seth was still living here in his own self-constructed purgatory. It didn't appear he was looking for a way out, either. He was settled in for the long haul.

Seth's lips twisted. "Listen, about earlier…"

Presley lifted her hands in surrender. "I get it. It was a mistake."

"Not a mistake, just…I think we should slow things down a bit, that's all."

It was strange to hear a man talk about slowing down when it came to sex. It wasn't just the woman's prerogative after all. Obviously, she'd gotten too close.

"We probably should. Maybe we should take a break from spending time together outside the office."

"I didn't mean we shouldn't see each other," Seth insisted. "I just meant we've only known each other a week. Maybe we should get to know each other more."

Presley didn't know an elegant way of saying what she needed to say, so she was simply going to put it out there. "I'm not sure it's a good idea for us to see each other at all. Shit, Seth, you're a buttoned-up control freak. My life is in chaos. Sure, I'm pretending while I'm here that everything is normal, but let's face it, it's not." She shook her head, thinking about how she lived her life in Tampa. "If I'm brutally honest, my regular life isn't all that in control. I've been drifting from job to job since I quit school. My sister says I have no direction. My friends say I'm trying to find myself. I can't even keep a houseplant alive. I wanted to get a cat and my friends talked me out of it, fearing for its life. If you're attracted to a woman like Eliza, I'd make you crazy inside of a month. I don't like rules. I don't like barriers. I do like you. That's why I think you should know what you're getting into. It won't be peaceful and sedate. It'll be a roller coaster ride. You have to really want that."

She blew out a breath as she waited for his response to her monologue. They weren't right for each other, but damn if she didn't really like this man. He wasn't only handsome and sexy, he was good. And kind. And she felt safe and protected when he was around.

Seth rubbed his chin. "Maybe today isn't the day to make decisions. Why don't we enjoy our food and the game? Nothing more complicated than that. There's time to figure out all the other things later. Neither one of us is going anywhere."

Presley slumped back into the booth. It sounded like a nice way to brush her off. He didn't want to hurt her feelings, which was so like Seth. She'd only known him a week but she knew he didn't like hurting people. She nodded in agreement, but inside wanted to crawl away and lick her wounds. Seth didn't want her the way she was.

She didn't know any other way to be, and she wouldn't, couldn't, change for him. She'd tried that once, and it hadn't worked out at all.

* * * * *

Seth couldn't sleep. It had been one hell of a day and although his mind was emotionally drained, his body was too keyed up to sleep. He put it down to Sunday Night Insomnia, but he knew who the real culprit was.

Presley.

His body still remembered being on top of her, stroking her soft skin, and breathing in her delicate scent. It was telling his brain he was a stupid idiot who ought to be with Presley now, deep inside her. Instead he was sitting in his kitchen eating cookies his mother had brought over earlier. She'd given him a look as if she'd wanted to ask him what was wrong, but she hadn't. They'd chatted about the weather and Eliza's new boyfriend. His mother had been waiting for him to say something, but the days of running to Mommy for comfort were long gone.

She'd been there for him when Trent was killed. They'd been like brothers so she'd loved Trent like a son. Seth hadn't really thought about that until this moment. She must have been as broken up as he was but she'd been the strong one. She'd been the one who dragged Seth's ass out of bed every day when all he wanted to do was sleep and forget. She was the one who had supported his decision to work in law enforcement when he returned from Iraq, over his father's objections. His mother had been there every step of the way asking nothing in return.

Like Presley. She hadn't asked for much tonight. Just his understanding of who she really was. Seth knew she was a bundle of trouble. The way she drank cup after cup of coffee all day long. The way she engaged with complete strangers all over town. She'd met a lot of people in the last week and they all loved her. Why not? She was sweet and kind and she made people feel good about themselves.

Even him.

She made him feel like a god. That day they'd found Millie, her expression had been filled with admiration. She looked at him as if he were some great protector. Seth knew the truth. When it came down to it, would he be able to keep Presley from harm or would he fail her as he'd failed Trent that day? He'd spent his entire adult life trying to make up for that moment. He wasn't sure if it was even possible, but he couldn't stop himself. It drove him every waking moment of every day. The need to atone was strong. And painful.

Whatever happened between him and Presley, Seth vowed he would do everything in his power to keep her safe and alive. She was so full of life and spirit. It would be wrong for it to be extinguished too early. She might decide not to be with him. He would keep her safe and alive and deliver her back to her old life.

He'd go back to the life he had before she came here only one week ago. Solid and controlled.

CHAPTER EIGHT

Presley pressed the button on the new coffee machine she'd picked up in the city on Saturday before heading back to her desk. She needed the caffeine. She hadn't slept well last night. It wasn't surprising but it was starting to wear on her. When she'd looked in the mirror this morning, there were purple shadows under her eyes. She'd spent an extra minute with the concealer, hoping no one would notice.

There wasn't much to do today. She'd spent most of last week re-organizing the office and it was much easier to manage now. Everything was at her fingertips and the paperwork was under control. Maybe she could talk Seth into letting her scan in the old paper records so they could be digitized. The printer was also a scanner so it wouldn't cost the city any money. She would need to set up a meta tag system so they could be searched, but she'd done it at one of her previous shit jobs. The bundled software the office used had the capability. It would be a challenge to figure out how to use it, and a nice present to leave Harper when she finally moved on.

She was absorbed in the software manual when the front door opened and Marion Reilly bustled in with a smile. Presley really liked Seth's mom but was instantly wary as to why she was here. It had been clear as a bell the night Presley had dinner at the Reilly ranch, Mom Reilly wanted her baby boy married off, and giving her some grandchildren. Several hints had been dropped Presley's way when they were touring the Elvis room.

"Mrs. Reilly! How lovely to see you this morning. Would you like a cup of coffee?"

"I certainly would, dear. It's chilly this morning. And please, call me Marion." Marion peeled the gloves from her fingers and shrugged off her coat, taking a seat on the other side of Presley's desk.

"How do you take yours?" Marion told her and Presley made two coffees, before settling back in her chair. "What brings you to town so early in the morning?"

Marion sipped at the hot liquid and her face split into a smile. "That's wonderful. It may be the best coffee I've had since our vacation three years ago to Seattle. We went to visit an old friend of George's. The coffee there was sinfully delicious."

"I bought a new coffeemaker when Eliza and I went shopping on Saturday." Presley waved to the shiny stainless steel machine with several buttons and levers. It was state of the art and the coffee she was now drinking was kick-ass. A huge improvement on the drip dinosaur Presley had shoved in the storage closet.

"As for what brings me to town this early, on Monday mornings I do my grocery shopping for the week. I like to get there early when it's not very busy and get it done. I'm making bread today. Do you like to bake?"

"I can make cookies," Presley laughed. "My talents don't run to something like bread. It sounds tasty, though."

"Why don't you come to dinner tonight and try some? I'm making lasagna and garlic bread. Do you like lasagna?"

Presley loved lasagna but she wasn't sure this invitation didn't come with strings attached. "I do, but I'm not sure it's a good idea. I'm not sure how Seth would feel about it, honestly."

Marion patted her hand. "I appreciate your honesty. It's one of the things I like about you. You tell the unvarnished truth. But you do it with love. It's a rare person who can do that."

Presley felt like shit. She was keeping a huge secret from Marion. Her real identity. She wasn't fighting crime like Batman to make it okay. Presley was just trying to stay alive.

"Thank you, I try. But no one is truthful all the time." She'd learned that the hard way.

"True. You're special, Presley. I think so, and I know Seth thinks so. I saw him last night when he came home. I know that haunted look in his eyes. Something reminded him of Trent. Did he tell you about Trent?"

Presley took a sip of the scalding liquid, letting the caffeine calm her nerves. "He told me Trent was his best friend and about the accident. He told me it was his fault."

Marion's eyes were bright with unshed tears. "It wasn't his fault. Those two boys and their friends were wild, no one more so than Trent. He was a sweet boy, a good boy, but he was a daredevil. Riding between two trucks was only one of the stunts he liked to pull on a regular basis. He drove his souped-up car too fast, and he rode his motorcycle too fast. He drank on the weekends and got in fights." Marion sighed and put down her coffee cup. "And I loved him. We all did. He was the nicest boy you'd ever meet. All the young men were a little wild, to tell you the truth. I probably don't know a fraction of the crazy things they did and that's just fine with me. I'm sure it would turn my hair gray. Well, grayer." Marion smiled sadly.

Presley frowned. "That doesn't sound like the Trent Seth described."

"Yes." Marion nodded. "He only thinks about the good in Trent, which was so many things, but he doesn't think about Trent's flaws. He had those too. We all do. No one was responsible for Trent's death that day. Not Seth, not Trent. It was an accident. A stupid, tragic accident."

"Seth's spent his life trying to make up for it, hasn't he?"

"He has. At first I encouraged it. I thought it would help him get over things. When he enlisted in the Army and then when he decided not to work the ranch but go into law enforcement, I supported those decisions. Unfortunately as the years have passed it doesn't seem to make any difference. He's still trying to make up for that day."

"We saw a bunch of teenagers doing that same thing yesterday. That riding between two cars thing."

"That's what set this off then?" Marion pushed away her empty coffee cup. "I'd wondered. Kids have been doing this for years, long before that movie showed it. They'll be doing it long after I'm gone. Seth's fighting a losing battle."

"You feel immortal at that age." Presley refilled Marion's cup and her own. She needed a second cup for this conversation.

Marion chuckled. "I know I did. Seth did too. Such memories of my youth. I wish Seth's hadn't been spoiled." Marion looked straight into Presley's eyes. "Since then he's been a different person. He tries to be in control of everything. He follows rules to the letter. He used to be more laidback and relaxed. He's not the same boy I raised."

Presley swallowed hard. "I'm trouble."

Marion looked at her for a long time before nodding. "Yes, and that's what makes you perfect for him. He needs someone to shake him out of his complacency. Eliza was a sweet girl but she wasn't for Seth. She and Seth both need someone to bring fire and passion into their lives. They couldn't do it for each other."

Marion knew her son. Presley found herself longing for a close family like the Reillys. She'd seen the love between them and it made her wonder why she'd never been able to inspire that kind of love in her own small and dysfunctional family.

"I'm not sure he agrees. We kind of decided last night to maybe take a break from spending personal time together."

Marion stirred her coffee, a smile playing around her lips. "I won't allow that to happen. You're the one, Presley."

Presley shook her head. "I'm not. I won't even be—" She broke off, realizing she couldn't say she wasn't planning to stay in Harper. "It's just that we met only a week ago. I'm not sure we know each other very well."

"You mean you haven't slept together yet," Marion stated, much to Presley's shock. "What are you waiting for?"

Presley tried to hide her smile. "I don't know, to be honest. I think we both want to."

Marion snorted. "All men want to, dear. Do you want to?"

Fuck yeah, she did. She'd never been this attracted to a man in her life.

"I think so. He's a complicated man, Marion. It might not work out."

"How do you know if you don't take a chance?" Marion stood and started to pull on her coat and gloves. "I'll text Seth and tell him to bring you to dinner tonight. If you want something, dear, you have to go after it. The more it means to you, the more you have to work for it. But it's worth it, I promise. Don't let Seth's melancholy and doubts drive you away. Don't let him fill you with his own pain. Sweep it away and replace it with something infinitely better."

"What?" Presley stood to see Marion to the door.

Marion smiled as she headed out. "Why, love, of course. Thank you for the coffee. See you tonight."

Presley fell back into her chair, almost choking on her own spit. Love was the last thing she needed.

* * * * *

His mother was up to her usual tricks. Seth had brought Presley to dinner tonight as requested. He wasn't sure it was a good idea though. The day had been long and awkward, broken only by the occasional visitor who stopped by to chat with Presley and have a cup of her coffee. She'd been proud as punch of her new coffeemaker and even Seth had to admit it made a damn fine cup of coffee. She'd even frothed his milk. At first, when she'd offered it to him, he'd thought frothed milk was some sort of euphemism. When he realized she was seriously offering him whipped milk in his coffee, he'd graciously accepted, remembering the fancy coffees he'd drank as a rookie cop in Denver.

His parents had kept the conversation flowing all during dinner and it was probably time for him to take Presley back to her apartment. Seth found her staring out the window of the family room. He walked up behind her, and was immediately surrounded by her soft, clean scent. He had to fight the urge to pull her into his arms. He wasn't sure what she wanted from him now. Yesterday had started so promising, but it had all gone to hell in a hand basket, and it was all his fault. He settled for placing his hands on her shoulders.

"What are you looking at so intently out there?"

She turned slightly so he could see she was smiling. "The snow. I'd never seen snow until I came here."

Sometimes he forgot she had another life away from here. One he wasn't part of and never would be. "It's just cold and white. Shoveling it is hard on your back and slippery under your feet."

She shook her head. "It's beautiful. I never thought snow could be beautiful, but it is. Look at the way the full moon reflects off the new snow. It's like something out of a movie or a painting."

Seth looked at the back yard through Presley's eyes. The carpet of white that sparkled under the moon reminded him of a book he'd read as a young boy. He couldn't remember what the title was, but he did remember one thing. People liked to play in the snow. He hadn't done it in years but he still remembered how.

"So you've never built a snowman?"

Presley chuckled. "Beach sand makes great castles. I haven't tried to make a person."

He grabbed her hand and pulled her toward the door. "We need to address these gaps in your education and there's no time like the present."

She gasped in surprise as he bundled her up in her heavy coat. He pulled on his own while she tugged on gloves and wound a scarf around her head and neck. She looked so cute, dressed like a little girl about to play in the snow. Seth wanted to make up for being a total prick yesterday and showing her the magic of snow seemed as good a way as any. He yelled into the living room that they were headed outside for a little while.

The evening was cold but not deathly freezing. He wasn't going to tell Presley the weather she was experiencing now was only going to get colder. As it was, she kept the space heater turned up next to her desk each day at the office. He flipped on the outdoor floodlights and led her to the middle of their large backyard. Gathering a mound of snow together, he started to pack it together to make a ball.

"Roll this along in the snow and it will grow." He pushed the small snowball toward her. "We do this three times, each one progressively smaller."

Presley was bent over, pushing the snowball through the snow. "I know what a snowman looks like, Seth," she huffed. He started on the second snowball, building it up much faster than Presley. She was scowling with her hands on her hips when he finished the second one before she was done with the first.

"Shit, how did you do that so fast?"

"Years of practice, honey. Let's get this old guy put together."

He helped her finish the last snowball, laughing at how lopsided it was before he smoothed it into an icy sphere. They stacked the snowballs one on top of the other and stood back to survey their work. Seth was about to commandeer Presley's scarf when his mother came out with an old cardboard box he recognized instantly.

"Mom, where did you find that?"

His mother laughed, handing him the box. "Mothers always have their secrets and we don't tell. Enjoy, but don't stay out here too long. The snow is really starting to come down."

His mother turned and hurried back into the house since she was only in her sweater. Seth held up the box triumphantly.

"Snowman supplies."

Presley peered into the box and smiled. "You have a box of things to dress a snowman? That's handy."

Seth grabbed up the pieces of "coal" to make the eyes and mouth, and handed another handful to Presley for the buttons.

"We used to make snowmen a lot when we were kids. Then Mom would make us hot chocolate with marshmallows."

"Sounds like Norman Rockwell would be proud." Presley had finished with the buttons and was attaching stick arms he and his brothers had whittled years ago.

"I guess I did have a pretty cool childhood. My brothers and I fought all the time and drove our parents crazy but we're very close. Are you and your sister close?"

He almost thought she didn't hear him but she had stopped decorating the snowman and was standing there with snow falling all around her looking thoughtful. Finally she shook her head.

"No, I wouldn't call us close. I've always wanted us to be, though. I've wanted a family like you have, but it isn't in the cards for me, I guess. When my mom married Nora's dad I was ecstatic. I thought I would have the family I'd always wanted. My stepdad wasn't what you would call a family man. Pair that with the fact Nora is tough to get close to. She tries, though. She just has trouble showing her emotions, that's all."

Seth didn't like the sound of it but kept his mouth shut. It took all kinds in this world, and not everyone's family was like his, always in his business and never leaving him alone. In fact, there were times he wouldn't mind trading her for a day or two.

Seth reached into the box and pulled out a scarf and a hat. He handed the hat to Presley and wrapped the woolen length around the snowman's neck while she placed the hat on its head.

"I think that's easily the best snowman I've ever seen. You have a real knack for this for someone from Florida."

She giggled and it made his heart beat faster. "Shhh! Do you want someone to hear you? I'm from Wheaton, remember?"

He shook his head. "There isn't a soul out here except for Frosty and he ain't talking." Seth reached out and plucked the pieces of charcoal from the snowman's smile, rendering him speechless. Presley laughed and then fell back into the snow on her bottom. Seth grinned and held out his hand to help her up. "What in the hell are you doing? You'll be covered in snow, woman. Take my hand."

She did take his hand, and tugged at his until he slipped in the snow, falling next to her with a bump. She was giggling and laughing and he couldn't stop staring at her, mesmerized by her beauty. He'd fallen under her spell with a little help from the glistening snow and the full moon. He should want to get them inside and dry. He should want his life to be orderly and peaceful, but next to this luminous woman, none of those things seemed very important. The only important thing at the moment was Presley.

He fell on his back and waved his arms and legs, making a snow angel. Presley watched in fascination as he stood up carefully, so as to not disturb the impression in the snow.

"You next," he urged. "Try it." She obediently lay in the snow, making the wings and dress of her angel. He reached out a hand and helped her up, lifting her so she wouldn't make foot impressions in the snow. He knelt down next to her angel and drew a gloved finger through the snow in a circle above the head.

"An angel needs a halo."

She pointed to his angel. "What about yours? It needs a halo."

He laughed and stood up, brushing the snow from his pants. "I lost my halo a long time ago, honey. Didn't we already talk about that night in the backseat of my dad's truck?"

Her eyes danced with merriment. She knelt down and quickly drew two triangles above the head of his figure. "Horns. For your snow devil."

He caught her hand in his and pulled her to her feet, stepping close so their bodies were touching. His gaze zeroed in on her full lips. He remembered well what it felt like to kiss them. He didn't know if he'd ruined everything yesterday, but he was going to go for broke.

"I want to kiss you, Presley."

Their lips were mere inches from each other. Seth could feel her warm breath on his chin.

"I want to kiss you, too, but what about yesterday? About slowing down?"

He shook his head. "I'm a dumbass. Forget everything I said yesterday. I panicked for a moment, but I'm okay now."

She looked at him as if she was trying to see his soul. "Are you okay with me? My life is what it is, Seth. It's out of control and there isn't much I can do about it. I'm not Eliza. I'm not peaceful and I sure as hell can't be described as serene. I make mistakes. I drink too much coffee and I laugh too loudly. And here's the biggie...I make bad decisions sometimes. Can you deal with that?"

Seth felt a moment of fear in his gut but ruthlessly pushed it away. He wouldn't let Presley down. He would keep her safe and make her smile. Nothing would happen to her on his watch.

"I can. Can you deal with me?"

She tapped her chin thoughtfully but her lips were curved into a smile. "I can." She ran her hands up his chest and around his neck, making every cell in his body wake up and take notice. "I think you should take me somewhere and get me warm."

He swept her up into his arms, her weight almost nothing. "Yes, ma'am. There's nothing I'd like better."

He knew just where to take her and just what to do. Presley would be his tonight. At least, while she was here. He wouldn't think about when she would have to leave.

One thing was for sure.

When she left, she'd never forget the time she spent with him. He'd make every minute memorable.

For both of them.

CHAPTER NINE

"We need to get you warm," Seth said, tugging at her wet coat and gloves.

"I can do it. You're wet too." Presley shrugged off her coat while Seth started a fire. She looked around the log home appreciatively. It was beautiful but simple, with gleaming wood and overstuffed leather furniture. With Seth's love of football, she wasn't surprised to see a large flat screen television on one wall. She was surprised to see the large eat-in kitchen with shiny stainless steel appliances and copper pans hanging from a rack over the large island.

"Do you cook?" Presley shook her long hair out and knelt by the fire. She sighed as the heat seeped directly into her bones. She held out her hands as if to absorb the radiating warmth.

"I do, but like you, it's not much fun to cook for one person. Maybe I'll cook for you sometime." Seth headed into the kitchen and pulled down a saucepan. "In fact, how about some hot chocolate?"

"That sounds yummy. And warm."

"Good," Seth nodded. "You're soaked head to toe. There's a robe on the back of the bathroom door." He gestured to a hallway. "Why don't you get out of those clothes and put that on? You'll be warmer. I can't have my fabulous secretary getting sick. How would I run the station without you?"

She chuckled as she headed down the hall, finding the bathroom with no trouble. The robe on the back of the door was flannel and from its size, clearly belonged to Seth. She pressed her nose into the fabric and inhaled his scent, letting it fill her lungs.

Damn, he smells good.

She stripped off her wet clothes and hung them over the shower rod, pulling the cozy robe over her nude body and tying it in place. The hem hung past her knees and she had to roll up the sleeves, but she was dry and warm. She winced as she caught a look in the mirror. Her hair was a rat's nest, curling all over the place with the moisture. She'd left her purse in the living room so she plucked Seth's brush from its spot next to the sink, hoping he wouldn't mind her borrowing it.

By the time she'd tamed her hair and returned to the kitchen, he'd also changed into a pair of blue sweatpants and a white T-shirt. The room was filled with the sublime aroma of chocolate and she followed her nose to the stove, where he was lifting the pan from the burner and pouring two steaming mugs.

"Marshmallows?" Seth rummaged in a cabinet.

"Heck, yeah. What's hot chocolate without the extra sugar?"

Seth dropped a handful of mini-marshmallows in each cup. "My mom used to put peppermint sticks in our hot chocolate at Christmas time."

"I'm waiting for Norman Rockwell to break down your family's door, wrestle you to the ground, and take your picture for some magazine cover or Christmas card."

Seth picked up both mugs and motioned for her to precede him into the living room. "Norman Rockwell is dead. At least, I'm pretty sure he is. Would that picture be with or without Dad's life-size cut out of Elvis? Grab those cushions and toss them on the floor, will you? We can be close to the fire."

They settled on the pillows and Seth handed her the mug. She sipped at the rich liquid and sighed with contentment. The chocolate slid down her throat and warmed her belly, relaxing every care away.

"Delicious. My compliments to the chef. I think the picture would be with Elvis. I bet Elvis liked Norman Rockwell."

Seth placed his cup on the side table. "From what you've said, your family life wasn't a Rockwell painting."

She fiddled with the handle of her mug. She had come to terms with it, and didn't want his pity. "It wasn't but its okay. It's just every time I'm around your family, they seem so genuinely nice." She didn't know how to describe it. "Your family are really good people."

"You haven't met them all. My brothers were real hell-raisers when they were younger."

"And now?"

A shadow passed over Seth's face so quickly she almost thought she imagined it. "Now they're devoted family men. They're very lucky."

"You're not lucky?" He seemed lucky to Presley. He'd had tragedy in his life, but he had family by his side.

"In some ways." Seth finally smiled. "I have the best secretary in town. The sexiest one too." His voice had deepened at the end and it sent shivers through her entire body straight down to her curling toes. Whatever it was, this man had it. She wanted to pull those clothes from his body, lick up his flat abdomen, and then move to parts further south.

He reached across the small space between them and plucked the mug from her fingers, setting it on the side table. He picked up her hands in his lifting them so he could place a kiss on each palm. "Presley..."

He didn't need to say any more. She nodded vigorously, wanting him more than she could remember ever wanting a man. "Yes. Yes, Seth."

She wasn't sure what all she was saying yes to, but she didn't have the capacity to say no to him. Yes to making love. Yes to stripping their clothes off and exploring private, sensual places on their bare bodies. If she was saying yes to more than that she would deal with it in the morning.

Seth pressed her back into the cushions, the heat from the fire nothing compared to the flames licking at her veins and building in her abdomen. His lips trailed a delicate path from her neck to her ear, nipping at the flesh and making her shiver. Her fingers gripped his shoulders, an anchor as the room started to spin. Her head fell back in invitation and his tongue traced a line up her jugular before capturing her lips in a kiss that seared her soul. His tongue explored every nook and cranny of her mouth as if he owned it. She gave in to his mastery, content to be a supplicant to the feelings he evoked. He tasted like sweet chocolate and she rubbed his tongue with her own to get more of his decadent flavor.

When he lifted his head, his expression was stamped with passion, his normally light blue eyes dark with arousal. Seth's hands parted the folds of her robe and his eyes glowed with pleasure. She felt her insides twist at his obvious approval of what he beheld. Her nipples tightened to taut peaks to entice his mouth and her cunt softened, leaking honey. She could smell her arousal in the air and feel his hard cock against her belly. She wriggled against him playfully and he groaned in response.

"Witch," he growled. "I know just what to do with you."

Boy, did he ever. His rough fingers were plucking and twisting at her nipples, then his lips and tongue were there, teasing and tormenting each in turn. He blew his hot breath over a wet nipple and it quivered under the attention, puckering tighter and harder. He smiled up at her and repeated his action on the other side.

"So responsive. I love it."

As long as he didn't love *her*, it would be okay. Further coherent thought was difficult as he kissed a damp trail down her stomach to her waiting pussy. He pushed her thighs apart and his eyes widened as he gazed down at her.

"Honey, I think you forgot something down here." His eyes were dancing and his grin mischievous. "You must be cold. I'll warm you right up."

Her playful lover had discovered her bare pussy. She'd been waxing for the last few years and then eventually simply had it lasered off. It was a common enough practice in warmer climates but it must be an anomaly in Harper.

"I am a little chilly," she giggled as his tongue swiped at her swollen clit. The sensations rocking through her stopped her laughter cold. She moaned and bit her lip as he made a meal of her cunt, running his tongue through every fold and tongue fucking her until she thought she might scream from the pleasure. He pressed one and then a second finger inside her, moving them in and out until he found a sensitive spot. This time she couldn't hold back her approval.

"Seth!" Her hands grabbed at the cushions and her fingers tightened as he continued to rub the sweet spot inside her while licking her clit with the flat of his tongue. He had her right on the edge of orgasm and he kept her there, teetering on the brink. He was in total command of her body. At that moment, he was every inch the alpha male, giving pleasure to his woman on his terms and no one else's. She wouldn't come until he decided she would come.

She closed her eyes and gave over control to this man. His body, lips, and fingers held the promise of pleasure and she had no doubt he would deliver. When his lips closed over her clit and he sucked gently, his teeth scraping the sides lightly, she screamed his name in a voice she barely recognized as her own.

Brightly colored lights played behind her lids and her body was wracked with intense pleasure. She'd never felt this much, and yet the minute it was over she greedily wanted more. Presley's eyes snapped open and she reached for the hem of his shirt.

"I want you naked, too."

"Easy, honey. You've got all of me tonight. Anything you want." His voice was like a soft caress and she let her hands glide under the soft cotton to find the ridges of his stomach. He sucked in his breath as she explored every inch of his torso. Her fingers lingered on a line of raised and puckered flesh over his ribs.

"Knife. I took it off of a perp when I was a cop in Denver my first year on the job. Luckily, he missed anything important." He gave her a crooked grin.

Presley pushed up his shirt and he grasped the bottom and tossed it away. The orange and yellow flames cast shadows on his muscular body and golden hair. She dragged her attention back to the scar and let her hands and palms run over the smooth flesh until she found another area on his arm that felt rough under her fingers. She lifted a brow in question.

"Fell off my bike when I was twelve. Trent and I built some ramps and we were trying to jump over the family pets. I managed to miss the dog but ended up sideways and ran into the garage door. It took fifteen stitches."

Her hands glided to his jaw and then up to where one of his brows had a slight mar where the hair didn't grow. "And this?"

Seth laughed. "I was showing off for Sheryl Albright. Damn, she was pretty but she only had eyes for Trent. I was giving her a ride on the back of my ATV when I wiped out. I cut my forehead and needed four stitches. Sheryl got her new outfit dirty and didn't speak to me for months."

It was hard to reconcile the calm, controlled man she saw in the office every day to the impetuous young man he had once been.

The girl's name caught her attention. "Wait. You said Sheryl Albright. Isn't she the girl you lost your virginity with in the back of your dad's truck?"

Seth's eyes widened. "Holy shit, I can't believe you remembered I said that. Yes, it was the same girl." He waggled his eyebrows. "She forgave me."

Presley shrugged. "I have a good memory." She pushed him back until he was lounging on the pillows like a sultan, his head cushioned on his hands. She straddled his thighs and pressed a kiss to his stomach, the muscles jumping under her lips. He watched as she kissed a trail up his torso and to his chin, tangy from his aftershave. She rubbed her mouth softly against his, but didn't deepen the kiss. "How many scars do you have, anyway?"

He quirked an eyebrow. "A few more. I have one on my thigh from a fishhook gone awry, and there's one on my back from when my brothers and I tried to build a tree house."

"A tree house? That sounds like fun." Presley nibbled at his ear and he grabbed her hips and ground her against his hard cock.

"It might have been if we had any damn idea what we were doing. Dad said he'd help us but we didn't want to wait. Jason shot a nail from a nail gun right into my back. Hurt like a son of a bitch. Luckily, nothing important got hit that time either. I guess I have been lucky."

She noticed he didn't talk about any injuries from his time in the Army and she didn't ask. It was okay with her if he had a few secrets.

Presley slid her hands under the waistband of his sweats and started tugging them down his legs. "You're about to get luckier, Sheriff."

"Wait," he held up his hand. "I need to get some protection. Are you on the pill, honey?"

She nodded. "I am, but I'm almost to the end of my prescription in my former name. I'll need to see a doctor or something."

"I don't mind taking care of things. I'd be wearing a condom until we were exclusive for at least six months anyway."

Would she be here in six months? She tried to picture her former home and some of her friends but the memories were already hazy and undefined. Everything seemed so much sharper and more real here in Harper. It was funny how she felt more alive when someone wanted her dead.

Seth rolled to his knees and padded on bare feet into the hallway, disappearing for a moment before coming back. He had a triumphant smile on his face and was holding up a strip of condoms. She raised her eyebrows at the number. There had to be six or seven there.

"You're anticipating quite an evening, I see."

He laughed, and it echoed off the walls. "I just grabbed a strip. I've wanted you since that first night, but even I don't think I'll hold out for more than, oh say, three or four times tonight."

Presley shook her head. "Are you always this...cocky?" She pressed her lips together to hide her smile but he saw right through her.

"No pun intended?" he grinned.

"Pun completely intended. Now let's get you out of these pants. I have plans for you." She tugged down his sweats as he stood before her, and she let him kick them to the side. His male beauty almost took her breath away. He looked like those hot man-candy pictures her friends posted on Facebook and she licked her lips as her gaze zeroed in on his impressive erection. He was hot and hard and ready for her.

Her hands slid up his muscled thighs and wrapped around him, her fingers barely touching. She laved her tongue around the purplish-red mushroom head of his cock and giggled when she heard him groan deep from his throat as if he was in real pain. If this hurt, she was about to torture the fuck out of him.

* * * * *

Presley's tongue was making him crazy and taking him right to the edge. She was running it up and down his cock and swiping his balls before returning to the head to trace the slit. His fingers tangled in her long hair to get some control, but her naughty mouth played by its own rules. By the time he pulled away from her hot, wet lips, his sac was drawn up tight. He'd be lucky to last a minute inside of her. He needed to cool down if he wanted to savor this first time.

"Easy, honey. I don't want to blow yet."

Presley stuck out her lower lip in a cute pout. "Then we get to start all over again."

"Next time. This time we're going to take it slow. Lie down for me, honey."

Presley settled herself on the cushions and held out her arms, making his heart lurch. She looked so fucking beautiful lying there, her lips swollen from his kisses and sucking his cock. Her creamy skin highlighted like pearls in the glow from the fireplace. Her hair was spread all around her like the halo on the snow angels they'd made earlier. She looked almost too wonderful to touch.

Almost.

He ran his hands up her body from her thighs to her breasts, cupping them and brushing the tips with his thumbs. Her lips parted and her eyes fluttered closed and he felt a surge of power. She was feeling this pleasure he gave to her. He leaned down and captured her mouth with his, letting his tongue delve into its honeyed depths. She tasted sweet and he drew out the kiss until they were both breathless, their hearts beating in time with one another. He grabbed a condom packet and ripped it open before rolling it on.

He eased between her silky thighs and looked deep into her eyes as he pressed forward into her welcoming cunt, her heat wrapping around him. He pushed in slowly, inch by inch, driving them both crazy. By the time he was in to the hilt, she'd wrapped her legs around his middle and dug her fingers into his shoulders. Her pupils had dilated and she sighed as he pulled almost all the way out and thrust back in quickly, making sure his groin rubbed her clit. He wanted her to come again while he was inside her.

Seth wanted to make this time with Presley last, so he started a slow, easy rhythm, determined not to give in to the voices in his head urging him to fuck her faster, ride her harder. Her nails dug into his back.

"Harder, Seth. Faster." Her voice was breathless but he felt her pussy contract around his cock, pulling his balls up tighter and building the pressure in his lower back. He sped up his thrusts until he was pistoning in and out of her, her cunt squeezing his dick as she neared her climax. He balanced on one elbow and reached his other hand between them to rub the swollen nub. With one touch, she went off like a rocket, crying out his name and clamping down on his cock.

It was all he needed to send him over the edge with her, his orgasm traveling from his balls out his cock. He dragged air into his lungs as he shot jets of cum into the condom, her tight pussy caressing him with each spasm. When it was done, he balanced over her, their breathing ragged and their bodies covered with a fine mist of sweat. He let his forehead fall gently against hers, pressing a kiss to her adorable nose.

"Honey, you just about killed me."

He felt her giggle against his body. "If we're dead, it's a hell of a way to go."

Seth levered up and rolled away. "I'll be right back." He headed into the bathroom and disposed of the condom quickly. Snatching the quilt from the back of the couch, he stretched out next to her, pulling it over them. She settled her head on his shoulder and sighed.

Seth stroked her hair and listened to the crackle of the burning logs. He'd had sex more than a few times in his life, but tonight felt different somehow. Presley was as playful inside the bedroom as she was outside of it. Sexy and giving, she'd blown him away with her open sensuality. He was a lucky man to be with her tonight. Seth couldn't predict the future, but they could have something good while she was here. He knew her real goal was to go home to Florida. He couldn't compete with that and wouldn't try.

Presley sat up. "Maybe I should head home. The snow was really coming down earlier. The roads might be bad."

Seth didn't analyze why he didn't want her to go. He had a warm, naked woman next to him and he simply wanted to enjoy it. "I learned to drive in bad weather years ago. But you don't have to go if you don't want to."

She was holding the quilt up to cover her breasts and Seth wanted to tug it down. "You mean spend the night? Is that a good idea? What if someone finds out?"

Seth laughed. "Honey, this is a small town. The town gossips probably already know we just had sex. No such thing as a secret in Harper. I'll get you back to your apartment before the sun comes up. How does that sound?"

"We're keeping a secret from the town. They don't know my real name."

This time Seth gave in to temptation and pulled the quilt away from her bare body. "I don't know your real name. You're Presley to me." He tossed the quilt aside and pulled her down on top of him. "I want you again."

His cock was already hard and raring to go. This woman was going to fuck him into an early grave. He was like a horn-dog teenage boy at the Prom. She placed delicate kisses on his chest and stomach. "I can take anything you got to give, Sheriff. Bring it on."

In the orange glow of the fire, Seth did exactly that until they were exhausted, sore, and barely able to speak. He carried Presley to bed, her head lolling on his shoulder, and tucked her in. He went back into the kitchen to grab a glass of water and stare out the large picture window of his home. The snow was starting to taper off and the moon hung low in the sky. He could have easily taken her home, but he liked it when she was around.

He walked over to the laptop on the kitchen counter and fired it up. When he opened the internet search page, he entered "Randall Simon." It was stupid to read about this guy, but Seth wasn't thinking too straight at the moment. He needed to see what Presley saw in Simon, and what might make a billionaire want to kill an innocent woman.

CHAPTER TEN

She needed another cup of coffee. It wasn't even the butt crack of dawn yet, and Presley was already up, showered, and dressed. Somehow Seth had convinced her to accompany him on his hunting trip this morning. He wanted to bag a turkey for Thanksgiving coming up in a few days and although it was the last thing she wanted to do, he'd promised to take her dancing at the roadhouse if she went with him this morning.

It wasn't the best deal she'd ever made but it was the best she was going to get. In the last month, she had learned quite a bit about Sheriff Seth Reilly. He was stubborn as a proverbial mule. He was also an amazing, passionate lover. She could deal with the former and bask in the latter.

Presley heard Seth's boots on the stairs and poured him a cup of coffee, refilling her own. This roadhouse better really be something. Eliza had been talking it up after going with Alex a few times, but Presley and Seth spent most evenings in low-key mode, watching television or just hanging out. A couple of times they'd gone horseback riding on the Reilly family ranch and she'd ended up sore, which of course necessitated a nude rubdown from Seth with fragrant oils and strong hands.

Seth pushed open the door, his wide shoulder taking up the entire space. He was already scowling and it was only five in the morning. She decided she'd tease him about being dressed head to toe in camouflage later in the day after his mood had improved. She handed him his coffee with a smile.

"What have I done now? You're already in a bad mood. It wasn't my idea to get up in the middle of the night, you know. I tried to talk you out of it."

"Your front door was unlocked. Did you leave it that way all night?"

Despite not a peep from anyone trying to kill her for over a month, Seth still fussed over her like a mother hen. "No. I unlocked it a few minutes ago. I knew you'd be here any second. You're always early for everything."

His scowl softened as he drank his coffee. He liked good coffee almost as much as she did. "I like to be on time, that's all."

Presley almost spit out her coffee laughing. "I sure as hell wasn't leaving without you. The only turkeys I know about are in the local store. And speaking of that, why are we braving the cold and the elements to kill a turkey with our bare hands when we can just buy one from Sue Ann?"

Sue Ann owned the local grocery and knew all the good gossip, Presley had learned. If anyone wanted to know something, all they had to do was talk to Sue Ann.

Seth gave her a look Presley had come to know as his "patience look." He wore it quite a bit around children, old people, and herself. "We are not killing the turkeys with our bare hands. I am using a bow and arrow. I thought this would be something fun for us to do together, but I see you're not approaching this with an open mind. Are you ready to go?"

"Yes, Kimosabi. Let me fill the thermos." Presley giggled. The thought of Seth shooting a bow and arrow was amusing and kind of hot. He was a man's man, hunting, fishing, and playing pickup football with his brothers, but watching him in action was something completely different. She filled the tall thermos, bundled up in her coat, scarf and gloves, and hoisted her purse on her shoulder. "If I didn't have an open mind, I wouldn't be up and dressed, babe."

She thought he might laugh too but instead he looked taken aback. "You aren't taking your purse, are you? You can't take a purse hunting, Presley."

She looked down at the large bag. Everything she needed was right there. "Why not?"

He shrugged. "We'll be walking. It'll weigh you down. Besides, what do you need with all that stuff?"

"There's stuff I need. I can switch to a smaller bag, I guess."

Seth waited, his toe tapping impatiently as she moved a few essentials from her large purse to a smaller bag that fitted across her body. She held out her hands so he could take a good look at the outfit she was rocking. He'd asked her to dress in greens and earth tones and she'd complied with khaki green pants and a beige sweater. "Ready." She poked his chest. Man, did he get a stick up his butt sometimes or what? "Stop being pissy. It took like one minute to do that. All the turkeys won't be gone by the time we get there."

Seth sighed, his features relaxing. "Sorry. I guess I'm a little intense when it comes to hunting. I'm very competitive. At least that's what I've been told."

"No shit." Presley snorted. "But it's just me this morning. I'm not going to shoot any turkeys."

Seth tapped her nose as he helped her into the truck. "No, you won't. You don't have a hunting license. This is simply for your Montana education. When I say I'm competitive, I mean with my brothers or my friends."

They drove for quite a while until they were even more in the middle of nowhere than they normally were. There wasn't much around but some trees and bushes. Once they stopped and got out of the truck, Seth pulled her behind a large bush and pressed his finger to his lips. "We need to be quiet and listen."

She nodded and he pulled out his bow and arrow, along with a strange box from his pocket. He rubbed the lid against the box and the friction, to her surprise, sounded just like a turkey. Presley slapped her hand over her mouth to hold in the laughter and shifted her eyes so she was looking anywhere but at Seth. If she looked at him, she was sure she would bust out laughing.

"What's so funny?" Seth's voice was a low hiss in her ear. She shook her head and her eyes widened innocently. She swallowed hard and kept the sleeve of her coat pressed to her lips. He obviously didn't see the humor in the situation. She, however, couldn't wait to write about it in her notebook. This was a gem of a story.

It felt like ten hours later but it had probably only been a fraction of that and Presley was getting antsy and bored. All they were doing was sitting on the cold ground, sipping coffee, and not saying a word. It was probably Seth's dream date since he wasn't hearing her voice ringing in his ears, but it wasn't what you would call fun for her. She was about to ask him if she could get up and stretch her legs when a bush about twenty feet away started rustling.

Seth was instantly on alert, going up on his knees, bow at the ready. She watched as a large brown and white turkey ambled into the open.

Turkeys actually do gobble.

The turkey ruffled its feathers wide and strutted toward them as Seth pulled on the bow and lined up for the kill. Something lurched inside of her and she tugged at his arm, knowing she couldn't allow him to kill the bird. It was just too cruel. The darn thing looked just like the turkeys she'd seen in pictures growing up.

Seth bit off a curse and lowered the bow, his brows drawn together and his mouth unsmiling. "What," he whispered, "is wrong? We're going to lose him."

She nodded, her eyes filling with tears. "Don't kill him, Seth." She kept her voice low when she really wanted to scream and flap her arms to scare the fowl away.

His eyes scanned her face and his expression softened. "Fuck, shit, Presley. You knew we were going hunting. You knew we were going to kill a turkey, honey."

She nodded. "I know. But thinking it and seeing it are two different things. He looks just like the turkeys I used to make with construction paper when I was in grade school. I bet he has a family, Seth. I bet they love him, like your family loves you."

* * * * *

Presley hadn't said how her family loved her. She'd said how Seth's family loved him. Seth set his bow on the ground in defeat, knowing he wouldn't be bagging a turkey today. How could he do it with Presley's tragic expression talking about familial love? Her own family was a piss-poor example of how a family should be. Seth's mother, seeing Presley's delight in the Reilly togetherness, had quickly taken her under her wing. Seth had considered discouraging it, after all, he didn't know how long she'd be here—but he hadn't. Presley simply seemed to fit in with his family, despite growing up three thousand miles away. His mother was teaching Presley to bake bread, for fuck's sake. Presley had managed to hook his mother on those fancy coffees. His mother, along with half the town, came by every day to have a cup of designer java with Presley. Seth's office coffee budget had doubled in the last month.

"Relax, honey. I won't kill the turkey." Seth gave the bird one last regretful look. The turkey actually looked like he was laughing at Seth's predicament before waddling away back under the bushes and brush.

Her bottom lip was trembling. "Are you mad, Seth?"

Seth rubbed his forehead with his hand and sighed. "No, I'm not mad. I am frustrated. Looking at this with hindsight, it was a lousy idea to bring you today. For some crazy reason, not clear to me now, I thought you would find this interesting."

Presley nodded vigorously. "It was. Very interesting."

"You are a terrible liar, Presley Lawson. I can see right through you."

She fell back on her heels. "Okay, it was dead boring. Are you happy now?"

He started packing his bow away. "Not particularly. It just shows that we don't have a lot in common."

She tilted her head in question. "Your other girlfriends went hunting with you?"

"Well...no." The question confused him for some reason, and he wasn't sure why. He'd wanted her to come today because, shit, he liked spending time with her. He wanted her to like the things he liked. She was completely hooked on Broncos football now, he was happy to say. She even liked the jalapeño poppers he favored as a game snack.

"Then why did you ask me to go with you?"

He opened his mouth to answer then shut it. He was a damn idiot and he didn't know why he'd invited her. He simply had. "I thought it would be something different than you were used to in Florida."

Her eyebrows went up. "You're right about that. Can we go? I'm hungry."

Seth nodded and led them back to the truck, tossing his stuff in the back before helping her climb in. It had been a waste of a morning.

"You're mad," Presley stated.

"I'm not mad," Seth said. "I told you I'm just frustrated. I'll be going home empty-handed, which means we'll be buying our turkey this year."

"Sue Ann will appreciate the business."

Presley was always thinking about the happiness of others. "I'm glad we could help."

He shoved the key into the ignition and turned over the engine as her hand covered his. His eyes widened as she swung onto his lap, straddling his thighs, her body tucked between him and the steering wheel. "I can't let this be a completely lost morning. I think I know by now how to make my sheriff smile."

He reached around her and flicked on the heater. If she was thinking what he thought she was thinking, they'd need it. He leaned over and moved the seat back, grateful he had purchased the double cab model.

She pushed aside his coat and ran her hands over his chest, making his cock hard behind his zipper. He tangled his fingers in her hair and pulled her down for a kiss.

He'd learned early kissing Presley was like kissing no other woman. She put everything, her entire body and soul, into her kiss, until he felt about ten feet tall. She acted as if kissing him was the most important thing in the world. She was like that about everything. Whatever she was doing, she did it all out. She was passionate and he drank up every bit of it with his lips and hands.

They were tugging at each other's clothes, their breathing getting heavy as they stole kisses and caresses in between a piece of clothing getting tossed away. It was colder than hell outside the truck but the temperature inside was zooming higher every minute. Seth cupped her breasts and lifted them so he could tease them with his tongue. The nubs tightened under his lips and he suckled first one then the other. Presley dug her fingers into his biceps and let her head fall back with a moan.

He loved hearing the sounds she made when they were like this. He was never in any doubt as to how much she wanted him or liked what he was doing. He pressed a finger inside her wet cunt and she clenched on him, letting him know exactly what she'd do when he was inside of her. Her cream dripped on his hand as he finger-fucked her, adding a second digit to find the sweet spot that sent her into orbit. He knew he'd hit the jackpot when her thighs tightened against his and she cried out with a mini-orgasm.

"Seth!"

Her pussy spasmed around his finger and he pulled it from her drenched slit. He needed to fuck her now. He reached for his pants and the condom stuffed in the front pocket, but came up with her pants instead.

"Shit." Seth leaned to the side, trying not to dislodge her on top of him. With his fingertips, he found his slacks and snagged the condom, ripping it open with his teeth. She plucked it from his fingers and rolled it on his hard cock trapped between their bodies. She lifted up and he grasped her hips, slowly lowering her onto him inch by inch. When Presley was stuffed full of cock, she locked her gaze with his.

"Fuck me, Sheriff." Her voice was husky and it amped up Seth's arousal even higher. Fucking Presley was sublime, her tight cunt hugging him. She rode his dick hard, their bodies slapping together in the close confines of the truck cab.

He could feel the pressure building in his balls, wanted to hold back, but Presley had other ideas. She leaned forward and bit down on his earlobe as he slammed into her.

"Yes," she hissed, her cunt rippling with her own orgasm, her body quivering. He couldn't hold back any longer, his own climax coming over him like a tidal wave. She tucked her head between his neck and shoulder as her shuddering subsided and his breathing grew more normal. He pulled her head back by her hair and grinned.

"Woman, I haven't had sex in my truck since I was in high school."

"Then you were long past due. I knew I could get you to smile." She grinned right back at him. "This is a pretty comfy truck. I wouldn't mind doing it in here every now and then."

Instantly, his mind conjured up a vision of Presley riding shotgun naked as the day she was born. He groaned and shook his head to clear his brain.

"You're trouble. I am a man in trouble." But he liked it, if he were honest.

She lifted herself off of him, wincing as she did so.

"Shit, did I hurt you, honey?" He was so much bigger and stronger than she was. Seth needed to be more careful. Presley was such a little thing.

"No." she shook her head. "Just a little sore, that's all."

Now he really felt guilty.

She pushed at his shoulder. "From horseback riding, you pervert. Not riding you. Although the way we go at it, it wouldn't be surprising. You're a horny devil." She waggled her eyebrows as she pulled up her panties and hunted for her bra in their pile of discarded clothes.

The decision to make love had always seemed mutual, but perhaps Presley felt pressure to fulfill what he knew was a strong sexual appetite. A sexual appetite that had only grown sharper since meeting this woman. Before her, he'd gone several months in between women without much thought about it.

He shifted in the seat, tugging on his boxers and jeans. "I guess I am." He couldn't meet her eyes.

She grabbed his shirt right out of his hands, holding it like a game of "keep-away". "For the record, I wasn't complaining. I like that you want me all the time. I want you the same way."

He breathed a little easier and motioned for his shirt. "I was worried for a minute you might feel, you know, pressured."

An eyebrow arched. "Do you honestly think you could pressure me into having sex with you, Seth Reilly? Really?"

It did sound absurd. She had him chasing his tail on a pretty much daily basis. There was no doubt Presley Lawson was a woman to be reckoned with. Seth reckoned with her on a regular basis.

"No, honey, probably not. I just needed to be sure."

She buttoned up her pants and found her bra wedged under the seat. "Then be sure to feed me afterward. I'm hungry, Sheriff."

He finished dressing and put the truck into gear. "I won't let you starve, honey. Breakfast coming up."

He headed into town feeling better than he ever had after a hunting trip and he didn't even have a turkey.

* * * * *

Presley patted her stomach, now pleasantly full of pancakes and sausage. The pancakes she'd ordered from the smiling waitress in the diner. The sausage was stolen from Seth's plate. She was enjoying her third cup of coffee when Seth's phone started buzzing on the table. He put down his forkful of hash browns and picked up the phone.

"Um, yeah, I can talk. Just let me get to a quieter spot."

Seth gave her an apologetic look and headed out the back door of the diner into the alley. The diner was busy and loud this Monday morning. Despite the snow and the cold, Harper was bustling with activity. Thanksgiving was this week and everyone was shopping and decorating. Seth told her it was easier to shop and prepare for Christmas now when the weather wasn't too bad than in a week or two when the snow and cold were worse. Presley had pointed to her laptop on the desk and replied she knew how to shop when the weather was poor. As for decorations, she was looking forward to putting up a small tree in her apartment and helping Seth decorate his home. She spent most of her time there anyway.

Trask came in the door of the diner and spotted her. He waved as he ordered his coffee at the counter before coming over to greet her. She'd grown quite fond of him. He had a sweet, old-fashioned way about him that always made her smile. He was also an incurable romantic, constantly hinting to her about how happy Seth looked these days. The whole town had turned into matchmakers, giving her and Seth indulgent smiles when they would walk down Main Street hand in hand or share a plate of fries at the barbecue joint. She felt like they were the reality television for this town.

"Hey, Presley. Where's Seth?"

Presley nodded to the back door. "He had to take a call and it's pretty loud in here. What brings you to town today?"

"I needed to restock the pantry. I thought the crowds wouldn't be too bad today but I was wrong. The grocery store was already busy this morning. I saw the Sheriff's station was closed. You and Seth taking the day off?"

Presley chuckled. "Apparently, this is normal on a holiday week. There are deputies on duty but no one comes into the office. Seth will be on duty tonight, but he told me not to worry about the paperwork and such until next week."

Trask winked at her and accepted his to-go coffee from the waitress. "Enjoy your time off. It sounds like you've earned it. You've revolutionized the place the way I heard it."

The office had desperately needed it. "I've tried. Seth didn't make it easy."

Trask laughed and headed for the door. "I'm sure you're right. Have a good day, Presley, and Happy Thanksgiving."

"Happy Thanksgiving, Trask."

Presley tried to relax and wait for Seth but her gaze kept falling on a man who appeared to be in his late twenties or early thirties. His hair was cut shorter than most of the men in Harper and his skin wasn't as tan. She signaled to the waitress for more coffee as Seth returned, an unhappy expression on his face.

"I thought I'd wiped that frown off your face earlier, Sheriff. You're all grumpy again." She nodded to the man in the corner booth. "Do you know who he is?"

Seth twisted around and quickly looked at the stranger. "Why do you ask? Has he broken the law? We do get people passing through town on occasion."

"No," Presley shook her head. "He doesn't look like the usual hunter or fisherman tourist, that's all."

Seth sighed. "He's not a tourist. He's a Fed. Every week or so, they send a Fed or two here to check on you. I get an email with their pictures so I don't freak out when someone is watching you."

"I've been here all this time and I didn't know? Why didn't you tell me?" Presley pressed her lips together. She didn't like Seth keeping secrets from her in the least.

"What would you have done with the information? Evan told you he would be checking on you. Would it make you feel more safe or less? Can you say you're surprised?"

"I thought they trusted you to keep me safe?" Presley traced a pattern in the sugar spilled on the table.

"They do, but they wouldn't be doing their jobs if they didn't see you with their own eyes every now and then."

Seth had effectively taken the wind out of her sails. He was right. She should have known they wouldn't drop her in the middle of nowhere and never check on her. She hadn't really processed Evan's statement that night. She'd had other things on her mind.

The waitress refilled their coffees and bustled away. Seth looked around the diner and then leaned forward in his chair. "That was Evan on the phone."

Her body stiffened in response. She'd almost forgotten why she was in this town. It was easy to forget as she became more involved in her new life and less enmeshed in the old. Tampa seemed very far away at the moment.

"What did he want?" She waited for the answer. Just when she thought her life was her own again, something came along to disabuse that notion.

"He said they're ready to convene the Grand Jury. They're ready to indict Simon. They need your testimony."

This was why they were protecting her. She'd always known that fact. She sipped her coffee and tried to appear nonchalant. "When and where?"

Seth was gazing at her, his eyebrows raised. It was clear he wasn't convinced she was as calm as she looked.

"Tampa Federal Courthouse. December tenth. He gave me the name of a hotel for us that will have their protection. We can fly you in and out quickly."

She nodded. "They get what they want and I get my life back. It's a fair trade."

Seth fiddled with his spoon. "Evan didn't say anything about you being released from protection."

"Did you ask?"

"No," Seth admitted. "I was busy getting the logistics for getting you in and out of Tampa."

"Out? Evan said back out then?"

"He did." Seth nodded. "I can call him back for you if you like."

She shook her head, holding her coffee cup with both hands and letting the warmth of the ceramic seep into her cold fingers. "There's no need. It sounds like he made things clear. It appears the plan is for me to come back here, at least for a little while. I just want to get this over with. I'm not sure I know anything that's going to help them."

Disappointment at having to come back to Harper warred with happiness at getting more time with Seth. When the time came, she had to admit she would miss him. She genuinely liked him and there weren't many men she could say that about.

Seth sipped his coffee. "Did you see anything that made you wonder what was going on? Anything at all?"

Presley felt a flash of annoyance. If she said no, she was an oblivious idiot and if she said yes, it made her look foolish and weak. It was a stupid, no-win question and she didn't like it at all.

"How do you want me to answer that, Seth? Would it be better if I was totally ignorant or if I suspected something but did nothing? Which is better to you?"

Seth scraped his hand down his face. "I'm not accusing you of anything, honey. It was just a question."

"It was a trick question. Like if I asked you if my butt looked big in these jeans. If you say yes, well, then I have an oversized load and you won't get sex for the foreseeable future. If you say no, well, do I have a big, fat ass and it just looks small in these particular jeans or do I not have a big butt? Either way? You're not getting laid."

That got a peek of a smile out of Seth. "I promise no matter which way you answer, I'll have sex with you."

She thought about kicking him in the shin but she wasn't the violent type. "I don't think I know anything. I clearly remember the invoices and emails, but I never saw anything that looked out of place. I'm going out on a limb here as I'm not a criminal, but I doubt they'd leave a paper trail of their illegal activities."

Seth nodded. "I've found that criminals are rarely very bright but I've never dealt with something like selling arms to terrorists. How does one even do that?"

Presley shrugged. "I have no idea. Nothing I saw in email or paper even hinted at something like that."

Seth stroked his chin. "I bet there were a lot of emails, though. It would be hard, if not impossible, to remember details like that months later."

Presley pushed away her empty coffee cup. "I have a good memory, Seth. I didn't see anything that raised any flags. Besides, the longer I worked there, the more Randall had me working on personal things. He was having his house renovated and he asked me to manage the project. It was practically a full time job. I wasn't in the office much the last four months."

She'd only worked for him for six. The fact was she hadn't spent much time at all in the office learning the business.

Seth picked up his hat. "My job is to make sure you get to Tampa safe and sound, not to try and figure out this case. That's Evan's job, thankfully. Are you ready?"

Presley pulled on her coat and gloves. "Where are we going?"

"To the store to buy a turkey, then to Mom's to tell her why we bought her a turkey."

Presley felt her face get warm. "Why don't you let me buy the turkey since it's my fault and all?"

"No way, honey." Seth laughed. "It wasn't your fault. It was mine. I should have known better."

He was taking the whole turkey hunting thing much better than earlier. "I still think you should let me buy the turkey."

"I have another way you can pay."

She heard the promise in his words and felt her body get very warm indeed. "Oh yeah? What did you have in mind?"

Seth leaned down and whisper raunchy, filthy suggestions in her ear. "Do we have time before your shift?" she asked.

He glanced at his watch. "If we buy a turkey, and visit with Mom for a little while, I'm thinking we'll have the entire afternoon to explore those ideas."

Presley grinned. "Let's get this show on the road, Sheriff."

She let Seth lead the way and watched the sway of his very fine ass in front of her. The day was turning out much better than it had started.

CHAPTER ELEVEN

Every member of the Reilly household was in attendance on Thanksgiving Day. Presley and Seth had shown up early to help Marion start dinner, or rather Presley had helped Marion while Seth had gone outside to chop some wood so his father wouldn't have to. It was fun to be in the kitchen cooking and talking with Sarah and Cindy, the wives of Seth's brothers.

Presley checked out the kitchen window to make sure Seth was still outside before turning back to the three women. "I was hoping you could help me figure out what to get Seth for Christmas."

Cindy, a pert redhead, smiled and shifted ten-month-old Amie to her other hip. Amie was in a phase where she only wanted to be held by her mother. Even her own father sometimes made her howl in outrage. "Seems to me, Seth has been smiling more in the last month than in the entire ten years before combined. He actually has fun every now and then. I think you've already given him a gift. All of us, really."

Presley waved off the praise. "He just needed someone to get him out of his routine. I haven't done anything special."

Marion shook her head and smiled. "You are special, Presley. You've worked a miracle with my son. You two are perfect together. He's the exact right foil for your sparkle."

"Sparkle? I don't sparkle." Presley wasn't even sure what it meant.

Sarah nodded. "You do sparkle. Everything seems to light up around you. You're fun, happy, and easy to be around. People seem to be drawn to you. I wish I was like that. I never know what to say to people."

Presley shrugged. "I never do either. That's why I just let them do all the talking. It's easier on me."

Cindy laughed. "Is that the secret? Letting them talk? If it is, I'm in big trouble."

Marion shook a spoon in Cindy's direction. "We wouldn't have you any other way, young lady."

Cindy popped a piece of cheese from a platter into her mouth. "Does your family mind that you're here for Thanksgiving, Presley? They must miss you. Will you be visiting them soon?"

Presley knew there would eventually be questions like this. She'd decided to stick as close to the truth as she could without telling the entire sordid story. "My parents are dead. Well, Mom is, and my real dad is somewhere, but I couldn't tell you where. My stepfather passed away a few years ago so that just leaves my stepsister and unfortunately, we're not close."

Marion's expression turned sympathetic. "I'm so sorry. Were you young when your mother passed on?"

"I was twenty." She didn't bring up how it was one more thing gone wrong in her life along with Oliver. Presley, or Katie, didn't make great choices in her life. Presley was trying to do better.

Cindy shook her head. "So young, but there's never a good age to lose someone you love. It's too bad you're not close to your sister. Are you near in ages?"

"She's five years older than me. I think I frustrate her, honestly."

Sarah popped the stuffing pan into the oven. "Why? You seem fine to me."

It was hard to put into words. Nora had never said anything straight out. Neither had her mother or stepfather. It had simply been a feeling Presley had had. "I'm kind of the screw-up in the family. I didn't do super well in high school, but my sister did. She's really smart. When I went to college, I didn't really know what I wanted to be when I grew up. I was kind of directionless, to be honest. Eventually, I took a break from it thinking I would go back. I never did, much to my family's disappointment. In the meantime, my sister got married to a successful attorney and started her own computer business. I just sort of drifted from job to job."

She didn't mention Nora's subsequent divorce. Presley had liked Nora's husband and always felt a little sorry for him. He let Nora boss him around terribly.

Marion smiled. "Then you drifted here. Thank goodness. I think we'll keep you."

Cindy sipped her iced tea. "I didn't do that well in high school either. Frankly, I hated high school."

Presley had loved high school. She'd dated every weekend, been Prom queen, and Student Class Vice-President. She hadn't done very well academically.

"I'm not very ambitious." Presley shrugged. "I think my stepfather wanted me to marry well. I remember him saying it didn't matter how I did in school as long as I married well. I'm still not sure what that means, but I think he wanted me to find a rich husband so my failure in academia wouldn't matter."

Sarah stuck a fork in the potatoes to check if they were done. "Money isn't everything."

"I think that would be news to my family," Presley said.

Marion opened the oven to check the turkey thermometer. "I'm glad you're here today. We're thankful you came into our lives." Presley felt a warmth in the vicinity of her heart. She adored Seth's family. Norman Rockwell couldn't have found more wonderful people. "Now, as for what you should get Seth for Christmas, I have an idea."

"Thank goodness. He's the man who has everything."

Marion wiped her hands on a dishtowel and joined her at the table. "He's been complaining that the case he carries his bow in is worn out. He needs a new one."

Presley remembered the case from earlier in the week. It had seen better days. "That's a great idea. Can I buy it online?"

Marion pointed to the laptop on the far kitchen counter. "I can show you a really nice one online and you can order it, if you like."

"That would be great. I don't have my own laptop yet. I use the one in the office."

Cindy laughed. "Now when Seth asks us what to get you, we know what to tell him."

Presley shook her head. "It's too expensive. I'll get one soon."

"What happened to your last computer?" Sarah asked, settling herself in a chair.

It was incinerated in a fire.

"It stopped booting up one day."

That's kind of the truth.

"Things just aren't built to last anymore," Marion said as she typed on the keyboard of the laptop. "Here you are. I think he'd love this one."

Presley peered over Marion's shoulder. The case looked sturdy and was reasonably priced. There was even an option to have his initials stamped into the leather.

"This is awesome. Thank goodness I asked you."

Marion stepped aside. "You can use this to order if you like. You'll just have to change who's logged in."

Presley nodded. "I have an account here." Luckily, the store was one of Presley's favorite online retailers. She clicked on the Buy button as Seth and his brothers were stomping in the back door. She couldn't let Seth see what she was doing. It would ruin the surprise. She quickly entered her login and password so the screen with his present would disappear. A few hurried clicks later the transaction was done.

And not a moment too soon. Seth was right behind her, wrapping his arms around her middle and kissing her neck. She slapped at his hands.

"Not in front of your mother."

His chuckle was warm and deep. "I think my mother knows we hug and kiss. If we didn't, she'd be pretty worried about us."

Presley turned in his arms and looked up into his face. This morning when he'd woken her to make love, his jaw had been covered with stubble and his hair askew. His blond hair was still tousled from the wind but he was now clean-shaven and smelled of soap and toothpaste. She couldn't decide which way he looked sexier. He was devastating to her equilibrium no matter what. It wasn't fair men woke up looking so damn hot.

She tugged at the zipper on his jacket. "Your nose is red from the cold. Can I get you some coffee?"

Marion laughed and waved the spoon she was wielding in a pot of cranberry sauce. "Don't spoil him, Presley. Make him get his own."

Presley hated to admit it, but she loved spoiling Seth. He certainly returned the favor in a myriad of ways. He was, after all, protecting her with his life, although there'd been nothing to protect her from since she came to town.

Seth shrugged off his coat. "In the interest of family harmony, I'll get my own coffee. I'll even get Jason and Sam coffee."

Sam shook his head. "None for me. I'm going to watch the pre-game shows."

Jason grabbed a handful of cheese cubes. "I'm right behind you, bro."

Seth gave her a pleading look and she shooed him away with her hands. "Go on. Go watch the game or whatever. The women will do all the real work."

Cindy grinned. "We didn't tell you? Reilly family tradition is the men do the dishes afterward."

"I like that tradition." Presley smiled at Seth, but he only grimaced.

"I'm going into the living room before I get roped into anything else," Seth said.

Marion watched her son leave the room. She motioned to Sarah. "They're all watching the game. It's time."

Sarah grinned and rummaged way in the back of the packed refrigerator before holding up a bottle of Chardonnay triumphantly. "I got it. You hid it really well this year, Mom."

"We don't want the men to horn in on this tradition. It belongs to the Reilly women alone."

Presley started to move toward the door. She wasn't really a Reilly woman, but Marion put her arm around Presley's shoulders and led her to the kitchen table. The wine was opened and everyone's glass was filled except for Sarah, who was given iced tea instead. Marion raised her glass.

"As is the tradition, the oldest Reilly woman goes first. We tell each other one thing we regret and one dream. I regret not going back to teaching after the boys started school. I dream about George and me having a vacation in Alaska." Marion drank the glass down before slapping it on the table. "Cindy?"

Cindy held up her glass. "I regret not going after Sam earlier. I dream about having six children." Cindy knocked back the glass of wine quickly. "Sarah?"

Sarah raised her glass of tea. "I regret not telling my brother I loved him that day that he died. If I had known I'd never see him again, I would have. I dream of becoming a successful graphic artist." Sarah drank the tea and turned to Presley. "Presley?"

Tears pricked the back of Presley's eyes. She hadn't really thought about it until this moment but she had so much to be thankful for. She raised her glass. "I regret not going back to college. That was a mistake. I let myself be intimidated." She hesitated but the feeling was too strong not to verbalize. "I dream about becoming a famous writer someday." She drank her wine down and smiled. She really and truly felt like a Reilly woman today. It was only temporary but there was no harm in enjoying it for a few hours. It wouldn't hurt anyone or anything.

Except maybe her.

She would miss these women when she left.

* * * * *

Nora Shefflin pushed open the door of her office and settled behind the desk. She'd only planned a half day today due to the holiday yesterday but some things needed to be done. She reviewed projected revenue and current expenses every Friday morning and today would be no exception. Her computer consulting business wasn't a gigantic money maker, but it did decently enough. She flipped open the laptop and opened the weekly reports but her concentration was jolted by a buzzing noise from the top of the file cabinet. Nora's assistant, Diane, had plugged in Katie's cell phone there. Of course, Diane had no idea it was Katie's phone. She probably thought it belonged to Nora.

She frowned and walked over, unplugging her stepsister's cell phone and sat back down at her desk. Nora wasn't sure why she was holding on to Katie's phone, but she couldn't seem to get rid of it. When the maître d at the restaurant had handed it to Nora the week after Katie had supposedly died in a car bomb, Nora had been shocked. It was the only thing left of her sister's. The bomb had taken care of Katie's car and a house fire had destroyed everything else.

But it didn't kill her.

Of that, Nora was sure. She hadn't believed for one minute the line the Feds had given her about not being able to see the body as it had been blown into pieces. Nora had specifically told Joe she wanted Katie dead, but she wanted to see the remains. Then and only then would she believe her stepsister dead.

There was also the question as to why the Feds were involved in the first place. When she'd asked, they'd said the city and county officers didn't have a bomb investigation squad so they were called in.

A bunch of fucking liars.

Katie was somehow still alive and probably on the run, perhaps with the help of the Feds. Nora was at her wit's end looking for her but it looked like her search might be coming to an end. Katie wasn't very smart and it had only been a matter of time before she showed her hand. Then Nora would make sure the job got done.

Katie would be dead, and Nora's life would be better. Much better.

Nora swiped the screen and pressed a few buttons. An email had come in. The first few weeks after Katie died, her phone had gone off a few times and emails still came in. After word was spread of her untimely death, the calls had stopped and the emails dwindled. The phone hadn't gone off for over a week. It had been hard to be patient, but Nora had waited this long. She could wait a little longer.

A quick look showed Katie had received an email confirming an order made the day before. Nora opened the email and smiled. Katie had finally used her account and credit card at a large online retailer to make a purchase. Nora tapped her fingernail on the oak desk before picking up the receiver of her desk phone and dialing an old friend.

"Jerry? It's Nora Shefflin. Happy Thanksgiving."

"Nora, I haven't heard from you in a long time. Happy Thanksgiving. To what do I owe the honor?"

She liked a man who got right to the point. "Jerry, I need a favor. You're still a detective with the county, right? My stepsister died a little over a month ago, as I'm sure you heard, and today she got an email confirming an online order. I think someone is using her account illegally. Can you check it out?"

"Sure. I'm actually off duty for the holiday. Do you need it today?"

Nora looked out the window of her office and over the calm waters of Tampa Bay. She needed the information yesterday. "If someone is using Katie's credit card, I don't want them to go on a Black Friday shopping spree. I know this is your day off, but it would mean a lot to me if you could find out what's going on with this. I would be grateful, Jerry."

There was a short silence. "Sure. It may take me a little longer, though, since so many people are off the day after Thanksgiving. You're right. We can't let some thief run up her card. Although, you know, Nora, you wouldn't be responsible for paying the bill."

She was well aware of that fact. The bill wasn't her concern. "I know. It's the principle of the thing, Jerry. I didn't even know about the account. I should have thought to cancel her credit cards but I never got around to it."

Jerry chuckled. "You are a principled woman. You can't think of everything in a time of grief. You've been through so much. Losing your sister had to be difficult. I'll look into it and call you back."

Playing the bereaved sister suited her. People always wanted to come to her aid.

"I appreciate your help. Thank you. I'll be waiting for your call." She gave Jerry the particulars of the account and the order.

Nora hung up the phone and picked up the cell phone. She studied the wallpaper picture on the screen of Katie and her two best friends posing on a girl's night out. They all looked young and happy, as if nothing in life could touch them. Nora had talked to those two girls at Katie's memorial service. They'd loved her, but then everyone had loved Katie.

Nora pressed the button at the top of the phone and the screen went blank. She sat back in her chair, propping her feet on top of the desk in satisfaction.

It was only a matter of time.

CHAPTER TWELVE

Presley was happily drifting in a dream state when a warm, male body pressed up against her back and an arm reached around her waist, pulling her close.

"This better be Channing Tatum," she mumbled, burrowing deeper into the warm covers. It was damn cold this morning. She felt and heard a chuckle in her ear.

"Channing Tatum, huh? That's the last time you watch Magic Mike with Eliza."

She wiggled her bottom against his groin and found him naked and hard. He'd worked the night shift after Thanksgiving dinner last night. Seth had insisted she climb into his bed to sleep so he could cuddle with her when he got home. It looked like he had more on his mind than simply a snuggle. With any luck, he'd fuck her brains out.

His hand came down on her ass cheek smartly and she yelped as the heat pushed the sleepy fog from her brain. "Ouch! Hey, that was mean."

She didn't really mean it. Seth had never given her an actual spanking, but he'd smacked her bottom a few times in and out of bed and it never failed to get her juices flowing. She wondered what she'd have to do to get him to give her a real spanking over his knee, just like in one of her erotic romance books.

"You were wriggling all around and grinding up against me. That's mean too. It's torture to a tired man who only wants to get a few hours of sleep."

She turned so she was facing him and reached down to encircle his cock with her hand. "This doesn't feel like a man who wants to get some sleep. This feels like a man who wants a sex slave in his bed."

She held her breath as she threw out the suggestion, unsure of his reaction. Seth was all alpha male in bed, but he'd very carefully stayed on the safe side of the line. She was hungry for him to take real control in the bedroom. She wanted him to give her a real spanking, and she definitely wanted to be tied up. There were so many things she'd read about that she was dying to try.

"What would I do with a sex slave?" His voice was tight and controlled.

"Anything you wanted to do. Your wish would be her command. She'd obey you in all things. In the bedroom. She'd be your sex toy."

There was a long silence and she only heard his breath going in and out. Finally, he eased her hand off of his cock. "You know, Presley, since the moment I met you I've been off balance. You're a woman who says what she wants and how she feels. Except for right now. You're playing a game and I'm not sure I know the rules, honey. Just tell me what you want. If it's in my power to give it to you, you know I will."

The morning sun was starting to slant through the windows and Presley propped up a few pillows and rested back on them. He was right. If she wanted something, she needed to fucking say it. Seth was many things, but he sure wasn't a mind reader. Not by a long shot.

"I've read some books," she started, "and some of the things I've read seem really exciting. I've never met a man I've wanted to do these things with until you. You're more like the heroes in the stories than anyone I've ever met before."

Even in the dim light she could see the color wash over Seth's cheekbones. "I'm not any kind of hero, honey. I'm just a guy."

"A swaggering, alpha male who likes to be in charge kind of guy."

He quirked an eyebrow. "I'm the first one of those you met? Welcome to Montana."

Presley rolled her eyebrows. "Yeah, I'm getting the idea. Talking with Eliza is the only way I've known you aren't a mutant from outer space."

Seth sat up in bed. "I'm trying not to take this personally, Presley. Are you saying we lack something in the sex department?"

"No!" Shit, she was handling this all wrong. "You're the best lover I've ever had. You're—" His grin started to widen and she realized she may have created a monster. "Stop smiling. I haven't slept with that many men so it's not that great of an achievement."

Seth was still smiling and she shoved his shoulder. "I mean it. Stop it. You asshole. What I'm trying to say, and badly, is that I'd like to make things even better and experiment."

"Honey, you are the only woman I know who would call a man an asshole and ask him to do kinky things in the bedroom all in one sentence. You're one of a kind."

"Will you?" She ran her toe down his calf and his cock jumped in reaction.

"Will I what?" Seth's gaze had landed on the swell of her breasts. He was clearly distracted from the original question.

"Do kinky things with me in the bedroom?"

Seth pushed her down into the mattress, his large body hovering over hers, and his arms caging her in. Her arousal immediately went into overdrive at his display of dominance, her nipples poking through the thin material of one of Seth's old T-shirts.

"Yes, I will. I take it you want me to take control? Give the orders? And the punishments?"

His voice deepened at the last sentence and she shivered in response, her pussy creaming at the promise in his tone. She nodded vigorously, her throat tight with excitement. Seth sat back up and she felt the loss of his body heat.

"Fine. My first order is for you to get out of bed. Stand right there." He pointed to a spot on the floor. "Stand there and strip for your master."

She opened her mouth but he placed his finger over her lips, shaking his head. "Sex slaves do not speak or get to voice their opinions. Their only job is to obey and be used for their master's sexual pleasure. Stand up or be punished."

The steel running through his voice overrode any desire to see what he'd do if she disobeyed. She scrambled out of bed, the cold hitting her as the covers slid off. Seth was fulfilling her greatest fantasy. She couldn't wait to hand him the control and simply relax.

She stood where he'd pointed and lifted the long T-shirt over her head and tossed it away. She hadn't put on panties last night so she was already bare to his hot gaze. He clearly enjoyed the view.

"Turn around." She turned so she was facing the window and Seth was looking at her ass. She felt his hand caress her bottom where he'd spanked her. "It's still a little pink from my hand. Disobedience will turn it bright red. Do you understand, Presley? Tell me what the price of displeasing me is."

She could no longer feel the cold air. Her body was on fire. "If I displease you, I'll be spanked."

"Hard. With my hand or my belt. It will be my choice as you have no choices to make during sex. Turn back around."

Presley managed to turn back around, her knees like jelly. Seth had moved so he was sitting on the edge of the bed. He pushed her legs far apart and placed her hands on his shoulders. "Balance yourself and close your eyes. Stay quiet."

Presley squeezed her eyes shut as his hand brushed her bare mound. His fingers traced the outer lips of her cunt and then tickled the inner depths without penetrating her or touching her clit. She bit her lip to keep from begging as he explored every fold of her pussy before pressing a finger inside her.

"Tighten on it."

Her body obeyed, not able to say no to his deep, commanding tone. She was dripping honey all over his fingers and hand, her pussy weeping with desperation. She wanted him inside her. Now.

Seth wasn't interested in what she wanted, apparently. He took his time, pressing a second thick digit inside her and stroked her sweet spot until she had to lock her knees in place to keep from falling at his feet. His thumb casually brushed her clit every now and then and she finally couldn't hold back her plea.

"Please!"

He withdrew his fingers, leaving her empty and bereft. "Please what, Presley?"

She kept her eyes closed but his tone was one of displeasure. Her pussy tingled at the thought that she might have earned her first punishment. "Please what, Presley?" he repeated when she didn't answer.

She kicked her dry lips. "I'm sorry, Seth. I spoke without thought. I wasn't trying to take control."

"That is not what I asked you. Answer the question, Presley."

She was going to be spanked for sure. "I was asking please so you would touch my clit. Make me come. I'm sorry."

She really was sorry. She didn't want to disappoint him. She peeked out with one eye and saw his expression. His jaw was tight but he didn't seem angry. He leaned forward and whispered in her ear. "Is this okay? Is that what you had in mind?"

She nodded. "Yes. I need more, Seth. Be more stern. Punish me."

Seth nodded and got up from the bed and stalked over to the dresser where he rummaged through a drawer before returning to her. He held up what looked like a bandana. "This should help keep you focused on me."

He disappeared behind her and her eyes closed of their own accord as he wrapped the soft cotton fabric tightly around them. A few thin shafts of light could be seen around the edges but for all intents and purposes, she was sightless. She felt him move in front of her, adjusting it until he was satisfied.

He leaned down and whispered in her ear. "Are you okay, honey? We can stop this anytime you want."

She shook her head. "No, please don't stop. I want to do this with you."

His hand stroked her hair and then drifted down her body, leaving a path of liquid heat wherever it went. He traced circles around her breasts and nipples, then pinched them until they were hard. Presley's legs were still spread wide and she shifted restlessly on her feet, needing and wanting something only Seth could give her.

"You displeased me. You asked me to take control then tried to take it back. What should happen, Presley?"

"Punishment. A spanking."

She felt her arms being pulled behind her back and another piece of soft cotton fabric being wrapped around her wrists and tied together at the small of her back. Another gush of cream from her cunt left her in no doubt how much she loved being at his dominant mercy. She only hoped the spanking would prove to be as pleasurable as she'd built it up in her mind.

Still behind her, he pressed on her back until her head and upper torso were resting on the bed, her legs spread wide, and her ass in the air. The actuality of how submissive this position was slammed into her like the proverbial freight train. She, Presley Lawson, feminist, was about to let a man spank her bare ass for displeasing him. She waited for the guilt and shame but they didn't show up at the party. She wasn't ashamed. Her entire body was on fire and her heart and mind was filled with trust. Seth wasn't going to try her order her around after this. Well, any more than he already tried. He wouldn't think less of her.

Because this was Seth. She couldn't do this with any other man. Stop. End of story. He was a man of his word, and if he said she could stop it any time, he meant it.

His hand was rubbing the cheeks of her ass and she silently pleaded for him to get on with it. She needed to know if she was going to like it or not. By the time his hand came down on her left ass cheek, her nerves were strung taut. He didn't go easy on her, but smacked the bare skin as if this were a real punishment.

The breath whooshed from her body and she was about to tell him to stop when the pain turned to a delicious heat that spread through her abdomen and straight to her pussy and clit. She felt him hesitate for a moment but she arched her back and stuck out her bottom, letting him know she wanted it.

Needed it.

Four hard spanks later she was breathing hard, with honey dripping down her thighs. She had to control her instinct to beg him to fuck her. Now. Hard and fast.

She'd handed him control because she didn't truly want it. She wanted him to make the decisions. It might mean at times she didn't like the decisions he made, but that was the price of asking him to do this for her. She couldn't beg for a dominant man and then whine when he gave her what she asked for.

Presley heard the opening and closing of the nightstand drawer and then the crinkle of a condom. She felt the brush of the hair on his legs against hers and the slide of his cock in her slit. He rubbed it back and forth a few times and his hands grasped her hips, pulling her knees up on the mattress.

"You are not to come until I tell you to."

She nodded, her face digging into the heavy winter comforter. "Seth, um, Sir? May I make noise or speak?"

"Yes, but you may not make any request for your own pleasure. Understood? Sex slaves don't think about their own satisfaction."

This one does.

"Yes, Sir."

His cock nudged her slick pussy and he slid in easily, stretching the elastic walls and rubbing over her sweet spot. When he bumped her cervix, she let out a moan of pleasure. Seth knew just how she liked to be fucked. He held her still, his fingers digging into the flesh of her hips and buttocks as he started thrusting in slow and deep. He built up speed quickly until he was pistoning in and out of her fast, riding her hard.

"Oh, oh, oh God," she chanted. The ridges of his dick ran over sensitive spots inside her with each stoke and her body was pulled tighter than the string on his hunting bow. Her skin was damp with perspiration and she wanted to scream with the pain and pleasure of arousal. Never had he held her on the edge so long. She felt the power of her release building inside her until she was terrified of what would happen if she went over. She might not survive the fall.

"It's okay, honey. You can do it." Seth reached around and played with her clit. "Come for me. Don't be scared. It's going to be a big one, I can feel it. You know how hard you come when you delay it a little."

His words of encouragement and his fingers on her clit were exactly what she needed. Her body exploded into a ball of fire, singeing her inside and out with the intensity. Stars shimmered behind her eyelids and her body contracted with the power of her orgasm. She vaguely registered Seth's own release, his cock slamming into her one last time and the heat of his seed inside of the condom.

She didn't move when he pulled from her, patting her on the fanny with a promise to be right back. She heard his footsteps as he went to the bathroom to dispose of the condom and then the running of water before he returned with a warm cloth to clean her sticky thighs. When he was done, he untied her wrists and removed her blindfold, massaging her hands and arms and inspecting her closely for bruises.

"Relax, I'm okay," she chided. "You worry too much."

He shook his head in amazement. "I worry too much? I just tied up my girlfriend, spanked her, then fucked her for my own pleasure. You better believe I worry, and you better be glad I do."

When he phrased it like that, she was kind of glad. She reached up and kissed him. "You're right. I am thankful."

"I'm right?" Seth laughed. "I better mark this day down on the calendar. Being submissive suits you, honey. You admitted I was right this time."

She narrowed her eyes and gave him her mean look. "Don't get too used to it. It was hot calling you Sir and letting you be the boss in the bedroom but don't expect it anywhere else, buster." She stuck her index finger in his bare chest.

"Believe me, I won't. How about we have some breakfast and then come back to bed for some sleep and maybe some more role-play games? I could get into that."

Presley slid out of bed and pulled on her nightshirt. "What kind of role play did you have in mind? Elvis and Priscilla? Do you think your parents play that game?"

She giggled as Seth groaned and pulled on his boxers. "Do not mention my parents and sex in the same breath. I wasn't thinking of Elvis and Priscilla, although that might not be a bad idea. I was thinking maybe cop and suspect."

Minutes later they were frying up eggs and bacon. "Which one of us is the cop?" Presley teased, knowing full well which one she wanted to be.

Seth tapped on her nose. "I'm the cop and you're the suspect I'll interrogate. Just as a warning, I'm planning to use some enhanced techniques I think you'll really enjoy."

Her body quivered as her mind went wild with the possibilities. "So it was okay? You know, being in charge? Did you like it?"

"I did. You know I like being in control of things. It's funny but I've always fought my need to control and be in command in the bedroom. I never would have asked you to do anything like that in a million years, but when you suggested it some switch inside me was flipped. It was like I'd never been more aroused in my life. The thought of being dominant with you was exciting. Very exciting."

Seth fiddled with the scrambled eggs, not looking at her when he answered. He might have found it hot, but he wasn't comfortable with it yet. She grasped his arm, tugging him so he was facing her. "I liked it too. It was amazing. I totally trust you, Seth. I know you would never hurt me."

He kept his gaze on his toes. "I spanked you. I bet that hurt."

How could she explain this? "It did but it didn't. It hurt at first, but then it felt really good. I loved it and if I'm really honest, I can't wait for you to do it again. And again. Just the thought makes me wet. I want you to do it with your belt or maybe a riding crop."

Seth finally looked her in the eye and rubbed his chin. "Dammit, Presley. As usual, your honesty does me in. I want to give you what you need, what I need, but I need to be careful for both of us."

She took the spatula from his hand and scraped the eggs onto a plate, followed by the bacon. "There are probably books and videos on the internet. We could do some research together. It would be fun."

Seth rolled his eyes and handed her a fork. "Only you would think that researching how to tie you up and punish you would be fun." They ate in silence from the shared plate until every bite of food was gone. She'd worked up an appetite this morning. "I don't want to do anything that will really, truly hurt you. I want to do this right. Since you're willing to research this with me, then we will."

Presley threw her arms around Seth's neck and kissed him hard. "This is going to be hot. We're going to have the best sex life in Montana."

"Honey, there are more cattle than people in Montana, so that wouldn't be all that difficult."

She nodded solemnly. "You're right. We already have the best sex life in Montana. Maybe Wyoming too."

Seth swept her up in his arms and strode toward the bedroom. "That's a lot of pressure but I think we can keep up. Let's go prove it again."

Presley leaned forward and nipped at his chin, the stubble tickling her lips. "Ravish me, Sheriff."

Seth dumped her on the bed, his expression wild with passion and desire. "Call me Sir in the bedroom."

She gulped as he reached down and dragged her T-shirt over her head, her eyes riveted to the muscular perfection of his bare chest. "Yes, Sir."

Presley and Seth proceeded to prove to the entire state what a great sex life they had on and off all day long. It beat fighting the crowds and standing in line at the mall Christmas shopping by a mile.

Black Friday? More like Wild, Kinky Sex Friday. Hot damn.

CHAPTER THIRTEEN

Presley was the first customer in Sue Ann's grocery store Monday morning. It was nice to be back on a regular schedule now that Thanksgiving was over but somehow they'd gotten dangerously low on coffee, necessitating Presley's early morning visit. She'd also picked up some donuts and bagels, knowing Seth and whoever else had been on duty, would be hungry when they finished their graveyard shift. She was always surprised by how much food they could put away, but then she found her own appetite to be more active than usual since coming to Montana. Perhaps it was the cold weather.

She exited the store, both arms full with her shopping bags. Luckily, the station was less than a block away, but the cold wind was bordering on bitter. She didn't think she'd ever get used to the frigid temperatures here. It was at least ten degrees colder this week than last, and Eliza told her it was only going to get worse before it got warmer. Presley headed down Main Street, her mind busy with the day's agenda. She had a stack of files she'd found in a storage area to scan into the new document system.

A white SUV suddenly raced out of the alley and swerved in front of her, effectively blocking her path. Anger and fear collided.

Asshole.

She was about to give the driver a piece of her mind when she heard her name being called from across the street. As Presley jerked back around to see Deputy Hank waving at her from the bakery, a blast rang out, exploding the bags in her arms into a million pieces. Coffee beans and donut bits rained down onto her and the sidewalk.

Frozen with fear, her heart pounded in her chest. What in the hell was happening?

I need to move!

Out of the corner of her eye, she caught the glint of sunlight off the muzzle of a gun as the shooter pointed it out of the rolled-down truck window. Adrenaline slammed through her veins, allowing her mind to kick in and her body to hit the ground, her hands over her head protectively, convinced they'd shoot again.

Fuck. Shit.

That bullet was for her and only by the grace of God had it missed. She flattened herself on the pavement as she heard the SUV peel away, accelerating down the street. Her heart was pounding against her ribcage and sweat had broken out over her body. She was literally shaking with fear. With her stomach still churning, she peeked up as Hank knelt down next to her, his police radio in his hand.

Fucking déjà vu.

"Shit, Presley, are you okay?" Hank's voice was urgent and breathless. He must have sprinted across the street at record speed. She nodded, not sure if her voice was working. She opened her mouth and was surprised to find words tumbling out.

"I'm fine. Go get them."

This could be their only chance to catch whoever Randall had hired to kill her. If they lost them, they'd be back to square one.

"I can't leave you. Are you hurt?"

She moved her arms and legs. "I'm fine. Go get them! Please! This is important, Hank!"

Hank looked torn but when the clerk at the bakery ran across the street, he nodded, knowing she wouldn't be alone. "Okay, I called Seth on the radio. He should be on his way."

Hank sprinted to his truck, which was parked on the street. Wheels squealing, he followed the shooters down the road and toward the edge of town. If Hank didn't catch up to them quickly, when the road split, the shooters could go in either direction and escape.

The clerk, a nice young woman named Sheri, helped her to her feet, exclaiming about the mess and asking what happened. From her angle, she'd only heard the shot and saw Presley hit the deck. Presley took a few deep breaths to try and calm herself. Now, more than ever, she needed to stay calm. She didn't have the luxury of fainting or making a scene. She'd been found and she needed to get into survival mode.

The safest place for her was probably the sheriff's station. She was only a few feet away and she could lock the door behind her. With her heart still in her throat, she thanked Sheri for her help and headed straight for the door. Seth's truck came barreling down the road and practically pulled up onto the sidewalk, making Sheri jump several feet away with an alarmed look on her face.

"Thank you, Sheri. Seth is here to take care of things now."

Sheri nodded as Seth jumped out of the truck, grabbing her arms and raking his gaze from head to toe looking for injuries. She pressed her fingers over Seth's lips when he started to ask her questions. She tipped her head slightly toward Sheri, who was still standing there taking the scene in. It was probably the most exciting thing to happen in Harper since the barn dance over a month ago.

Seth seemed to get her message and led her quickly her into the station, not giving Sheri a second thought, and locking the door behind him. His chest was heaving and she realized, for once, she was calmer than he was. She held up her hand.

"I'm okay. I'm not hurt."

Seth was running his hands all over her arms and legs. "Hank said you were shot."

He sounded desperate and she stilled his hands with her own. "I was shot at. There's a difference. Hank called my name from across the street and I turned at the last minute. They hit the grocery bags instead of me. Then I threw myself onto the pavement in case they decided to shoot again." She squeezed his hands, looking deeply into his eyes. "I'm okay, Seth." She said the last very slowly and deliberately and the air seemed to go out of him. He pulled her down into a chair, settling in the one across from her. His hand scraped down his face.

"When I got that call…Fuck, you can't imagine, honey."

"I think I can. They were shooting at me." She tried to smile but it was more like a grimace. She pressed a hand to her forehead, feeling the sweat gathered there. "How did they find me? How could they find me?"

Her heart was starting to slow down but her nausea was only increasing. The full import of what had happened was starting to sink in. Everything was as fucked as it could be. They'd found her and now she would have to get another identity and hide somewhere else. She was tired of playing hide and seek with Randall. She had to get to that appointment in Tampa alive so she could testify in front of the Grand Jury. She wanted Randall put away forever, and she wanted her life back. She clapped her hand over her mouth and barely made it to the toilet before losing the frozen waffle and orange juice she'd had for breakfast.

Seth was behind her, holding her hair and pressing a cool, damp washcloth to her face. He tossed the cloth into the sink and pulled her into his arms, holding her tight. She stayed there for a long time, leaning on his strength. She'd come to depend on his quiet steadiness, knowing all would be well if Seth was there. Having his arm around her settled her stomach and after a time she reluctantly pulled away.

"Thanks, I may not be as alright as I said I was."

Seth's forehead touched hers. "Honey, I think we're both shaken up here. I need to think about this. I need to think about what to do. I have to keep you safe."

He pulled away and paced around the office, his expression pale and grim. She was silent while he seemed to be working on something in his mind. He finally whirled on his heel and placed his hands on her shoulders. He'd turned from lover to warrior.

"I have to get you away from Harper."

* * * * *

"I think you have enough fire power," Tanner Marks casually observed. After Seth made his pronouncement seven hours ago to Presley, he'd called the only people he knew he could trust - Tanner Marks, Logan Wright, Griffin Sawyer, Reed Mitchell, and Jared Monroe. They were the best lawmen Seth knew and they'd done what great friends do. They'd showed up not long after his call with exactly what he needed, and a few things he didn't know he needed but was damn glad they'd thought of.

Seth tucked one of the handguns into a shoulder holster and another into his boot. He'd put a shotgun into the vehicle along with another handgun. Logan had brought Seth enough ammunition to start World War III, despite the fact that the Sheriff station was fully stocked for the apocalypse.

Jared watched the street through the blinds, a loaded Glock in his hand. Griffin, a shotgun leaning on his shoulder, gazed out the back entrance, guarding the RV that Tanner had brought with him. Seth had assumed he'd take Presley out of town in his own vehicle, but this was even better. They would be able to avoid the usual hotels along the highways and keep a low profile by staying at campgrounds.

Reed counted out the last bill in the stack of money. "Five thousand. That should get you down to Tampa. If you need more, you can call us and we'll wire the money to you."

Seth nodded grimly. "I'm going to try not to use my cell and I'm damn sure not going to use my credit cards. They can easily trace us through those."

Tanner shook his head and dropped a box on the desk. "Almost forgot these. Jared picked these up at the discount store on his way here. Throw-away pre-paid cell phones. There's four here so if you think one's been compromised, just switch to another. I wrote down the phone numbers if we need to get a hold of you. Don't answer them. We'll send a text if we need to talk to you and you can call us back."

Seth felt a rush of gratitude. If he'd had to do all of this himself, it could have taken days, not hours. As it was, they would be leaving soon after sundown. The RV had been stocked with groceries and filled with gas before Tanner even hit town.

"You're not going to call the Feds, are you?" Tanner asked.

Seth sighed heavily. "No. I want to trust Evan Davis. I really do, but as much as I trust him I can't trust the organization around him. Somehow this Simon guy found out where she was, and as far as I know, the Feds are the only ones who knew. I can't take a chance with her life. Presley is more than just a woman I'm protecting." He looked Tanner right in the eyes. "She's my woman, Tanner. I'll die before anything happens to her. I have to take her under until I know who I can trust or they stop this guy."

Seth waited for the fear and dread to overtake him, but nothing happened. It felt right, calling her his woman.

Tanner nodded. "That's what I figured. You're going to need help to keep her safe. That's what we're here for."

"There's no one I trust more in the world. Shit, you're the only ones I do trust. I should have told you about Presley before."

Logan turned from the window. "It's no big deal. We know why you couldn't. You like to play by the rules." Logan picked up his abandoned coffee cup. "Your girlfriend sure does make good coffee. She seems to be holding together pretty well."

Presley was holding together. She was a strong woman and Seth couldn't help but admire her resilience. She was upstairs in the apartment packing her few belongings and hopefully getting a nap. They'd be driving a good portion of the night and she'd need her rest. Seth stood up, needing to move around. "You don't have any use for rules," Seth stated.

Logan shrugged. "They've never been much use to me, personally, but I don't judge you, buddy. The fact is, you're going to break a few of those rules if you're going to keep that woman safe."

Logan spoke the truth. Yet, Seth was actually feeling more optimistic. With the help of his friends, he knew they could keep Presley safe from harm. Things were starting to be put in motion and they would build momentum quickly. But they had to hurry. Whoever wanted Presley dead wasn't going to sit back and give up. They'd be coming after her until they'd killed her. He had a small window to get her out of here and to safety and there was no time to waste.

"How long do you think it will take for you to get to Tampa?" Jared asked.

Seth shrugged. "Depending on weather, I'd say three days. I'm planning to take Ninety South to Seventy, then Seventy East to St. Louis. From there, it's not far to Seventy-five South."

"What did you tell your family?" Logan asked.

"The story about the shooting is all over town by now so there was no point in lying to them. I told them as much of the truth as I could. My deputies will keep an eye out on the ranch in case they look for her there. The rest of the time? My men will take care of the town while I'm gone."

"What's her real name?" Tanner asked abruptly.

Seth blew out a breath, trying to keep his adrenaline under control. He didn't have the luxury of crashing later. "I don't know," he admitted.

Logan quirked an eyebrow. "Is there more you don't know? Some of it might be important."

Seth shook his head. "I know she's in danger. Fuck, they shot at her today. Hank tried to follow them, but said the shooters abandoned the car. There were tire tracks there, which told him they switched cars. They had a car waiting, Logan. They're professional. They won't give up until she's dead, and I can't let that happen."

Jared was sitting next to Griffin but pulled the back door closed and locked it before stepping into the middle of the room. He reached into his jacket pocket and pulled out an envelope, holding it out to Seth.

"I think you might need these. It was the best I could do on such short notice."

Seth opened the envelope and the air was sucked right out of his lungs. Jared had procured a couple of driver's licenses. Seth's actually had his picture on it, probably taken at a cookout or beer bash in the last year or two. Presley's didn't have her picture, of course, but it was a fairly close likeness.

"How did you do this?" Jared had only had a few hours.

Jared smiled. "Let's just say I have friends in low, dark places. I'm sorry Presley's isn't her picture but I got one that was close, based on your description of her. Women change their look all the time, so maybe no one will say anything." Jared picked up Seth's new identification. "Mister Steve Rodell traveling with his wife, Missy Rodell."

Seth fell into a chair. "Shit, this better work. I'm breaking a few major federal laws taking Presley under with me. Evan's going to fucking have a cow."

Griffin shrugged. "Evan will have to deal with it. Listen, a few of us are going to follow you for awhile to make sure you get out of town and the bad guys aren't tailing you."

Seth shook his head. "I can't ask you to do that. I know you have your own towns to take care of."

Logan smiled. "You didn't ask, we offered." He shoved Tanner's shoulder. "Me and Tanner are coming. I got a shit-load of vacation coming to me and seeing the Midwest with this ugly asshole is my dream holiday."

Tanner's lips twisted. "I'm feelin' the love." He looked back at Seth. "We'll stay back a ways. Logan and I are each taking a car so we can take turns in the lead, and all that jazz. We'll follow at least until Denver."

"Seth?" Presley's tentative tone made all the men turn around. Her face was pale but her lips were firm. She was going to be okay. He would make sure of it. He got up from his chair and pulled her into his arms, not caring if any of his buddies saw him.

"Yeah, honey? Did you get a nap?"

She nodded. "For a little while. I'm all packed. When are we leaving?"

She was so subdued, and Seth wasn't used to his little firecracker being so quiet. He wanted to see her happy and smiling again, lighting up like a beacon.

"After sundown, so we have a few hours. Are you hungry? We should eat before we go."

Reed stood up. "I'd be happy to go pick something up. I'm getting hungry myself."

Presley shrugged, a far cry from the gutsy woman he'd encountered right after the shooting. She seemed to be beaten down by the events and Seth didn't blame her one bit. She looked up at him.

"What about Evan Davis? When is he meeting us?"

Seth looked over her head at his best friends. Tanner nodded to him and Seth nodded once back. Keeping things from her at this juncture wasn't a good idea. They were a team now and they needed to start acting and working like it.

"I'm not telling Evan anything." He guided her to a chair and helped her sit down. "Evan's part of a large organization that he can't control. They are, supposedly, the only people who know where you are. Someone must have told Simon your whereabouts. You didn't tell anyone, did you?"

Seth finally saw a flash of fire in her eyes. "No! I didn't tell a soul. That's a shitty thing to say, Seth Reilly."

His friends grinned at her feistiness and Seth smiled. This was a Presley he knew how to handle. "I was only seeing if you were paying attention. You seemed a little sleepy. But it begs the question, doesn't it? If you didn't tell anyone, and I didn't tell anyone, well, that only leaves the Feds to have leaked the information."

Presley crossed her arms over her chest and glared, much to the other men's amusement. "You have a point. I'm paying attention, rest assured. Did I hear that some of you are following us to Denver?"

Logan nodded from his post at the window. "Tanner and I are."

Presley nodded. "Thank you. I feel safe with Seth, but with both of you, I'll be triple safe."

"We won't let anything happen to you." Seth stroked her silky hair, watching it curl around his fingers. "We'll get to Tampa so you can testify, I promise, honey."

Jared cleared his throat. "Speaking for myself, if you were testifying against me, I'd be scared to death."

Seth saw the first real smile from Presley all day and silently thanked Jared. He had a way with people.

"Randall should be. I want him behind bars for good."

Seth patted her shoulder. "He will be. Don't worry."

"What would make me not worry is if you would go over all the things you've done and prepared to keep me safe. I saw the RV out back and I see you're all loaded for bear." Presley pointed to Seth's shoulder holster.

Griffin gave her a crooked smile. "Let me give you a tour then...Mrs. Rodell."

Presley frowned. "Who's Mrs. Rodell? My name is Presley."

Seth smiled. "Wait until we show you what the guys brought. I think you'll be impressed."

"Do I get a gun of my own?"

"No," the men all said in unison. Seth rolled his eyes. "Have you ever shot a gun? At all?"

"No, but it can't be all that hard. You aim and pull the trigger. Seems pretty straightforward, Sheriff."

"If you don't know what you're doing, you can hurt, or even kill yourself." Seth sighed. "No gun for you."

Presley pouted. "How am I supposed to protect myself?"

"You're not." Seth pointed to his chest. "That's my job. Got it?"

"Seems unfair. What else do you want to show me?"

Griffin held up the box of pre-paid cell phones. "We'll start here."

Seth paced the room while Griffin showed Presley every precaution they'd taken. Seth was ready to go. He could feel the anticipation and drive to leave building in his gut. He needed to get Presley out of this town as soon as possible. Her life depended on it.

* * * * *

"You're incompetent," Nora roared into her cell phone loud enough that her assistant hustled into the office to see what was going on. Nora waved her away and the woman ducked out as quickly as she came, clearly recognizing she was not needed nor wanted.

"It wasn't our fault," protested Joe Gartner, a man Nora had found a few years ago with not much brains, and even fewer scruples. He was clearly worried about his job and he should be. If he couldn't carry out something as simple as this, then what was she paying him for? "Some guy called to her and she turned at the last minute. It was a cop so we needed to get the hell out of there, Nora."

Nora's temper flared, but she needed to get a firm hold on her out of control emotions. Katie was like a fucking cat with nine lives who fell from the staircase but landed on all four paws. The visual of Katie making that same fall but breaking her damn neck made Nora smile with pleasure. Perhaps she needed to stop trying to kill Katie by remote means and get up close and personal.

Nora hadn't planned on getting her hands dirty with the deed but it was starting to look like she didn't have a choice. She turned her attention back to her failing employee.

"What is she doing now? Why haven't you tried again?"

Silence.

"She's gone." Joe's voice bordered on whiny and if there was one thing Nora hated it was a whiny man.

"What do you mean '*she's gone*'? Where is she?"

"I don't know. She's just disappeared." Nora's fingers tightened on the phone and she had to talk to herself to calm down. Anger wasn't going to solve this. Being calm and in control was what was called for at a time like this.

Nora sat up straight in her chair. "Find her," she hissed. "Find her and kill her, for fuck's sake."

"I don't know where she is," Joe whimpered so pathetically it almost made Nora sick. Fucking gutless wonder. He was why Katie was still breathing. After what Katie had done, she didn't deserve to breathe.

"Come back to Tampa." Nora made an instant decision. She always trusted her gut instinct at a time like this. "Get back here. It would be stupid to roam around trying to find her when we don't know where she is." Nora didn't wait for Joe's reply. She simply pressed the End button and tossed the phone on the desk.

She stood up and looked out the window of her office at the bright Florida sunshine. Through important contacts locally, Nora had learned Randall's Grand Jury hearing would be in less than a week. Katie had been his assistant and would surely be on the list to testify. It was the perfect opportunity. There was no need to go find her.

Katie would come to Nora. How convenient. Then Nora would end Katie's life, once and for all.

CHAPTER FOURTEEN

Presley had to admit the RV was certainly luxurious for a home on wheels. The kitchen had an oven and a microwave, and the refrigerator was as large as her own at the apartment. The sitting area had an oversized flat screen television and the back of the RV was a bedroom with a comfortable king-sized bed. The bathroom was small and it appeared she'd be taking a shower while straddling the toilet, but at least they had one.

"I feel like a rock star traveling around in this. Whom does it belong to?"

Seth didn't take his eyes off the road. It was after nine o'clock and the highway was deserted but she could easily see he was still tense. "Tanner's parents bought it for their retirement. When his mother's health took a turn, they stopped traveling. It was just sitting in a barn."

Presley's passenger side chair swiveled so she could look back into the RV. "Well, it's fancy. I think it's about the size of the apartment I lived in with my mom before she married my stepdad."

"Were things tough before your mom got married again?"

Presley unclipped her seat belt. "You're assuming mom was married the first time. Do you want a soda?"

"Sure, be careful, though. I don't like it when you're not buckled in. I'm not following you. What do you mean I'm assuming your mom was married?"

Presley grabbed two sodas from the stocked refrigerator and headed back to her seat. "I'm saying my dad never bothered to marry my mom. Never met my biological father but I hear he was a real piece of work. Liked to use mom for a punching bag." She popped open Seth's can and slid it in the cup holder before opening her own.

Even in the dim light, she could see Seth scowling. His family was so wonderful that sometimes he had a hard time wrapping his mind around the dysfunctional ones. She'd seen it often enough in Harper when he'd gone out on domestic disturbance calls.

"So your mom left him?"

"He left my mom. Decided being a father was a hassle. Thank God."

Seth turned to look at her briefly. "Why 'thank God'?"

Presley looked out the huge windshield at the desolate landscape, lit only by the headlights and the occasional streetlight. "Because if he beat my mom, he probably would have hit me. If that had happened, maybe I would have thought that was normal and ended up with a guy who liked to beat on me."

"Never, honey. I could never see you taking any crap from some guy."

Presley smiled to herself, thinking about what could have been. "I'm like that now, but we don't know what I would have been like if my dad had been around. Luckily, I saw my mother stand up to my stepfather. He was a jerk but she gave him shit for it. She didn't let him blame her for his faults. I heard him try to once."

"He blamed your mother for his cheating?"

"Yep, said she wasn't sweet enough to him." Presley snorted. "My mother laid into him good. She'd been a victim of my father but she sure wasn't going to be a victim again."

"She left him?"

"She did, then got sick right after. They tried to keep things together for me and Nora during that time."

"Nora's your sister?" Seth paused. "What's your name? I mean your real name?"

Presley twirled the can in the holder. She wasn't sure why she was reluctant to tell him, why it felt wrong to say her given name.

"Katie. Katherine Johnson, actually, but all my friends call me Katie."

"Katie," Seth said it slowly. "That's a nice name. Do you want me to call you Katie?"

"No," she answered. "I think you're supposed to call me Missy."

Seth laughed. "And I'm Steve. With all these names floating around, I think it would be easier if when we're around people we don't use names at all. I'll call you honey and you can call me babe or something."

"You don't look like a Steve." Presley liked teasing Seth. "Maybe like a Harvey or a Milton, but not a Steve."

"I'm going to pretend you didn't even say that." Seth handed her the large Atlas. "We need to stop in about three hours. Find a small city and see if it has a campground we can park in. Pick one of the phones from the box. They all have internet access to do the research."

It felt good to have something to do. She flipped on a small light to see the map. They were already in Wyoming and they had a three-day drive ahead of them, trying to stay one step ahead of her killers.

She set the map down and looked at Seth, his chiseled profile outlined in the low light. "Thank you."

He flicked a glance her way. "Thank you for what?"

Her heart felt very full at this moment for this man. "For everything. Protecting me. Dropping your whole life and hiding me. Just everything."

There was a long silence. "You're welcome. I wouldn't do anything less, honey. We're a team now. We take care of each other. That's how it will be from now on."

She really liked the sound of that, but she had to press him just a little. "Then can I have a gun?"

"No." He smiled, though, so he knew she was teasing.

"You're no fun."

"I think you know that's not true."

She couldn't leave it like that for some reason. She was becoming sentimental after everything she had been through today.

"Okay, you are fun."

"So are you, Presley. More fun than I've ever had, frankly."

His voice was warm and soft and she wished they were anywhere but in an RV running from people who wanted her dead. She exhaled slowly, trying to push those thoughts from her mind. Dwelling on her situation wasn't going to make anything better.

"You needed fun more than anyone I'd ever met, Sheriff."

Seth didn't reply this time. He simply kept driving into the night, putting more and more miles between them and Harper, and hopefully getting closer to safety. She picked a town on the map and fired up the phone, hoping her search would turn up an acceptable RV park with a vacancy. They could stop for the night and get some sleep before continuing their long journey.

When she was safe, everything would go back to the way it was. Seth would go back to Harper and Presley would go back to Tampa and resume her life. Such as it was.

Presley didn't expect the wave of sadness that poured over her, but she didn't push it away. Instead, she let herself feel it completely, knowing that losing this man was more than just breaking up with some guy. This was losing somebody who meant something.

She'd tried to keep it casual and light, but as usual, she'd screwed up.

* * * * *

The day was bright and sunny and Seth was almost cheerful as he drove the RV down Highway Ninety, nearing Denver. Since they hadn't stopped until after midnight, they'd slept late this morning, not getting on the road until ten. It was around noon now and Seth was thinking they could pull over for a late lunch once they got through Denver. He talked to both Logan and Tanner on the radio and so far there had been no sign of a tail. Seth's worst worry was the winter storm planning to blanket Kansas.

Seth glanced down at the gas gauge. Damn, this home on wheels guzzled fuel. He needed to stop and fill the tank. He'd seen a few signs for a good exit up ahead.

"Honey, we're going to stop for gas in a few if you want to get out and stretch your legs."

Seth picked up the handset of the radio. "This is Abe, calling Chris and Mercury."

Static and then Tanner picked up. "This is Chris. Is everything okay?"

"We're just going to make a fuel stop. Wanted to let you know."

More static. "We'll slow down. I'm about a mile behind you and Mercury is about a mile ahead of you."

"Gotcha. I was thinking we'd stop after Denver for lunch."

"Sounds good. Ten-four."

"What's with the Chris and Mercury stuff? And who is Abe?"

Seth chuckled. "I'm Abe. My middle name is Abraham. Tanner's is Christopher so he's Chris. Logan's middle name is Mercury. Don't think we didn't give him some shit for that."

"I thought you might have cool CB radio names."

"Like what?" Seth mocked. "Lone Wolf, Fighting Brave, and Dances With Wolves?"

She giggled and the sound squeezed his heart. The thought of anything happening to her was unthinkable. "Those are kind of cool. Would you be Lone Wolf or Fighting Brave? I know you wouldn't be Dances With Wolves as I practically have to beg you to dance with me."

"I've danced with you."

"A slow one, nothing else."

"That's all there is, honey." Seth grinned. "I can slow dance and I can line dance."

"I didn't get to go to the roadhouse, you know. You owe me, Sheriff."

"When we get back I promise I'll take you." He would get her back in one piece.

"I'll hold you to that." Presley stretched and yawned, setting her book down. She'd been quiet this morning, reading her book, but she didn't seem depressed or sad as she had yesterday. "I could use some exercise. How far are you planning to drive today?"

Seth glanced up at the still clear sky. "I was hoping Kansas City, Missouri, but there's a winter storm threatening. We may need to pull over for a day or two and wait it out."

"Can we get ahead of it?"

He liked the way her mind worked. She was full speed ahead. "We might be able to if I can stay awake that long to drive."

"I can help you drive."

Seth turned on his turn signal for the exit before answering. "I'm not sure that's such a great idea. Have you every driven anything this big before?"

"No. Have you?" Her eyebrows were raised in question.

"Well, no. But I've driven trucks hauling a horse trailer so I'm more experienced." It sounded lame even to him.

"How much experience do I need to keep it in the right lane? I promise I won't even pass anyone. Let me drive."

She was challenging him and his mind was whirling trying to think of a good excuse for her not to drive the RV, other than he was a male chauvinist who didn't think women were good drivers.

"I've never seen you drive."

She rolled her eyes at him as he pulled in to the combination gas station and convenience store. "I have a driver's license. Actually, I have three. One in Katie's name, one in Presley's name, and one in Missy's name. That's one more than you have."

He sighed heavily, knowing he was beat, but not wanting to give in too easily. "We'll see. I may not get tired."

She smiled triumphantly. "You'll let me drive. I can't do any worse than some of the people on these roads. They're crazy."

He was probably crazy as well but instead of saying something that was going to get him relegated to sleeping on the couch, he pulled up to the diesel pump and put the motor home in park.

"I'm going to fill up. Stretch your legs while you can. If we're going to get to Kansas City, we have a long drive ahead."

Presley headed to the convenience store, probably to use the facilities and stock up on snack food, or maybe grab a magazine. Seth went into the store to pre-pay since he was using cash and by the time he came out again, a county sheriff's cruiser was pulled into the pump next to his.

Seth tried not to even look its way, going straight to the side of his own RV and starting the pump. He watched the numbers whirl but kept a close eye on the cop putting gas in his own vehicle. Seth wiped at his brow, sweaty despite the frigid temperatures. He didn't know if the Feds realized Presley wasn't in Harper yet, but once they knew, they would be sure to put a BOLO out for them. He pulled his hat down further over his eyes and cursed the size of the gas tank. It took too fucking long to fill it.

"That's a beaut you got there."

Aw, fuck it. The deputy was talking to him now. Seth's heart was pounding but he schooled his features and smiled. "Thank you. It belongs to my in-laws. We're taking a little vacation." Seth was glad he'd rehearsed questions and answers with Jared.

The deputy laughed. "Hell of a time to be taking a vacation. Ever heard of summer?"

Seth tried to laugh along with the lawman. "It's tough to vacation in the summer. Besides, I like the snow."

The deputy looked around appreciatively at the snow piled up where the plows had been through. "Must say I do too." He walked up to the RV and patted it with a smile. "What kind of mileage you get in this thing?"

Seth leaned against the side of the vehicle trying to appear nonchalant when he really wanted to grab Presley and drive away as quickly as he could. "About ten miles per gallon, give or take. It's pretty bad." Where the hell was she anyway?

The older man shook his head and laughed. "Hell, I remember when I was a kid my old man's Chevy got about the same and he didn't have a can on board." The deputy gave him a hopeful look. "Don't suppose you'd show me inside? I've never been inside one of these fancy dancy ones. You got TV in there? I saw a satellite on top."

Seth grew up in a small town and wasn't surprised by the request, but he felt his stomach twist in fear. The cop seemed innocuous enough, completely unaware of who Seth was or what he was doing, but there was always that small chance he was being played. Still, he couldn't think of one legitimate reason to say no.

"Sure. Let me finish this and I'll show it to you."

They chatted about the weather while Seth finished pumping gas, then he led the way into the interior of the RV, his heart pounding so loud he was sure the deputy could hear it. "This is the living room and kitchen. There's a bedroom back there and a bathroom. It's pretty comfortable. Plenty of room for just the two of us."

The deputy whistled as he took in the flat screen television. "Nice. Very nice. I won't invade your privacy by looking at the bedroom but I'm sure it's as nice as this. Maybe someday when I retire the wife and I will get something like this and travel around the country."

Too bad that day and moment wasn't right now. The lawman appeared to taking his time, looking at every detail, in no hurry to leave. Seth was sweating up a storm in his heavy jacket and wasn't sure how to move this along when Presley opened up the door.

"Hey, I got us more sodas— Oh, I'm sorry." Seth saw the flash of fear in her expression but to her credit, she hid it quickly. She smiled at their visitor. "Hello, I'm Missy."

Seth took the bag of snacks from her and set it on the counter while the deputy held out his hand with a grin. "I'm Otis McRae.

Nice to meet you. Your husband was kind enough to show me around this palace on wheels. Very fancy, I'll say. He says it belongs to your parents."

If she was surprised by that statement, she never let it show. "It does." She pointed to his badge. "Are you in local law enforcement here, Mr. McRae?"

Otis beamed with pride. "I am. Twenty-two years on the job. Hoping for twenty-two more." He looked around the room. "I best let you two head on down the road. Drive careful now. There's bad weather coming our way. Which way are you heading?"

"South," Seth answered quickly. "New Orleans. We're visiting friends."

Otis's head bobbed. "Never been but I heard it's nice. Good luck and happy driving." The deputy climbed out of the RV and headed for his car. Seth felt the roar of blood in his ears as he sagged against the refrigerator. Presley pressed a hand to her forehead.

"What was going on in here?"

Seth wiped at his brow. "The deputy pulled up and started a conversation. Then he wanted to see the inside of the RV. He said he'd never seen one this fancy. Son of a bitch." Seth groaned as the full horror of what could have happened hit him. He could have lost Presley to the Feds and ended up separated from her, unable to keep her safe from the leak inside the agency.

Presley wrapped her arms around him while his heartbeat returned to normal. She patted him on the butt with a smile. "Close call, but we're fine. We need to get on the road or Tanner and Logan will be halfway to Kansas City before we even get to Denver."

Seth took a deep breath and nodded. Presley was right. They were fine, and as long as he kept alert they would stay fine. He couldn't afford to relax for even a moment. Presley's life hung in the balance.

"Let's get going then." Seth straightened and headed to the driver's seat, only to have Presley beat him to it.

"Let me drive." Presley gave him a beguiling smile. He shook his head and jerked his thumb toward the passenger seat.

"No way, honey. I'm in control of this vessel today."

She pouted but relinquished the seat easily. She'd probably just been busting his balls for fun. "Maybe we should sing or something. Do you know Ninety-Nine Bottles of Beer on the Wall?"

Seth started up the engine and pulled out in to traffic. "Never heard of it. Maybe if you sing it to me, I can pick it up."

He should have known not to challenge his Presley. She launched into the song at the top of her lungs. This was going to be an interesting drive for sure. He'd never met anyone like Presley Lawson.

A feeling of sadness came over him, sending a pain directly to his chest. When she was gone, he would never meet anyone like her again.

* * * * *

It was almost one in the morning when they pulled into an RV park outside of St. Louis. They'd had to drive over twelve hours to get ahead of the winter storm but they'd made it, exhausted and ready for bed. Tanner and Logan had turned around a few hours past Denver when it was clear the weather was turning bad. If they didn't turn around then, they were going to be stuck for a few days. Presley and Seth had bid the lawmen farewell at a rest stop on US Ninety. She'd miss the comforting presence of knowing they were around but she trusted Seth to keep her safe and alive.

He was now curled up behind her, a portable furnace, keeping her warm. Presley could feel his heartbeat against her back and his breath on her shoulder. He was idly stroking her skin.

"Can't sleep, honey?" He pressed a kiss to her hair.

"I'm almost too tired to sleep. Isn't that weird? I've heard of that but never experienced it myself until tonight. I'm exhausted but my mind is wired."

"It might be all the sodas and coffee we drank to stay awake." Seth chuckled and she felt the vibrations on her skin. She loved his deep, husky voice, especially in the morning when he was still half-asleep, his eyes heavy-lidded until he'd had his coffee.

She turned in his arms and pressed her head to his chest. "I was scared today."

His arms tightened around her. "At the gas station, when we saw the deputy?"

She nodded her head, her cheek rubbing the sprinkling of gold hair on his chest. "If we were separated I don't know what I'd do. I trust you. I don't know who else I can trust."

Seth rubbed her back. "If they separated us, I would get back to you. Know that. I would get one of my lawmen friends to help me. I would find you, honey. I will always find you."

She swallowed the lump in her throat. "You mean something to me. More than anyone has ever meant. I want to tell you that, Seth. If something happens to me, I don't want you to think that no one loves you." She took a deep breath, ready to plunge off a cliff. She was the queen of bad decisions and this one was probably the mother of them all. "I love you."

He tilted her chin up but it was too dark to see his expression. He captured her lips in a kiss that took her breath away. It was slow and sweet and told her he wasn't unhappy she'd declared herself. He rubbed his stubbly cheek against hers.

"I love you, too."

She pushed at his chest. "That's not why I said it. I wasn't trying to get you to say it. I just wanted you to know in case they find me and kill me."

Shit, saying it sounded bad. She didn't want to die.

"Nothing's going to happen to you as long as I draw breath, Presley. I mean that."

She believed him and it scared her. She squeezed her eyes closed and a few tears escaped down her cheeks. Love shouldn't be this painful.

"It doesn't change anything. Somebody's trying to kill me and when this is over—"

Seth pressed his fingers to her lips, his hand warm. "I know. We don't need to talk about it or anything. We have now. Fuck, it's more than I thought we would have. I sure as hell didn't intend to fall in love with you and I know you sure as shit didn't intend to fall in love with some cowboy sheriff from Harper, Montana, but here we are. I made a promise to you and I won't break it, honey." His voice was urgent and it made her heart hurt so badly she thought it might burst into a million tiny pieces. She now knew what they meant by heartbreak. "Let's be grateful for what we have now. Nobody knows what the future holds, right?"

She didn't answer him. Talking would get them nowhere. Instead she ran her hands up his chest and down his muscular arms, feeling the heat radiating from his skin. Her mouth sought and found his and she plunged her tongue deep into the cavern of his mouth. He tasted like the mint of his toothpaste and she rubbed his tongue until he groaned, his arms wrapping around her fully and his body rolling hers under him.

God, she loved this. She loved feeling his big, hard body on top of hers. It made her feel feminine and sheltered and she reveled in that, letting her fingers explore the dips and ridges of his body while he explored her mouth. She was fascinated with the differences in their bodies, his so strong and hers so delicate.

Her palms glided over his wide shoulders, down through the silky, golden hair on his chest, over his hard, flat stomach, then around to his tight, muscular ass, gripping him and pulling him closer so his hard cock nestled between her legs. She breathed deeply of his scent, spicy and clean. He smelled like a man should, not sweet, but like the outdoors he was so deeply a part of. She pulled her mouth away and licked at his neck before nipping it with her teeth gently.

She was already wet and slick for him and she rubbed against the hardness in his boxers, the friction sending frissons of arousal through her body and making her toes curl. Seth cursed and his hands slid under her T-shirt, tugging it over her head before his fingers curled around the elastic of her panties, dispensing with them deftly. She didn't care where he had tossed them, too lost in the pleasure he was evoking with a simple touch. Her hands pushed down his boxers, needing to touch him.

His head dipped and his mouth captured an already beading nipple in his mouth. Seth took a wrist in each hand and pressed them to the mattress so she was helpless under his erotic assault. His teeth scraped the sides of the hardening bud and she gasped at the heavy arousal building in her abdomen. Her pussy clenched with need and she arched her back, inviting his attention.

His tongue snaked out and circled the peak, driving her crazy with need. She pressed herself closer to his hard cock and he chuckled at her predicament, knowing what she wanted but obviously determined to make her wait. He repeated the nipple torture on her other side and she struggled in his gentle but firm hold. She wasn't going anywhere unless he released her wrists, and the thought amped up her excitement tenfold. She was desperate to come now, heated blood flying through her veins and electric sparks playing in sensitive nooks and crannies.

"Seth!" She cried out as his mouth blazed a hot, wet trail over her quivering abdomen. He moved her wrists from beside her head to the sides of her hips then to her inner thighs, but never lost control of them. With his shoulders pushing her legs apart and her arms trapped at her knees, she was thoroughly and completely under his control. He insinuated himself further, pressing her legs even farther apart, his hot breath on her clit. The room was dark and he wouldn't be able to see the honey dripping from her slit, but he could smell her arousal easily. It was perfuming the bedroom with sex and musk.

She tensed, waiting for the first touch of his tongue. When it came, she shuddered with pleasure as it traced a pattern around her clit, but never directly on it. He'd restrained her too well with his body weight for her to be able to move her hips to get more of his tongue. She had to take his teasing and licking, sending her tip-toeing on the edge of orgasm but never going over. She'd asked for a dominant man and Seth delivered in every way imaginable.

White lights danced in front of her eyes when he finally closed his mouth over her clit and sucked, releasing her wrists so she could grab onto the blankets. It sent her flying into the night, tumbling and rolling through the stars. She heard herself call his name, aware of her own breathing and heartbeat, as she came down to earth reluctantly. Her eyelids fluttered open but the room was still dark. Presley could hear Seth's ragged breathing as he rummaged in the nightstand for protection.

The crinkle of the wrapper and the snap of the rubber had her reaching for him, needing the contact of skin on skin. She wrapped her legs around his waist as he plunged inside her in one deep, satisfying stroke.

"Fuck, honey, you're so fucking tight and hot." Seth's voice sounded like ground glass. He hovered over her, pulling out almost all the way before pressing forward until he was in to the hilt. His cock stretched the walls of her cunt and ran over her sweet spot, sending her to the precipice again almost immediately. He thrust so deeply she thought she could feel him between her ribs. She grasped his shoulders to help steady the spinning room but each stroke simply sent her higher and higher, her body tensing and coiling, waiting for release.

She ground her pussy against his cock, her clit getting kisses from his groin. That was all it took for the climax to shatter her. She felt as if pieces of her body were fracturing into shards of light, spinning around the room, then coming back together in a completely new form. She felt changed, transformed by their lovemaking. There was no doubt of their feelings for one another. They'd been laid bare in the most elemental way possible between a woman and a man.

Seth's orgasm came closely after hers. He buried his face in her neck, biting gently at the sensitive skin, making her shudder and quake. His cock seemed to swell even larger inside of her and she could feel the heat of his seed, despite the barrier. She felt something primitive inside her wishing there was nothing between the two of them.

She ran her hands down his back, now covered in sweat. Their breathing was ragged and she could feel the racing of his heart against her own. Neither one of them wanted to move, but Seth did reluctantly, pulling from her swollen flesh with a kiss to her lips.

He was only gone a moment before he returned to drag her into his arms so her head was cradled on his chest. She heard the heavy thud of his heart under her ear but sleep still wouldn't come and she was perversely grateful. She wanted to stay awake. She didn't want to sleep and lose a moment of being held in his strong arms. This was truly heaven and hell and she didn't want to miss a minute of it. Dawn would come soon enough and remind them of all the things they needed to do.

Tonight she would simply lie in Seth's arms.

CHAPTER FIFTEEN

The next day, neither one of them mentioned their declarations of love. It was as if they'd made a silent bargain to agree the words had never been said, although Presley would never forget her rush of emotion when Seth told her he loved her. She doubted she would ever forget no matter how old she lived to be. It was the first time in her life she had loved and allowed herself to be loved in return, not for any other reason than it felt natural and right. Seth wasn't her mother or father or anyone who was supposed to love her. He loved of his own free will with no obligation.

They'd slept late again, both of them bleary-eyed this morning. Seth had declared a short driving day and they'd stopped just south of Nashville, too tired to continue. The RV park was pleasant and clean and the weather not as bitterly cold as the day before. Presley grabbed her iPod and started for the door, only to be stopped by Seth.

"Where do you think you're going?"

His jaw was set but she was even more determined to get some fresh air and exercise. They'd been stuck in the RV for two damn days and she was going stir crazy.

"I'm going for a walk. I need to get outside and stretch my legs."

He shook his head. "No way. I can't let you go alone."

She loved spoiling Seth but she wasn't giving in to him this time. "I need to get out of here for my mental health, Seth. I can't stay cooped up like this. Tanner and Logan said no one was tailing us and you haven't seen a sign of anyone following us, have you?"

"No, but that doesn't mean we don't have company. I said I'd keep you safe and dammit, Presley, I will." He wrapped his hand around her upper arm as she started toward the door again.

She was tired and stressed. Her temper frayed at his dictatorial words. "Then come with me!"

"Do you want to die? Is that it?" His face was red and she realized they were taking things out on each other. She didn't want things to be this way with him. He'd given up everything to protect her, asking nothing in return for himself.

She placed her hands on his chest to calm him. "No, I don't want to die. I want to live very much." She took a deep breath, exhaling slowly. "Seth, I'm getting cabin fever. Will you please walk with me so I can get some fresh air? I would very much appreciate that." She kept her tone even and friendly.

He ran his fingers through his blond hair. "I'm sorry. I guess I've got cabin fever as well. I think a walk is a good idea. Let me get my coat."

He didn't just get his coat. He put his shoulder holster with his gun underneath it, apparently wanting to be prepared for any eventuality. They locked the door behind them and headed toward the small lake, the sun starting to dip below the trees.

"We'll need to be back at the RV before the sun goes down," he warned.

"Okay, I don't need a long walk. It's warmer here, but still cold."

They walked in silence, smiling and waving at some of the other campers, but not stopping to engage in conversation. Presley was naturally friendly so it went against the grain to walk by but she understood they needed to keep a low profile. When they reached the lake, they sat down at a picnic table to watch the ducks swim in the icy water. Seth's pocket vibrated and she jumped. His phone hadn't gone off once the entire trip. From the look on his face as he scanned the text message, it probably wasn't good news.

"Griffin wants me to call him." Seth punched a few buttons and had Griffin on the line in less than a minute. "What's up?"

Seth listened, his expression grower darker. "Are you sure?" He flicked a glance at Presley, shaking his head. He listened some more before ending the call. "Okay, thanks for letting me know. If you hear anything else, give me a call."

Seth pressed the End button, a muscle working in his jaw. "I take it that wasn't a social call? Griffin wasn't inquiring into our health?"

Seth shoved the phone back into his pocket with a curse word. "You would be correct. He has contacts in the Marshal Service. Seems they've figured out you've disappeared and are none too happy about it. They've put out a BOLO nationwide. Shit. Shit. Shit."

Seth hopped to his feet, pacing in front of her. She reached out and grabbed his hand. "Do they know what we're driving? Do they know where we are?"

"No. Luckily, all they have is our physical descriptions, although they might guess we're headed to Tampa. They know you were shot at."

Presley chewed on her lip. "Should you call Evan? He's a good man. I don't want him to worry. He was really nice to me."

"If he knows you're with me, and Griffin says they do, then he knows I'll protect you. I'll think about whether we should call him. I'm not ready to say yes or no yet. I trust him. I don't trust anyone else in the Bureau." Seth looked up at the sky, the sun moving lower. "We need to get back to the RV, eat dinner, and get some real sleep tonight. Maybe in the morning we'll call Evan. I'll think clearer if I'm rested."

He pulled her up from the bench and they headed back to the RV, the temperature dropping as the sun set lower in the sky. By the time they reached the motor home and locked the door behind them, Presley was ready for some food and television time. Trying to keep things as normal as possible, she headed to the kitchenette to start dinner.

"How about a frozen pizza? Or I could make some chicken and veggies?"

Seth shrugged out of his coat but didn't remove the shoulder holster, even when he settled down to watch television. "Don't go to any trouble. Pizza's fine. Do we still have ice cream?"

"We do, and some of those ready-made cakes." Seth had a sweet tooth and liked his desserts.

"That sounds good. Since you're making dinner, I'll make breakfast." He grinned and she laughed as she warmed up the oven. He made terrific bacon and eggs. She was going to get fat at this rate, or at the very least have a cholesterol problem.

As she prepared dinner, she studied him as he watched the news. Even at rest, his body was tense, constantly alert. There would be no tranquility for him in the foreseeable future. Now there were more than just killers after her. Now the federal government had joined in.

She wasn't sure it was fair to ask one man to keep her safe and hidden from all of them. Maybe she should disappear on her own and let Seth go home to his life and his family. If she loved him, she should let him go. It was the right thing to do. He didn't ask for this and he didn't deserve it.

* * * * *

Presley pulled her coat and gloves on, trying not to make a sound. It was five in the morning and she'd managed to dress and pack a small bag all without waking Seth. She really wanted to take a shower and brush her teeth but she'd make too much noise. She tiptoed to the leather pouch where Seth carried most of the cash and, using only a small penlight from her purse, carefully counted out five hundred dollars. She wouldn't take much but she did need enough to get a bus ticket to Tampa, food, and a cheap motel.

She'd thought about it all night and came to the painful decision they would both be better off if they were separated. Whoever was looking for them was looking for both of them. Together. If they were apart, then it would be harder to identify them. Presley also planned to cut and dye her hair at the first opportunity.

She dug deeper into the leather pouch and pulled out the extra handgun. She didn't know how to use it but she was a quick learner and she might need it. She wrapped it in her scarf and shoved it to the bottom of her handbag. She hoped it was loaded but if it wasn't she was shit out of luck. She didn't have a clue of how to accomplish that task and she wouldn't have access to any You Tube videos to show her how.

Her hand hovered over one of the pre-paid phones they were carrying. It would be a lifeline to Seth and the other men but she'd heard them say cell phones could be tracked with GPS. If they knew where she was, they would feel honor-bound to find her and protect her, and that was something she was trying to avoid.

She was in love with Seth. She hadn't planned it but there it was. Despite the fact he was a little uptight and sometimes had a big stick up his butt, he was the man she loved. A truly good man. One she could lean on and trust. A man who deserved to live.

When she hadn't known him very well, it hadn't seemed normal for a stranger to vow to protect her with his own life. Now he wasn't a stranger and it felt very wrong. She loved him more than she loved herself. She wouldn't let him be killed trying to save her. He had a family who loved him, people who depended on him. What did she have? Not much in comparison. Everybody already thought she was dead. For them, nothing would change.

She shook her head and left the cell phones in the leather pouch. She walked slowly toward the door, her eyes now adjusted to the dim light of pre-dawn, jumping only once when the floor creaked. She pushed the door open and shut it quickly behind her, trying not to let the cold in to the RV. That would wake Seth up for sure. As it was, her heart was thumping so loudly it sounded like a rock band was playing inside the motor home.

She hiked her purse and bag up on her shoulder and zipped her jacket up as far as it would go, pulling the hood over her ears. When the sun came up, it would be warm into the forties, but for now it was downright freezing. She trudged through the park toward the main road. It was a long walk to the nearest bus station, but hopefully she could catch a city bus to the center of Nashville and from there a Greyhound to Tampa.

She was almost out of the park when she saw an older couple packing up their camp in preparation to leave. Her instinct was to smile and wave but she was a fugitive as of about fifteen minutes ago, so instead she ducked her head and plowed forward.

"Goodness, it's early to be out walking, isn't it?" The woman's voice seemed to boom in the silence. Presley inwardly groaned. She'd been so close. Her heart accelerated and she felt the clamminess of sweat under her jacket. She stopped and turned to find a smiling grandmother type and her equally happy grandfatherly husband.

"Are you one of those exercise people?" the older man asked. "I see them out in the morning in our hometown." He stuck out his hand. "I'm Harry Porter and this is my wife, Doris. We're from Green Bay, heading to Huntsville to visit our daughter and our grandchildren. How about you? We saw you last night arriving with your husband. Does he get up this early too?"

Presley had no choice but to shake their hands, glad she was wearing gloves so they wouldn't feel her sweaty palms. "Missy Rodell. Nice to meet you. No, he doesn't get up this early."

She hoped they'd accept her abbreviated answer. She would be polite and perhaps they might give her a ride into the city or at least to a bus stop. The only problem would be thinking of a valid excuse to need a ride. Currently, she was so cold and scared her mind was a blank.

Harry looked over her shoulder and grinned. "Looks like he does get up early. There's your husband now."

She whirled around, her body stiffening as Seth, looking wide awake and dangerously pissed, strode up to them. A muscle was working in his jaw but he smiled charmingly to the Porters before turning to give her a brief kiss. He leaned down so he was whispering in her ear. "You are in so much trouble."

He straightened and held out his hand to Harry. "Pumpkin, have you made a couple of friends? Hi, I'm Steve Rodell and it looks like you've already met my lovely wife, Missy."

Harry pumped Seth's hand. "I'm Harry Porter and this is my wife, Doris. Yes, we just met your wife while she was out for her morning walk."

Seth put his arm around her shoulders, pulling her close. His body was tense and stiff and she could feel the anger radiating from him. Luckily, the Porters appeared to be oblivious. Seth smiled down at her, but it didn't reach his eyes. "You should have woken me up, pumpkin. You know I love to walk in the early morning."

His hand squeezed her shoulder and she licked her dry lips. Seth was in a dangerous mood. "I wanted to let you sleep in, sweetheart." She congratulated herself that her voice was more than a croak. "You looked too peaceful to wake."

Seth's teeth were gritted together. "Always thinking of my wellbeing." He beamed at Harry. "I'm a lucky man."

The Porters smiled and linked hands. "You'll be celebrating forty years together before you know it," Harry declared. Doris shivered and looked up at the sky, the sun starting to peek through the trees.

"We need to get this campsite packed up and get on the road before the traffic gets bad. It was so nice meeting a young couple in love. Are you on your honeymoon?"

Seth nuzzled against her temple. "Not really but every day feels like a honeymoon with Missy."

She was going to kick him straight in the balls when they were alone if he didn't turn her over his knee and spank her first. She looked up at him, making cow eyes. "That's so sweet. I feel the same way, babe."

Harry winked at Seth. "You both have a safe trip wherever you're heading. Nice meeting you."

Harry and Doris bustled back to their RV to finish making preparations to leave. Seth none too gently grasped Presley's arm and firmly led her back toward their own motor home. The tension between them was almost unbearable. Seth didn't say a word, his mouth pressed into a grim line. She didn't say a word either, not sure what to say or how to explain what she was doing. He was clearly furious, although she had been doing it for his own good. He probably wasn't going to be too appreciative of that fact, though.

* * * * *

Seth needed to control the white-hot rage and fear tightening his belly. When he'd woken up alone in bed, he'd heard her moving around, and foolishly thought she was trying to start the coffee without waking him. One glance at the clock told him a different story. Presley wasn't a big fan of mornings and she didn't get up at five without a good reason. She was up to something. He listened as she rifled through his things and then snuck out of the RV.

He'd quickly pulled on his clothes and followed her. She had her purse and a small bag and, despite the Porter's declaration she was going for her morning constitutional, she was clearly flying the coop.

What was she thinking?

The sheer lunacy of what she'd done floored him. He'd busted his ass, risked everything to keep her safe, and she'd decided to leave him while he slept. He couldn't begin to wrap his mind around her logic. Was she that tired of him? Was he that difficult to be around?

He marched her into the motor home and pointed to the couch. Her lips were in a mutinous line but she slumped against the cushions, defeated. As always, Presley was a walking contradiction.

He shrugged off his coat and tried to calm himself. Yelling wasn't going to solve anything and might just make her cry. Her tears never failed to fell him to his knees, and now was the time to stay firmly in command.

He crossed his arms over his chest. "Why were you leaving?"

Her full lips trembled and her color was high. "I thought you'd be safer if I was gone."

Of all the things he expected her to say, those words weren't it. He sat down next to her on the couch, but not touching her. He was still mad as hell.

"Please explain your thinking to me," he said evenly. He congratulated himself on not pulling her over his knee and spanking her ass to a bright red color.

She plucked at the zipper of her coat. She was probably baking in that thing, but Seth wasn't in the mood to make her more comfortable. She should be sweating this interrogation out. In fact, if he had a set of spotlights, he'd turn them on her face.

She blinked rapidly, probably trying to hold back tears. *Shit.*

"I thought if I left you could go back to Harper and be safe. I don't want you to die because of me. Your family will be really upset if you die. My family already thinks I'm dead."

She fell silent but her fingers still played with the tab of the zipper. She hadn't looked him in the eye yet. He captured her chin and turned her to face him. Her eyes were dark and troubled.

"So you want to die then?" He challenged.

She shook her head. "They're looking for a man and a woman. If we split up, then we would be harder to spot." She ran her fingers through her hair. "As soon as I had a chance I was going to cut and dye my hair."

"How could you possibly take care of yourself?" Seth released her chin and rubbed his aching temple.

Her eyes shifted downward. "I took five hundred dollars and the other gun."

He jumped up from the couch. "I don't care about the money but a gun? Fuck, Presley, you could have really hurt yourself. That gun is loaded. Where did you put it?" He scanned her up and down and didn't see where she could have hidden it.

"I put it in my purse." She dug into her bag and pulled out something wrapped in her scarf, holding it out to him. "If you're really mad, you can just shoot me with it so we can be done with this."

Her little chin was lifted and she looked gloriously rebellious.

He carefully took it from her, unwrapped it, and inspected it for damage. "Don't tempt me, honey." He slid the gun back in the leather pouch and took a deep breath. "I don't even know what to say or do about this. Do you have any idea how worried I would have been if you had succeeded? I would have had to call all of the guys down here to help me look for you. I would have gone crazy wondering if you were lying dead in a ditch somewhere, for fuck's sake."

He hated playing the guilt card but he didn't have an ace up his sleeve. He would have had a stroke if she'd left. Period.

Her lips started trembling again and her eyes were bright with unshed tears. "I don't want you to get hurt or killed." Tears spilled and ran unheeded down her cheeks. "I love you."

He scraped a hand down his face. "Aw, fuck." He sat back down beside her and tugged her into his arms, rocking her while she cried. It looked like she'd been as scared as he was. He patted her back and stroked her hair. "I love you too, honey. That's why you have to let me protect you. If I lost you, well, everything would go to shit. Got it?"

She sniffled and scrubbed at her cheeks. "We weren't supposed to fall in love."

He sighed and rubbed his chin on her silky hair. He couldn't argue with her. "That's true, we weren't. But we did. Now we're a team and we need to stay together to be safe. We're stronger together, Presley, than we are apart."

She looked up at him, her expression sad. "If they don't think I'm safe after I testify, they're going to try and take me from you. Give me a new name and a new identity. I don't want them to do that."

Seth nodded. They'd never said it out loud, but he was sure it was what Evan would do. If Presley were still in danger, Seth would want her to be safe, even if it was without him.

"If they think it's not safe, you need to go back into hiding. Promise me you will, honey."

She shook her head. "I don't want to."

He pushed back an errant strand of hair. "Maybe I can come with you to the next place."

She looked hopeful for a second then back to sad. "You can't give up your life in Harper. You have a family that loves you. Friends. A town that needs you. That's why I wanted to leave. So you could go back home and be okay."

Deep in his gut, he knew she was right. He had a life in Harper and she had one in Tampa. The fact that she'd had to abandon it didn't make it less important than his own. The depth of her sacrifice hit him broadside. She'd been willing to give up her own safety for his. He might expect love that deep from his parents, but he'd never expected it from a woman. He was humbled and thankful all at once, and his anger drained away. She'd tried to do something she thought was right, only for all the wrong reasons.

He couldn't say she hadn't warned him about making bad decisions. She had and he'd said it would be okay. He leaned back so he could look into her eyes.

"Don't do that again, understand? If I lost you, if something happened to you, it would hurt me. I'm going to keep you safe. After you testify, if someone is still after you, you will go into hiding. As long as I know they can't get to you, I'll be okay." She started to shake her head but he stopped her. "No, honey. I love you and you love me. You want me to be safe. Well, I want you to be safe even if I can't be there with you, too. I'd rather have you alive and away from me, than dead with me."

Understanding crossed her features. "We have now."

He nodded. "Yes, we do. We have a few more days until the world gets crazy and we lose control of the situation. Let's enjoy this time together." Neither one of them finished his sentence.

It might be the only time they had left together.

After she testified, he might never see her again. He felt a sharp pain twist his heart. Being with Presley was the most exquisite pleasure-pain he'd ever known. He wouldn't trade it for the world.

CHAPTER SIXTEEN

"I can't believe how warm it is here," Seth said for the umpteenth time. He'd had to turn the air conditioner on in the RV and she'd been hearing about it since they hit the Florida state line.

"It's in the eighties which isn't unusual. I've done Christmas shopping in shorts all my life. I've broken a sweat decorating the tree."

He shook his head. "That's wrong about eight different ways."

Presley shrugged. "It's better than freezing your butt off trying to do anything outside. We can barbecue year-round down here."

He laughed. "You can barbecue year-round in Montana. You're just going to be cold doing it."

"You'd have to scrape the icicles off the steaks," she giggled. She looked out the window at the road signs. Seth told her he thought it might be good to spend the time waiting for the day of her testimony close to Tampa, but not too damn close. Orlando fit the bill. Seth flicked on his turn signal at the upcoming rest stop and smoothly parked the motor home.

He went back to the refrigerator and pulled out two sodas, handing one to her. "Time to call Evan," he said.

Her eyes widened. She'd thought he'd decided against it. "I'm surprised. I didn't think you were going to do it."

"He's probably worried. I didn't want any Feds in our way getting here, but I'm okay calling him now. You need to testify in a couple of days and we need to let him know you're going to be there."

Seth punched in the number and drummed his fingers as he waited for Evan to pick up, pressing the speakerphone button when he answered.

"Hello?"

"Evan? It's Seth Reilly and Presley, I mean, Katie."

She heard a loud exhale of air. "Son of a fucking bitch, Seth. Where the fuck have you been? I've got fucking agents looking for you fucking everywhere. When I see you, I'm going to kick your fucking ass—"

"I get the picture," Seth interrupted. "Listen, Presley's here so keep your language PG rated."

"Where the fu—I mean where in the hell are you?" Marshal Evan Davis sounded frustrated and pissed. She was glad they were only on the phone and not in person.

"Close," Seth replied. "Presley will be at the courthouse to testify on Monday. Don't worry."

There was rustling in the background and she could hear a door being closed. "You need to bring her in. Now. You're in big trouble, buddy."

Seth's expression hardened. "No can do. You've got a leak in your organization. I won't risk Presley's life just to follow procedure."

Evan was quiet for a moment. "Never thought I'd hear that from you. Are you sure you're Seth Reilly?"

"Meet the new and improved Seth Reilly, courtesy of Presley Lawson. I won't get her killed, Evan. I won't let her out of my sight."

"Holy shit, are you two—? Never mind, I don't want to know. I can protect her, Seth. You can stay with her."

Seth shook his head, even though Evan couldn't see him. "Someone found her, Evan. Your organization didn't keep the secret. You've got a leak, buddy. Have you found it yet?"

Evan sighed. "No. Everyone appears to be clean."

"Then she stays with me. No one dies this time, Evan."

Presley didn't know what that statement meant but Evan must have. "Can I talk to Presley?"

"I'm here, Evan," Presley replied.

"Are you okay? Are you hurt or anything?"

"Other than being shot at on the streets of Harper, I'm fine. I can't wait to testify so you can put Randall behind bars and I can breathe easy again."

"Do you want to stay with Seth?" The question sounded reluctant but she had to give Evan credit for even asking it.

"I only feel safe with him. No one else. I'm sorry, Evan." She smiled at Seth. "We're a team, and we're better together than apart." Seth grinned.

"Okay," Evan conceded. "I can't keep the agents off your back. You're on your own there. I can keep this call to myself. No one will know you phoned in."

"Where are they looking for us?" Seth asked.

"We have a set of agents in Tampa, another outside of Harper, and a third detail in Denver."

Presley frowned. "Denver? Why Denver?"

Evan chuckled. "Well, I know you're not in Denver. Seth has lots of friends in Denver from when he was on the force there. It seemed a logical assumption he might ask them for help."

"Let's just say I'm not worried about your agents." Seth smiled.

"I guess, hypothetically speaking then, you're not in any of those cities. If you were going to lay low until Monday, hypothetically of course, where might you do that?" Evan asked.

Seth's eyebrows went up. "Somewhere near Tampa but not too close. Hypothetically, of course."

"Hypothetically, the best place to blend in to the crowd would be where there's a crowd, Seth. I don't know any bigger crowd than at Disney. Take off the western wear, put on a couple of Mickey shirts and act like tourists."

"You're kidding," Presley groaned. Like many Florida residents, she held the tourist areas in disdain during the busy times of the year, and December was one of the busiest.

"I'm not. No one will look for you there and better yet, no one will find you. It's the last place anyone would look but the absolute best place to blend in and be hidden. Ride some rides, see some shows. Have a good time. Then get your ass here to the Federal Courthouse, Monday by eight in the morning. We need to talk about your testimony before you go in there." Evan's voice had gone from light-hearted to just plain hard.

"Thank you, Evan. Will you get in trouble for this?" Presley hoped he wouldn't. He was a nice man.

"Probably. Seth's in bigger trouble than I am. However, it will all be made better when you show up alive on Monday and testify. The brass will get the hell over it and be happy you're there, okay? I need to go. Do you guys need anything?"

"We're good," Seth answered. "See you Monday. Thanks, Evan."

Seth hung up the phone and gave her a lopsided smile. "Missy Rodell, you've had three days in an RV, traveling over three thousand miles. What are you going to do next?" Seth's voice was booming like an announcer's and she was glad the rest stop was deserted.

She laughed at the irony of her situation. "I'm going to Disneyworld."

* * * * *

Seth and Presley had some trouble finding an RV park near Disney that wasn't completely full, but they finally found one about five miles from Disney. Seth had been shocked at the traffic on I-4 and International Drive and more than once he'd let a few curse words fly as tourists with their heads bent over maps turned in front of him or drifted into his lane.

"I told you December is a busy time in Orlando," Presley said. "Did you think I was kidding?"

Seth swore as a car pulled out in front of him and he had to quickly hit the brakes. "Shit, when you said a lot of people, I couldn't even picture this. There are more people here than in the entire state of Montana."

He was probably correct.

At least they were now safely in the park, the RV hooked up. Presley breathed in deeply, the air warm and the sun high in the sky. It was a typical gorgeous Florida day - warm, with no humidity to speak of. This kind of weather was why people flocked to the state when the rest of the country turned cold and snowy.

"Hey, honey," Seth called. He was standing in the doorway of the RV looking completely out of place in his denim jeans, cowboy boots, and button-down shirt. Yes, he rocked those clothes, looking sexy and hot, but it wouldn't do here in Florida. Her first task was to change his wardrobe. Evan had been specific. Look like tourists. Seth looked like a tourist all right. From Montana. He'd stick out like a sore thumb among sunburnt tourists in shorts and Mickey ears. "Are you hungry?"

"I am." Presley was happy to be back in Florida and warm. It felt damn good. The Feds looking for them were nowhere near them, and it didn't appear that her killer knew where she was either.

Seth tipped his head. "You're very smiley. Is it because we're going to the happiest place on earth?"

She shook her head and spread her arms wide as if to encircle the sun. "I'm warm. Isn't it wonderful?"

Seth grinned. "That's all it took? Some warmth? Come here. I can keep you warm."

"If I come over there we won't eat dinner. We need to shop too. You can't walk around looking like the Marlboro Man. We have to blend in."

"We can go to dinner and then shop. Grab your purse."

Presley followed Seth inside the RV. "Why do I need to grab my purse? Aren't we going to dinner?"

They were tired of cooking for themselves and in a city with this many people, no one was going to notice them. Evan knew what he was talking about.

"We are." A smile played around Seth's lips.

"But we're all hooked in. How are we going to go to dinner?"

"We're not taking the RV."

Presley rolled her eyes, impatient with the game. "How, oh wise one, are we going to eat then?"

Seth reached down into a cabinet she'd never opened and pulled out two helmets. "Apparently, Tanner's parents used alternate transport when they parked somewhere for a while. Grab your purse."

This time she did and he led the way outside, locking the camper door behind them. He walked to the rear of the vehicle and began pulling a black tarp off something attached to the back. "Grab that end, honey."

She caught the fabric in her hands and helped him tug it, revealing a shiny motorcycle sitting on some sort of platform connected to the back of the RV. She put her hands on her hips as she surveyed his grin. "I never even noticed this."

"You've had quite a bit on your mind. Let me get this down and we'll go eat."

It didn't take him long to free it from its bindings and soon they were zipping along the streets and pulling up in front of one of Presley's favorite steak houses.

Seth looked around as they were seated and handed menus. "This has an Aussie theme? I've seen these in Billings, but never been to one."

"Yes," she nodded. "You should try the onion appetizer. It's really good. They have a great chocolate dessert too." Seth loved dessert. They ordered and then sipped at their iced tea while his eyes scanned the room.

"You never truly relax." Presley nudged him with her foot under the table. They might only have a few days left together and she wanted to make the most of them. She wanted to have fun with Seth.

"I'm trying." Seth captured her hand with his. "I still can't get over all these people in one place. The restaurant is packed and so were all of them up and down this road. There were people walking in crowds down the street and cars three lanes deep. That's a lot of people."

"If we'd been here in October it would have been better. There's less people that time of year." She was getting a little tired of defending her home state. She hadn't gone on and on about the cattle in Montana.

As if he could read her mind, he relaxed and smiled. "I guess it's just that time of year." The waitress plopped down the onion appetizer between them and Presley's stomach growled at the delicious aroma.

They demolished the appetizer, two steaks, and dessert. Presley groaned and patted her stomach. "That was so good. But now I need you to take me someplace. I saw it on our way here."

Seth's brows drew together. "Where are we going?"

She tugged at his hand as he threw some money down on the check. "Let's go."

Within ten minutes, Presley was sitting in the chair of a hair salon with a plastic cape wrapped around her. Seth was scowling but she knew what needed to be done. The killers knew her as a blonde and as a brunette. They had yet to see red. She gave the smiling stylist her request and the woman beamed as she clipped and fussed at her hair.

Presley knew what cutting and coloring her hair was going to do, but Seth was clearly shocked. Her hair was now bouncing in auburn curls and waves just above her shoulder. The stylist whipped off the cape with a flourish. It had taken over an hour and a half but the results were well worth it.

"Ta da! You look great. The long hair was lovely but this really looks good on you," the stylist enthused.

Seth reached out and pulled at a curl, watching it spring back. "Your hair's curly. Really curly. I had no idea."

The woman laughed. "The longer the hair, the more it pulls at the curl. If she went shorter, the curls would be even tighter."

Seth stared at Presley in the mirror. "You look so different."

Presley smiled and paid the woman. "That was the point, wasn't it?"

"I guess it was."

They walked outside, the sun starting to sink in the sky. They needed to get a move on if they were going to pick up some new clothes. "Are you okay? Do you hate it? Is that it?"

"No," Seth denied. "It's just you don't look like you. I can't imagine you blonde either, if that helps."

She entwined her fingers in his, leading him down the sidewalk to a large tourist trap shop. "I'm still the same person. Look at it this way." She waggled her eyebrows. "You can pretend you're with another woman tonight and you won't even get in trouble for cheating."

"I like the woman I'm with just fine. I don't need anyone else."

Presley felt a warmth in her heart and another place further south. "You are so getting lucky tonight."

Seth pointed to a liquor store on the corner. "I'm not that easy. I need to be romanced first."

"Come on." Presley giggled. "Let's get you some clothes and then a bottle of wine. I think I know how to romance my man."

CHAPTER SEVENTEEN

Presley certainly knew how to get Seth's motor running. They managed to compress an hour of clothes shopping into forty-five minutes of giggling as they modeled hideous T-shirts, bright shorts, and various cheap flip-flops. After grabbing a decent bottle of Chardonnay, they'd headed back to the RV with much more on their mind than having a drink and discussing religion and politics.

Seth was in the mood to seduce his woman and she seemed to be of the same mind. He dug into a drawer for a corkscrew while she closed the blinds. The neighbors weren't going to get a show tonight, although they might hear her when she screamed his name during her orgasm. Scratch that. Orgasms, plural. His beautiful Presley was going to come more than once.

He poured the wine and handed her a glass. She twirled the liquid, her eyes already warm with emotion and passion, then lifted her glass in a toast. "To now."

His heart lurched in his chest. He wouldn't think about what would happen after Monday. "To now." They clinked glasses and sipped at the fruity elixir. He was more of a beer kind of guy but he liked a good glass of wine every now and then. It seemed to fit their mood tonight for some reason. Seth switched on some music and one of the languorous melodies from Presley's iPod filled the air. He re-filled their wine glasses before taking a seat on the couch.

Presley was still standing, swaying to the music, her eyes closed, the wine glass dangling from her fingers. Her body moved sensuously, the burnished curls dancing around her head. He couldn't take his eyes away from her mouthwatering curves. Everything about her was beautiful, sexy. Her jeans hugged the curve of her ass and the shirt pulled tight over her round breasts. He knew what she looked like without her clothes. He shouldn't be this hot and hard from a tiny woman dancing fully-clothed in the living room, but he was.

Why this woman, at this time? It was messy, dangerous, and damn inconvenient but he didn't care. At that moment, he would have crawled naked across burning hot coals to get to her.

Her eyes opened and Presley smiled at him. She must know what he was thinking. Heat swept through his veins and his cock swelled in his jeans. He shifted to relieve the pressure and continued watching his brown-eyed witch gyrating to the music. She glided over to the iPod and rubbed her thumb over the wheel until a new song blared from the dock speakers. By the time he realized the song was Joe Cocker's 'You Can Leave Your Hat On,' Presley was already pulling up her shirt in teasing manner, exposing the bare skin of her midriff.

His cock jerked in his pants and his breath became shallow. Damn woman was doing a strip tease right in front of him. She shimmied out of her shirt, tossing it in his face, before turning her back and swaying her heart-shaped ass not three feet from him. He could have reached out and dragged her down on to his lap, caveman style, but he forcibly kept his hands on his thighs. His palms were covered in sweat and he rubbed them on the denim as his heart accelerated to the beat of the music.

When Presley turned around, her pants were unzipped and she was pushing them down her legs. She kicked them away with a flourish, her hands over her head, rocking to the beat. She flashed him a smile and leaned forward so he had an eyeful of her generous cleavage.

Holy fuck, his dick was as hard as a fence post. He could feel the blood rushing to it, leaving his brain too little to function. She was only in a bra and a ridiculous pair of panties, hardly more than a scrap of material. She went to her knees and reached behind her back, shaking her breasts so the bra slid down her arms.

Where the fuck did she learn to do that?

She giggled, her face pink, but his gaze was riveted to her breasts bobbing as she smoothly stood but bent over him so her nipples hovered over his mouth. He dipped his head and captured one between his lips but she danced away before he could suck on it. Blood pounded in his head, and he felt a wave of lust he could barely control. He dug in his pocket for a condom just as she turned her back again and tugged her panties down her thighs. He stood up with a roar and grabbed her around the waist. She yelped in surprise and then moaned in pleasure as he pushed two fingers inside her hot cunt.

Seth wrapped his hand around her trapped panties and ripped them from her body, crotch first, the flimsy material giving way easily. He turned her head so he could capture her lips even as he held her back to his front. He bent her over the back of an easy chair, her spankable bottom raised up, her toes off the ground, and the wet pink of her pussy peeking out at him. He smacked her bottom and she moaned in response.

"Yes, Seth. Yes." Her voice was a throaty whisper but the pleasure was in no doubt. He smacked her bottom a few more times, leaving red handprints behind on the creamy white flesh. He jerked at his zipper and pushed his jeans and boxers down far enough to roll on the condom. His fingers were clumsy but the minute he was sheathed he thrust inside of her in one stroke.

"Seth!" Presley cried out at his possession. He reached down and found her nipples, pinching and rolling them between his fingers. He kissed her spine, then nibbled at it as he fucked her hard and fast from behind, their breathing labored.

"Fuck me, fuck me, fuck me." Presley chanted. Damn, he loved how she loved sex. She didn't act all coy and shy. She liked it and she let him know he was all man. She was certainly all woman. He kept up the blistering pace, slamming into her over and over until the pressure in his lower back and balls was too much to bear.

He found her clit with his fingers and massaged circles over the swollen nub until her body stiffened and she lifted her head back, calling his name. Her pussy clamped down on his cock, the muscles squeezing his own orgasm from him. His balls erupted, practically turning his body inside out. He shouted her name as his seed shot from his body, the pleasure radiating to every muscle and deep into his bones. This is what he and Presley were made for. This was what they were born to do, to love each other in this most basic way.

Seth slumped over her back until he had control of his arms and legs again. He pulled from her body regretfully and she hissed, obviously sore from their rough and tumble ride. He rubbed her back and leaned down to kiss her neck. "You okay, honey? Was I too rough?"

She reached back and wrapped an arm around his waist. "At the time it was awesome, but I'm definitely going to be sore." She giggled, though, so it set his heart at rest. He wouldn't hurt her for the world.

"I wish we had a bathtub in this thing so you could take a soak."

With another kiss to her shoulder, he straightened up and headed for the bathroom to dispose of the condom. He was turning around to return to her but she was right behind him.

"I could use a shower. I know we try to conserve water but I'm all sticky."

He laughed and snagged two towels from the under sink cabinet. "We can save water by showering together. I'm sticky too."

"Only a shower," she warned, shaking her finger, but there was a big grin on her face. "No funny business, buster."

"I wouldn't dream of any funny business. We wouldn't have been involved in that funny business if someone hadn't performed a striptease in the living room," he countered.

Her expression immediately turned serious. "Did you like it? Was it trashy? Oh God, even worse, stupid looking? Tell me the truth. I can take it."

He shook his head. "Honey, I can honestly say it was hot. Very hot. Why do you think I rushed you like a bull at a red flag? You definitely made me forget things like foreplay and finesse."

Her smile came back. "Good. That's what I was going for."

"You wanted me to lose my cool?" He turned on the water, adjusting the temperature.

"I did," she nodded. "Wasn't it fun?"

He didn't answer. Instead he lifted her so she was under the warm spray. It had been fun, and he would miss it when she was gone. Their time together was ticking away.

* * * * *

It was their last night in Orlando. Tomorrow, Presley and Seth would drive to the outskirts of Tampa. She needed to go clothes shopping so she would have something presentable to wear to court, although Seth was determined she wouldn't be doing the shopping herself. He was bound and determined to do it for her while she stayed locked up in the motor home, twiddling her thumbs.

They decided to visit Disney's Hollywood Studios to see the dancing Christmas lights on the back lot. She'd visited a few years ago, but the display had grown quite a bit and the New York-themed back lot was packed with people. There were lights and hot chocolate and even snow. Presley found herself getting in the holiday spirit despite what she was facing on Monday. With any luck, she'd testify, they'd arrest Randall, and she would be free.

She looked up at the lights strung overhead as the snow drifted down around them. "Isn't it beautiful? Snow in Florida. We didn't even have to freeze to get it."

The evening was cool and they were both wearing Mickey sweatshirts, but the weather was still mild. Seth rolled his eyes as he shuffled his feet to avoid the crush of people. He looked distinctly uncomfortable.

"There are too many damn people. We can barely breathe. And it's fake snow."

She was determined he wouldn't bring her down. She was having fun. "It's as real as it gets here. Besides, it's pretty and festive. Isn't that enough?"

The multi-colored lights were perfectly synchronized with the music and it was an amazing spectacle to behold. She'd read it took months to put it all together, starting in August. Seth's mouth twisted.

"I guess. It seems kind of artificial to me."

She could barely hear him over the blaring music. She leaned forward so she wouldn't have to yell. "Artificial? How so?"

Seth shrugged, obviously uncomfortable with the topic. Too bad. "It's commercial. Christmas isn't about flashing lights and characters dressed up in holiday wear."

He just couldn't relax and enjoy it for what it was. She tossed her paper cup in the trash bin, her hot chocolate suddenly losing its appeal. "Thank you, Linus. This Charlie Brown has just been schooled in the meaning of Christmas. Geez, I was simply enjoying the lights and the happiness around me. Way to bring it down."

A muscle ticked in his jaw. "Presley," he began, but she was in no mood to hear it. She was trying to have a good time and he was being a prick. She turned to move toward the exit. He easily caught up with her, his long strides matching her much shorter ones.

"Presley," he started again. "I'm sorry, okay?"

She rounded on him, causing a group of people to bump into both of them.

"What are you sorry for?"

"I'm sorry that you're mad." He didn't sound sorry.

"But you're not sorry about why I'm mad?" She crossed her arms over her chest and tapped her foot on the pavement.

He mirrored her body language. "Honestly, I'm not sure what your issue is. You asked a question and I answered it. If you don't like my answer, I'm not sure what I can do about it."

"You were lecturing me," she accused. "You were looking down your nose at people, like me, enjoying this. Like you were too good to have fun at Disney. You've been doing it all weekend, if the truth be known." There, she'd said it. He'd been uptight since they'd arrived in Florida, as if he didn't dare allow himself to have fun and actually enjoy warm weather and relaxation. "You're pulling away from me, Seth. I can feel the distance between us growing. It's getting even bigger as we speak. Are you trying to piss me off so we won't be sad if I have to go back into hiding?"

From the expression on his face, it was clear that was exactly what he'd been trying to do. Tears sprang to her eyes and she turned on her heel to move toward the exit again. She wanted to get back to the RV and begin preparing to testify. They were starting to unravel these last few days. He was pulling away. She could feel it and there was nothing she could do about it. Perhaps it was the wise thing to do, put distance between them so the inevitable parting wouldn't hurt so much.

But it was going to hurt like a bitch no matter what.

He caught her arm and led her to a quiet corner away from the stream of people. His color was high and he looked like he would rather be any place but here having this conversation.

He opened and closed his mouth several times. "Maybe. Shit, I don't know. Maybe I was trying to pull away a little." His expression was fierce, his eyes blazing. "Am I supposed to be happy about this? Well, I'm not. Every moment brings us closer to the time we might have to leave each other. I'm not happy about that. I'm trying to have fun and enjoy myself, but it keeps hanging over me like a cloud." His face gentled. "It's easier for you, honey. You know how to have fun. It doesn't come as naturally to me."

Presley sighed. "You need me to help you."

"I do," he nodded. "I'm sorry. And this time I know what I'm sorry for. Come on, let's go back and see the lights."

She shook her head. "You don't really want to. You don't like Florida. You don't like Disney."

"I do want to. I may not be the biggest fan of Florida, but I'm the biggest Presley Lawson fan there is. Come on."

She turned and nodded in the other direction. "I'm tired. Let's just go back to the RV."

He looked like he was going to argue but then he wrapped an arm around her shoulders and they walked through the park. There were thousands of people all around them but she felt alone. He could deny it all he wanted, but Seth was distancing himself from her ever so subtly. It wouldn't be long until she lost him altogether.

CHAPTER EIGHTEEN

"I'm fucking everything up, Tanner."

Seth blew out his breath and gripped the cell phone until his knuckles were white. It was Monday morning and they would be leaving for downtown Tampa in a few minutes from the RV park they'd found yesterday just outside the city proper. The last thirty-six hours had pretty much sucked and he knew it was all his fault. He was acting like an ass but he couldn't seem to stop himself. It was like driving at an unmovable brick wall in slow motion. It menaced closer and closer but he couldn't turn the wheel from his inevitable slaughter.

"Probably you are, buddy. What have you done this time?" Luckily Tanner wasn't laughing at him. Seth glanced at the door to the RV where Presley was getting dressed inside. They had gone shopping in an out-of-the-way outlet mall in Orlando before heading to Tampa yesterday. She'd wanted to look professional and none of the jeans and shorts fit the bill.

"I'm being a jerk. All I did while we were at Disney was act like it wasn't good enough. Presley took offense. She called me on it, asking if I was pulling away from her. I couldn't say no, Tanner. There was a part of me that was trying to piss her off so it wouldn't be as big of a deal if I lost her after she testifies."

"Can't you go with her? This is Presley we're talking about, Seth. Would it be so bad? Would it kill you?"

Being with Presley would be heaven, even in this flat state with no seasons.

"We've talked about it. Presley wants me to go back to Harper and be with my family. I want to be with Presley. I love her. It's all fucked up, Tanner. I can't force myself on her. Maybe...maybe she really doesn't want me with her."

"Your head is screwed on wrong, buddy. She's just trying to be noble and all that shit. Of course she wants you with her. She's scared, Seth. If she has to go back into hiding, she's going to continue to be scared. I can't imagine you letting her walk away knowing what she's going to."

Seth wanted to love and protect Presley. He was thinking in terms of a lifetime with her. It was something he'd never contemplated before, but a future without her yawned empty and cold.

"I want her to stay alive, first and foremost. We can't think about anything past that. If she's not safe after today, they're going to take her and I may never see her again."

Tanner snorted. "Then you better make sure she knows you're going with her, no matter where they send her. I'd give everything I own to have a woman who loves me a fraction as much as Presley loves you. Stop being an ass and tell her. Your friends and family will understand. If they don't, well, they probably aren't your friends. Can you find another Presley?"

"No." Seth shook his head. "There is no other Presley. Fuck, Tanner. But I can't imagine never seeing my family or friends again. I don't know how Presley did it, walking away from everything. She's stronger than I am, that's for sure."

"She did it to stay alive. Think about it, Seth. Think really hard about this. Once she's gone, she's gone. You won't see her again if you don't go with her."

"If you're going to be so supportive and cheery, I'm going to hang up."

"If you called me to tell you you're doing the right thing holding back, you called the wrong guy. Maybe Logan's home. You could try him. He'd probably be more sympathetic to your problem."

"You're an asshole."

Tanner laughed. "Never said I wasn't. Hug Presley for me, will you? Tell her good luck today. Don't fuck this up, Seth." Tanner's voice went down an octave. "Don't be your usual self and try and get Presley to tow some invisible line you've drawn. I need to go. I'm on duty in a few. Call me later after she testifies. I want to hear all about it."

"Will do."

They said their goodbyes and Seth hung up, Tanner's words ringing in his ears.

* * * * *

Presley resisted the urge to rub her clammy hands down the thighs of her conservative navy blue pantsuit. Seth's eyes had widened when she'd walked out of the RV dressed in professional clothes with her hair wound in a sophisticated chignon and her makeup applied with an understated hand. She looked cool, calm, and ready for anything. Which, ironically, was exactly the opposite of what she was in reality.

She was a quaking mass of nerves.

The waiting room she was in was sterile looking, the beige furniture adding no character to the drab interior. She'd been waiting for several minutes inside this room, deep in the bowels of the Federal Courthouse, and at this rate she'd be a puddle of sweat and adrenaline by the time she actually had to testify.

She wished Seth was there to hold her hand, but Evan had caught Seth's arm and dragged him away even as the other agent, Marisa, was escorting Presley into this room. She'd protested but Marisa had assured her Seth would join her soon. Now the only question was, when was soon? There was a small niggling fear in her heart she wouldn't see Seth again. What if Evan kept them apart?

She straightened her spine when the door swung open. Evan and another man with a briefcase bustled in, smiling and shaking her hand.

"Miss Johnson, I'm Art Lancaster, the prosecutor for this case. Thank you for coming today."

It was jolting to hear anyone call her by her former name. She took a deep breath and nodded. "I'm glad I could be here. I'm honestly anxious to get my testimony over with."

The door swung open again and Seth came in with four coffees. Presley wanted to jump up from the table and kiss him. She needed him and she needed the caffeine. He passed out the coffees and settled in a chair next to hers.

Presley didn't miss the glance Art gave to Evan. It didn't look like a happy one. "Is there something wrong, Mr. Lancaster?"

"Call me Art." Art looked over at Seth, who was serenely sipping his hot coffee. "It's unusual for another party to be included in these preparations."

She had never met Art but he appeared to be a by-the-book kind of guy. Seth would love him. Presley, however, wasn't going to be dictated to. She'd been through too much in the last two months to let anyone intimidate her. "Seth is an involved party. Can we get started?"

She smiled sweetly but she kept her tone even and firm. Art's eyebrows shot up but he nodded and pulled a stack of papers from his briefcase.

"First, here is the subpoena from the Grand Jury. It's a moot point now since you're here of your own volition, but you may want to read it over." He handed her a set of folded papers, which she passed to Seth. She trusted him to look through them while she listened. Art didn't miss her action and frowned. "You, of course, should not discuss your testimony with anyone."

Seth held up his hand. "Excuse me, but she doesn't have to keep her testimony a secret. There's no law or obligation to do so. I'm not saying she wants to talk about it, but telling her she has to is a misleading statement."

Art's face turned a shade of red. "You are correct. I was asking as a courtesy."

Presley's respect for Seth grew exponentially. His law enforcement background made him a good ally. Evan leaned forward, his brows drawn together. "He's right, Art. Presley's here of her own free will, but let's keep what's legal separate from what we're asking her to do as a favor. I didn't encourage Presley to get an attorney since I thought this would be a friendly exchange. If it's not going to be, she needs counsel."

Art's brows drew down even further. "Who's Presley?" He shuffled through papers as if looking for the reference.

Presley placed her hand on top of the papers, the rifling grating on her nerves. "I am Presley. It's my new identity. Katie Johnson was killed in a car bomb in south Tampa."

It was quite freeing to say it. Katie was gone and even when she was free from Randall, she wouldn't be coming back. Presley was alive, however. It was a watershed moment and she snuck a look at Seth, but he seemed to be unaware of the gravity of what had just happened.

Art shook his head and turned to the first paper on the pile. "Fine. This is a friendly discourse. I'll just prepare you for testifying." He picked up a picture from the file folder. "Answer the questions truthfully. Listen closely to the questions, and answer only the question I ask. Give no extra information. Don't go off topic and don't speculate. Keep your answers short, simple, and to the point. For example, if I hold up this picture and ask you if you know the person in the photo what do you say?"

"Yes." She'd seen every episode of Law and Order ever made.

Art nodded approvingly. "Good. I didn't ask you who it was, only if you knew him. Excellent. Keep that up and you'll do fine. Now let's go through some of the questions I'm going to ask you."

An hour and a half and two more coffees later, Art turned over the last piece of paper in the stack. Presley sighed and rubbed her neck. She'd been sitting too long in one place.

"Are we done? When do I testify?"

Art's expression was concerned. "We're done." He seemed to be looking for the right words. "Ms. Johnson, are you being completely truthful today? I asked you questions regarding documents and incidents that happened months ago, the only two months you were actually in Simon's office. Yet you recalled them as if they were yesterday. No juror is going to believe your memory is that clear. You seem quite genuine, but I have trouble understanding how you could remember something from that far in the past. Most people can't remember what they ate for lunch the day before yesterday."

She felt Seth stiffen in the chair beside her and placed a soothing hand on his thigh under the table. "I understand your concern. I have an excellent memory. Better than average. My stepfather once had me tested for an eidetic memory."

Evan pursed his lips. "Eidetic? That's like a photographic memory, right?"

Presley shrugged. "Something like that. I didn't score high enough on the test, but they did say I was close."

Seth shook his head and smiled. "That's why you're such a damn good secretary. You remember everything. Every damn detail."

"I'm good because I'm organized and know my job." Presley sniffed in disdain. "Having an excellent memory simply makes it easier to get everything done."

Art stroked his chin. "Can I give you some advice? Don't answer so affirmatively when asked a question involving the past. Say something like, 'as best as I can recall' or something to that effect."

Seth growled. "Maybe you shouldn't ask her questions she shouldn't be able to answer in the first place?"

Art stood and began shoving the papers back in his briefcase. "I do intend to edit my questions to Ms. Johnson." He snapped the case shut. "Be ready to testify at two o'clock. You're the last one to give your testimony. Remember, your role is to corroborate Mr. Simon's links to illegal arms dealers that the other witnesses have already testified to." He headed to the door, but paused before leaving. "Frankly, Ms. Johnson, I'm puzzled by why Mr. Simon singled you out to kill. There are several witnesses who knew much more about his business dealings than you appear to. You are, however, an expert in his home renovations, which you managed the majority of the time you worked for him. Architectural Digest would be happy to interview you regarding Simon's mansion on the water. Today, I feel like this has been a waste of my time."

Art hurried out of the room leaving only Presley, Seth, and Evan. Presley grimaced at her empty coffee cup. "That guy's a real charmer."

Seth scowled. "He's a jerk."

Evan chuckled. "He's also one of the best Federal Prosecutors in the country. He's lined up a star-studded gallery of witnesses. We've piled on the evidence so thick Simon's expensive legal team is shaking in their Armani suits. It doesn't matter how much money he has. He's going down."

"He's still a jerk." Seth stood and tossed his paper cup into a trashcan. "What do we do now? Just sit here for the next four hours with our thumbs up our asses?"

Evan grinned. "That's what I love about you, Seth. You're always so eloquent." He stood up and pointed to another door in the back of the room Presley hadn't noticed. "No, we are not going to sit here. We're going to get some lunch in a private area of the courthouse." Evan lifted his hand as Seth opened his mouth to object. "There are guards on both doors and there will be guards on her at all times. You are coming with her, don't worry. The only time she'll be out of your sight is when she's actually testifying. No one can go with her."

"Then what?" Presley asked.

"Then I take both of you back to the hotel," Evan answered. "You'll stay there in our loving embrace until the indictments come down. Once Simon is arrested, you should be safe from harm."

Presley breathed a sigh of relief. They weren't planning to send her away with a new identity again. She sagged against the back of the chair, her entire body relaxing for the first time in days.

"What if he runs?" Seth crossed his arms over his chest, his eyes narrowed. "A billionaire must have resources to get out of the country."

"He's surrendered his passport and a good portion of his assets are frozen." Evan slapped Seth on the back. "Once we indict him we can freeze everything except the minimum he needs for his defense. We've already started talking to his defense team about a peaceful surrender to authorities when he's indicted. He knows this is coming."

Evan opened the door and ushered them into a hallway where three very large, fierce, and armed men stood waiting. Presley looked around her nervously, a prickle of fear in her gut.

"Is he here? Is Randall in the courthouse? Does he know I'm here?"

Evan led them down a long corridor. "No, he's not here. The Grand Jury has been convened for several days. He may think you're in the area, but he wouldn't know which day or when. We've kept the security heightened all last week and this week as well so he wouldn't be tipped off when you were going to be here."

Evan opened a set of double doors and motioned for them to precede him. This room looked much more comfortable with leather couches, a television and a conference table in the middle.

"I've got several papers here if Presley wants to catch up on the local news, and I've ordered from a nearby Italian place for lunch. It will be here in about forty-five minutes. There's cable and video games. Make yourself at home."

"Is there coffee?" Presley's gaze ran over the room.

"There is." Evan pointed to a fancy setup in the corner. "Help yourself."

Presley headed straight for the caffeine. She was one step closer to having her freedom back, and a great cup of coffee would only make it better.

* * * * *

Seth rubbed the back of his neck. He was going stir-crazy stuck in the conference room with Presley and Evan but he wasn't about to complain. Presley was obviously nervous about her upcoming testimony and didn't need him bitching about a small inconvenience. Luckily, it was almost two o'clock. Soon she would be done, and they could start looking forward to planning the rest of their lives.

Just what they were going to plan was, of course, a mystery. Bringing two separate lives together wasn't going to be easy. Shit, maybe they could split the difference and live in Kentucky. A discreet knock on the door had all three of them turning toward the sound. Evan stood and nodded. "It's time. Are you ready, Presley?"

"Yes." Her determined little chin lifted. He caught her hand in his and tugged her closer so he could wrap his arms around her.

"Good luck, honey. I can't be there with you in body, but I'll be there in spirit. This will all be over soon. I love you."

She smiled up at him and his heart squeezed in his chest. Damn, he loved this woman. She made everything seem brighter. He'd never realized what a rut he was in until this tiny woman came into his life and dragged him out of it

"I love you, too. Lots and lots. I'll be back before you know it."

Evan stood at the door. "I'll take her down the hall and come back here with you to wait. Give me a minute."

Evan and Presley disappeared and it was all Seth could do not to run after them, his instinct to protect Presley strong and absolute. He had to trust Evan at this moment, and although Seth would trust Evan with his own life, Presley's was infinitely more precious. He poured himself another coffee but Evan was back before Seth had a chance to even add cream and sugar.

"Relax, Seth. She's going to be fine. They'll start her testimony in a few minutes."

"Is she safe?"

"I've got six agents surrounding her. No one's getting to her unless they go through them. We've had bomb-sniffing dogs all week. She'll be okay."

Seth nodded reluctantly. "When do you think the indictments will be handed down?"

Evan grinned. "Anxious to get Presley back to Harper? I never thought the great Seth Reilly would be felled by something as basic as love."

Seth smiled. "Have you spent any time with Presley? She's something else. I'd be a fool to let her go. You might want to take some time and find a woman for yourself, Ev. I highly recommend it." He gulped at the hot liquid. "I'm not sure we'll go back to Harper, actually. Presley loves Florida. I may need to find a job down here. Got any openings?" Seth joked.

Evan's eyes went wide. "Fuck, I'd love to have you down here. You could definitely get a job with the Marshal Service. Are you really thinking about moving?"

Seth shrugged. "Whatever Presley wants, Presley gets. That's my motto. When she's happy, shit, I'll be happy."

"For someone who has a killer after her, she looks pretty happy, buddy. She sure as fuck looks happier than the day I handed her over to you."

Seth remembered that first day. He'd had no idea how that day was going to change his life forever. Evan's phone started going off, and he jerked it out of his front pocket with a curse.

Evan's expression turned from annoyed to disbelieving to incredulous. He glanced at Seth and shook his head.

"Got it." Evan hung up and ran his fingers through his hair making it stand on end. "They're bringing Presley back here. Her testimony's been cancelled."

Seth wasn't sure his ears were working correctly. It sounded like Evan said Presley's testimony had been cancelled and they drove three thousand miles and risked their lives for nothing.

"What did you say?"

"They're bringing her back. She doesn't have to testify."

"Why the fuck not?" Seth voice got loud but he didn't give a damn if everyone in the entire building heard him. Coming here today had been a risk to her life and now they'd decided she didn't need to testify. They should have fucking decided that a few days ago when they were miles away from Randall Simon.

Evan looked slightly sick, his complexion pale. "They don't need her testimony because they won't be indicting Simon. The evidence was overwhelming and I guess he got scared." Evan ran his hands through his hair again. "He's turned state's evidence. He's rolling over on his partners and apparently singing like a bird. He also swears he never tried to kill Presley."

CHAPTER NINETEEN

Presley paced back and forth in the small living area of the hotel room she and Seth had been taken to after her aborted testimony attempt. Evan had ordered room service but she barely glanced at the tray of finger foods, too agitated to eat. Everything since the bomb had gone off, destroying her life and her car, had been leading up to this moment. A moment that had been abruptly taken from her.

"So he just gets away with everything? He goes free and I just have to suck it up and deal with it?"

Evan winced. "His testimony will hopefully allow us to go after even bigger fish in the arms business. It could save thousands of lives. He won't go to jail, that's true. Although a billionaire like Randall Simon isn't going to find his new life in Witness Protection nearly as cushy or glamorous. He'll be living a very small, quiet, ordinary life."

"Not being rich is hardly a punishment," Seth retorted. "He tried to kill Presley. Twice."

Evan shook his head. "He says he didn't. He told the prosecutor he liked Presley and didn't want her caught in all this."

"Why should anyone believe him? He's a criminal." Presley shook her head and evaded Seth's hand that was trying to tug her down in the chair with him. She was too upset to sit.

"Apparently, he's admitted to everything, giving them information we had no clue about. The one thing he says he didn't do is try to kill you. Since he's admitted to everything else, and has immunity, there's no reason to lie about this, Presley. We believe he's telling the truth."

"Then who tried to kill me?" Presley cried in frustration. She didn't have any enemies.

Evan looked distinctly uncomfortable. He fell into the couch with a heavy sigh. "Simon says the attempts on your life had nothing to do with the illegal arms business. It was personal."

Presley stopped in her tracks. "Personal? Who hates me enough to kill me?"

Evan's lips curled as if he was about to take a bite of something really distasteful. "Simon says your stepsister, Nora, is the one who wants you dead."

The world seemed to tilt and Presley reached out blindly for something to hold on to. Suddenly, Seth was by her side, holding her in his arms, and she leaned against his strength, desperately needing him at this moment. He turned to Evan. "That's quite an accusation, Ev. I don't suppose Simon has any proof of this? It's her stepsister for fuck's sake. Family doesn't bomb one another."

"We're checking out everything he's telling us, but at this point, I think we have to give some credence to what he says. Early intelligence said Simon was making Presley the fall guy for everything. Then suddenly he moves her out of his office and assigns her to manage the renovations on his house. He says he got to know her and liked her. He couldn't go through with setting her up."

"Why do it in the first place?" Seth scowled.

Evan shifted his gaze to the windows, not able to look Presley in the eye. "Simon said it was Nora Shefflin's idea to use her sister as their fall guy. Apparently, she lured him into the scheme."

Presley knew her mouth was hanging open but she couldn't seem to close it. His words were thundering through her brain like the beat of horse's hoofs.

Nora's idea. Nora's idea. Nora's idea.

"Why—" Presley's voice came out like a croak. "Why would she want me dead?"

Evan finally looked Presley in the eye. "Simon said Nora ranted about how her father married a whore and the daughter stole his love and attention. She said you deliberately set out to steal her father from her."

Presley's knees gave way under her. Luckily, Seth was holding on to her tightly and he swept her up in his arms and placed her gently in a chair, kneeling close on the floor and grasping her hand in his.

"Presley would never do that," Seth declared.

Evan nodded. "We know that. Simon said when he met Presley it was clear Nora was delusional about the situation. That's why he backed out and sent her to work at his home."

"But he didn't back out of arms dealing?" Seth asked, his hand stroking her arm. Presley was shaking with the effort to not scream. Everything she'd thought she knew was a lie. It was like being betrayed all over again and this time it hurt a thousand times more. This was her sister.

Oops. Stepsister.

She could hear Nora's voice at the restaurant that day correcting Presley about their relationship. Could Nora really hate Presley enough to want her dead?

"Simon had this patriotic idea he was arming militias and keeping the checks and balances on the government. He swears he had no idea the weapons his company manufactured were being sent to foreign terrorists."

Seth snorted. "Right, no idea. Maybe at the beginning, but when the money started rolling in did he honestly think it was from local militias?"

"Probably not," Evan agreed. "I'm betting when the cash started to pile up Simon decided not to ask too many questions. No sense ruining his vision of himself as a hero."

Presley swallowed the lump in her throat, her stomach in knots. She licked her lips and tried to put her words together so they would make sense.

"I want to talk to Randall." There. She'd managed to speak an entire sentence. She didn't feel any better. In fact, she maybe felt even worse. Talking to him was the last thing she wanted to do, but she needed to hear these words directly from his mouth.

Seth was shaking his head. "No way. You're not going near that guy."

Evan shook his head as well. "I'm with Seth on this one. Why talk to Simon?"

She raised a shaky hand and tucked her hair behind her ear. It was a nervous gesture but she had quite a bit to be nervous about. "I need to hear this from him. I can't totally believe what you're saying. Nora and I have had issues throughout the years, but trying to kill me is taking things to a whole new level. Even for her."

Nora could be a bitch, but a murderer? Presley needed proof.

Seth captured her chin so she was looking him in the eye. "Presley, I do not want you anywhere near Simon, whether he tried to kill you or not. He's an admitted criminal. Let the Feds do their job and investigate this."

"No." Presley firmed her lips. "I want to talk to Randall. I won't believe this until I speak with him." She looked up at Evan. "Can you arrange it? Please, Evan? I think he owes me this much. He was going to set me up for a crime I didn't commit."

Evan rubbed the back of his neck. "Okay, I'll talk to his handlers and see what I can do. It may take a day or two. We're starting to investigate the new information he's given us, including your sister's involvement in the illegal arms trade. We'll know more very soon either way." Evan popped open a can of soda. "In light of the new information, technically, we can't hold you here. We'd like for you to stay under our protection for a few days longer until we figure this out."

"Do you think her sister will make an attempt on Presley's life?" Seth asked.

Evan nodded. "I do think it's possible. I can't stop you from walking out of here, but I'm asking you to stay. We'll have audio surveillance on your sister within hours. At that time, we'll see what she's up to and what her plans are. If she's tried to kill you twice, once as far away as Montana, we have to assume she's determined to succeed at some point." Evan sighed. "We also have to concede that somehow she knows you're alive and that she knows you're in Tampa. As much as we've tried to keep the Grand Jury proceedings under wraps, the media has been a circus."

Seth's expression was grim. "We're no better off now than we were this morning." Seth gripped her hand. "We need to keep you under wraps for a few more days, honey. Until we know more about what and who we're dealing with."

Presley nodded and leaned back in the chair, her arms wrapped around her body, her eyes staring into space. She wouldn't believe any of this until she talked to Randall. Hopefully, it would be soon.

* * * * *

The SUV pulled up in front of the Spanish style house near Moon Lake in Pasco County, just north of Tampa. It was a sparsely populated area with the privacy a federal agency would want to hold a witness. This house didn't have a neighbor for miles in any direction. The grim-faced agent in dark sunglasses stopped the vehicle.

"I'll wait here," the driver said. Evan was in the front seat with the driver and Seth was in the back seat with Presley. The men hopped out and Seth came around to help her out. She took a deep breath as they approached the front door. The home looked like any middle class house in any neighborhood. She wasn't sure what she expected but there weren't any cannons in the front yard or black helicopters hovering in the sky.

Presley had spent the last twenty-four hours showing Seth the Tampa Bay area from the privacy of a bullet-proof SUV. Evan and the sour-faced agent had driven them all the way down to Anna Maria Island and as far west as Clearwater Beach. She'd stayed in the vehicle at all times, although when no one was around she was allowed to roll down the window. It had been fun showing Seth her old stomping grounds, and he'd had a much better attitude about it this time than at Disney a few days before.

Evan pushed the bell and the door was opened by another man with hair clipped short and a gun in a shoulder holster. Another agent.

"Evan, you made good time up here. Simon is in the living room waiting for you."

Seth had insisted on coming with her and Evan had never intended for her to see Randall by herself either. In a way, it felt stupid for them to be there since she didn't feel threatened by Randall, but if it kept the peace it was a small price. They wouldn't be here long anyway. She had a few questions and then they could go. This wasn't a social call.

Evan and the other agent led the way through an entrance hall into a large living room. It was the middle of the day, but the blinds and curtains were drawn, and every lamp in the home was illuminated. Evan indicated she should sit on the sofa. She moved to do that but the man occupying the chair opposite caught her eye. It was Randall. Or it appeared to be someone who looked like him. This man was much grayer and much older.

She sucked in her breath and sat down heavily. She stared at the man and he gave her a weak smile. It was Randall. Her fingers gripped the handle of her purse and her heart beat loudly.

"How are you, Katie? I thought you were dead. You can't imagine how relieved I was when I found out you were alive," Randall said. He was drinking from a Pepsi can, his hand shaking slightly, but his voice sounded the same.

She lifted her chin. "I didn't come here to exchange pleasantries or pretend we're friends. I wanted to hear the truth from your own mouth. Talk."

Her words made him smile wider. "But we are friends, Katie. I'm the reason you're not in jail for selling arms to terrorists. In a way, you should thank me."

Seth stiffened next to her and she put her hand on his. This was hers to do and do alone.

"I think I'll pass on thanking you. You've told the Feds quite a tale. Is any of it true?"

His expression grew sad. "It's all true. It's part of my deal with the government that I tell the truth, but I would have anyway. This has all gotten out of control. All I wanted to do was be a patriot. A good

American. You know how important that was to me, Katie." His voice was urgent and she nodded.

"I remember, Ran." She didn't say anything more. He was the one with a story to tell.

He fiddled with the can. "I've known your sister for many years. We traveled in some of the same circles."

Presley was getting impatient. "I know. That's how I got the job with you."

Randall shook his head. "No, you got the job with me because Nora suggested you as the patsy for everything. We were going to frame you for what we were doing."

Presley felt herself tremble all over at the thought of what might have happened. She could have been thrown into a dark jail cell for the rest of her life, never understanding what had been done to her. In a way, the car bomb was a blessing.

"Why, Ran? What did I do to you that would make you want to send me to prison for the rest of my life?"

He smiled sadly. "You could never do anything like that. That's why I pulled the plug on the idea and sent you to manage the renovations on the house. I liked you, Katie. You were a sweet girl and we had fun, didn't we? I tried to protect you from her, but I guess it didn't work. She hates you, you know."

Presley shook her head and leaned forward, scooting until she was barely sitting on the sofa. Seth tried to pull her back but she pushed at his hands. This shit was important and she didn't want to miss a word or a flicker of his expression.

"Why does she hate me? What did she tell you, Ran?"

Randall tipped the can back and took a gulp of the soda. "You took her father's love away from her. Apparently, he loved you more than he loved her."

"That's not true," Presley protested. "He loved Nora."

"Maybe," Randall shrugged. "The reality isn't what's important. It's what she believes. She says her boyfriends would talk about how pretty you were and her father would say how you were going to snag yourself a rich, handsome husband. He bragged about you being Homecoming Queen."

"So she tried to kill me?" Presley was incredulous. "That's a reason not to invite me for Thanksgiving dinner, not trying to blow me up or send me to prison."

"She was very upset when her father left you one of his houses. She said you didn't deserve it."

Presley pressed her face into her palms. Her home hadn't been burnt down to destroy evidence, it had been burnt down because Nora was throwing a fucking tantrum. She felt Seth's hands on her, lifting her from her perch on the edge of the couch cushion and setting her further back, his arm wrapped around her shoulders. She twined their fingers together.

"I'm okay, Seth. Just trying to wrap my mind around this. I never realized my sister hated me so much. It seems unreal."

Randall frowned. "I honestly thought you knew Nora hated you, Katie. She never really tried to hide it in front of you. It just went overboard when her husband divorced her. She blamed you for that."

"What?" Presley jumped up from the couch, shaking Seth's arm from her. "How am I to blame for that?"

Seth stood and placed a hand on each of her shoulders. "Calm down, honey. Stay with us here."

Presley took a deep centering breath. Seth was right. She was getting too upset. She needed to stay calm and in control. She could scream later when Randall wasn't around.

"Her husband liked you," Randall explained. "That was all it took. In her mind, if he had loved her, he would have hated you. She's pretty twisted but I never thought she'd try and kill you. When I saw that car bomb on television I was shocked. It was over the top even for Nora."

Presley thought about all the years she'd struggled to stay close to her sister and make them a family. "Nora's always been over the top. I've been closing my eyes to things I didn't want to see."

"No one could foresee a sister trying to kill them." Evan finally spoke from his spot on the couch arm.

"There were signs of how she felt. I just didn't want it to be true." Presley could see it now. Hindsight was always twenty-twenty. Little digs from Nora whenever she had the chance. Slights when their parents were still married. Nora had tried many times to blame things on Presley when they were kids. Looking back, she realized her stepfather had rarely taken Nora's side. It must have infuriated her.

"All that hate festering away for years. Growing and deepening every day until she just couldn't take it anymore." Presley was shaken, and she leaned into Seth, needing his strength.

Presley turned back to Randall. He was far from the eccentric billionaire now. He looked old and worried, his face deeply lined and ashen. "What happens to you now, Ran? Do you get off scot-free? Does money buy everything, even justice?"

Randall's eyes were haunted. "No. I'll get a new life, a new name, but nothing will ever be the same. I'll always be branded a traitor and not a patriot. I'll spend the rest of my life looking over my shoulder. I'm glad I got to see you again, Katie. I've missed you."

Revulsion at what he'd done made her stomach curdle. He hadn't tried to kill her but he'd been willing to bend the law and throw his lot in with her batshit, crazy sister. It made her bad decision history look pretty good in comparison.

"My name is not Katie. Katie's dead."

She turned on her heel and started for the door. She'd heard what she needed to hear and she never wanted to see him again. Evan and Seth caught up with her before she hit the front porch and all three of them were silent as they loaded into the SUV and drove away.

Presley couldn't take the quiet any longer. Her skin was prickly and she wanted to jump up and pace, or run. She needed to move. She also needed to end this chapter of her life.

"So Evan, what do you have planned to catch my sister and how can I help?"

CHAPTER TWENTY

"Have you lost your mind?" Seth thundered. He scraped his hand down his face in frustration. They'd returned to the hotel suite minutes ago and Evan had wisely and discreetly excused himself while Seth tried to talk some sense into the woman he loved.

Presley was going to send him into an early grave. Now she wanted to help Evan get evidence against her sister.

"No, I think I'm finally making a good decision." Presley's expression was serene. "Finding out the truth about Nora has set me free. I can finally stop trying to create a family with her and move the hell on with my life."

"That's a good idea. Let's move on with our lives, honey," Seth urged. "We can head back to Harper. You're out of protective custody and it won't be long before Evan has Nora behind bars."

Presley rummaged in the honor bar and pulled out a soda, holding it up in offering. He shook his head, but she opened it anyway, taking a long drink.

"For how long? She sent killers after me to Harper. I'm done with looking over my shoulder, Seth. I want my life back, dammit. If I can speed up this process, well, why not? Don't you want us to be a regular, normal couple? Wouldn't you like our biggest concern to be what movie we're going to rent for a Friday night? I'd like that."

That made Seth smile. "Honey, you and I will never be a regular, normal couple. I don't think it's in our DNA."

Presley smiled back. "As normal as we can be then." She stepped in front of him and went up on her tiptoes so she was looking up into his eyes. "I'll be surrounded by agents. From what Randall said, it sounded like she hates me so much she'll love to tell me all the stuff she's done in the name of revenge. They'll get it on tape and then they'll arrest her. Piece of cake, Sheriff."

Seth wasn't sure it would be that easy, but he could see the determination in her eyes. She wanted this and he needed to find a way to keep her safe. "There will have to be some precautions. We need to have a foolproof plan, Presley. I'm not risking your life after I've protected it all this time."

There was a soft knock on the door. It was probably Evan back from making his phone calls or whatever he'd been muttering about when he'd hurried away from the blast zone of the impending argument.   Seth peered out the peephole and confirmed Evan's identity before opening the door.   Evan's expression wasn't any happier than before he'd left.

"What's going on, Ev?" Seth hated feeling helpless and he sure felt that way right now. Everything was spinning out of his control and he didn't know how to stop it. Seth offered Evan a soda, hoping he would reveal what was bothering him. Evan nodded absently, his mind obviously elsewhere.

"This case has been a bear from day one.   We put audio surveillance on Presley's sister and we intercepted a phone call between her and one of her minions. She's hired a couple of guys with long rap sheets and violent pasts. They're sniffing around the courthouse and the hotels nearby. Nora didn't tell them directly to kill Presley but with what Simon told us, we can infer it. It's not enough to arrest her, but it's enough for us to know there's still danger."

Seth closely watched Presley's reaction. Other than a small flinch at the word "kill" she remained composed. His woman was tough, but all he wanted to do was make this go away. Fix it. Wasn't that what a man was supposed to do? Protect his woman and keep her from harm?

Damn woman has me talking to myself.

"All the more reason for me to go to her instead of waiting for them to come to me," Presley stated. "I don't like feeling like a sitting duck."

Seth looked at Evan. "I don't suppose you have a plan?"

"I've got some ideas." Evan's eyebrows went up in surprise. "I'd like to run them by you. Get your input." Evan leaned over the back of the chair casually, a smile playing around his face. "You know, a Federal Marshal has the power to deputize local law enforcement and even civilians, if needed."

Seth grinned. "Deputize me."

Presley's gaze shifted back and forth between Seth and Evan. "Wait, you can make Seth a Federal Marshal? Really? Does he have to take a vow or something?"

"He has to take an oath," Evan replied with a smug smile. "If you get to be a part of the operation, will you let us use Presley as bait? I swear as God as my witness we will keep her safe, Seth."

Seth rubbed his chin. Presley's eyes were alight with excitement. She wanted to do this and technically he couldn't stop her. At least if he were a part of it, he could watch over her.

He turned to Presley. "Do you really want to do this? It's risky, honey. This woman may be your sister, but she wants you dead. Very dead."

Presley nodded. "She won't stop. We have to do this. I have to do this. If I think the plan is too risky, I won't do it, okay?"

Seth sighed. He knew when he was beat. Besides, she had a point. A good offense was the best defense. He wasn't a big fan of sitting here and waiting for this woman to make another attempt on Presley's life. It was better to have control of the situation and be the initiator, take this Nora person by surprise.

"All right, honey. Let's catch us a criminal."

Evan grinned and Presley beamed. Seth felt the familiar rush of adrenaline as if he were preparing for battle. It felt good and right to be doing something constructive rather than sitting around waiting for shit to happen. That was unnatural for any man. He'd lost sight of it because he'd been so worried about Presley.

Seth went to the bar and grabbed a soda, this time for himself, popping it open. "Let's hear what you have in mind. I've got a few thoughts of my own."

* * * * *

Presley had acted pretty macho and brave for Seth but the fact was she was fucking nervous. She checked under her armpits one more time, sure she had a growing damp spot on the cotton shirt. Evan had dressed her in a long sleeved rugby-type shirt, not too form fitting and thick enough to conceal the wires taped to her skin. The agents and Seth would be recording everything said between her and Nora.

As long as she didn't sweat the tape off before the mission began. She reached for her coffee cup and cursed when she realized it was empty.

"Nervous?" Evan smiled sympathetically. "We'll be with you every step of the way, Presley. If she tries to pull a gun or anything, we'll have a sniper pointed at her and we'll storm the place as well. Just make sure the drapes stay open so we can see in."

"You can change your mind, honey. You don't have to do this," Seth said. He was sitting next to her in the SUV with dark-tinted windows down the street from Nora's home. They had a small car Presley would drive to the house since she couldn't arrive in the SUV with the Marshals. There were already agents surrounding the house. Federal agents had taken over the houses on both sides of Nora. Even if Presley couldn't get a confession out of her stepsister, she'd probably have to move out of her snooty neighborhood. Nora's friends and neighbors liked to gossip about one another and Federal agents with a sniper rifle pointed at one of your own was too juicy to hold back.

"No." Presley shook her head. "I have to do this. You were right, Seth. We have to take the fight to them." She reached over and squeezed his hand. His palm was as sweaty as her own. "I'm the only one that can do this. I have to do this."

"Remember what we talked about, honey," Seth coached. "Get her to talk about what she did and why. Talk about the car bomb and Simon. You have the element of surprise. She's not expecting you to waltz into her home."

Evan's phone rang and he pulled it from his pocket. He listened and nodded before hanging up. "Okay, she's stepped out onto the back patio and is having a glass of wine. It's the perfect time for you to go. The sniper can get to her unobstructed if need arises, and we doubt she has any weapons on her verandah. Remember to keep her talking. Try to get her to say as much as possible. The more details we have the easier it will be to find hard corroborating evidence, and the harder for her to recant when she lawyers up."

Presley didn't really want to think about having her sister, scratch that, stepsister, shot in the head while Presley looked on. She hoped Nora wouldn't do anything stupid and simply cooperate.

Because Nora is sooo cooperative.

The three of them stepped out of the SUV and Evan handed her the keys to the small car she would be driving. "We'll be right outside. Good luck. Stay calm and focused. If you want us to rush in, all you have to do is say the word 'coffee.' Got it?"

She nodded. Seth had chosen the trigger word and he had chosen well. Seth wrapped his arms around her and pulled her close. "I'll be right outside the door, honey." He pressed a kiss to her lips. "No heroics. If something isn't going right, you say the trigger word. I mean it."

Presley rolled her eyes but inside she was a basket case. "I got it. You worry too much."

"I worry about you. I love you, remember?"

She smiled and kissed his rough chin. "I love you too. When this is all over we can start our life without looking over our shoulders."

"I can't wait. We'll go somewhere quiet, just the two of us, and talk about our future."

Evan looked impatient but she needed to say this before she went in. "I've been thinking about that. I think we should live where there are family and friends who care."

Seth nodded. "Then that's where we'll be. We'll live in Tampa."

She shook her head. "No. I was talking about Harper. I don't have any family here that cares about me. I have your family though, and I know they care. I have friends there that make time to stop by to talk to me and have coffee every day. I have friends here in Tampa, and I miss them, but I miss Harper more."

She'd surprised the man she loved. His mouth was hanging open but his expression was one of joy. They were going to go home.

She just had this one thing to do first.

"I'm ready. Let's do this." Presley got into the subcompact car, started it up, and headed up the road to Nora's house.

"I hope you can hear me. I'm almost there. I'm parking in the driveway now and I'm heading directly to the back patio."

Presley paused as she exited the car, taking a deep breath. Her hands were shaking and her heart was pounding. She'd never been big on confrontation, but this was probably the most important one of her life. It was time to deal with the specter of her lame-assed family at last.

Her tennis shoes didn't make any noise in the grass or on the concrete and before she knew it she was standing on the patio looking directly at her stepsister and would-be killer. The patio was large, taking up half of the manicured back yard. The other half of the yard was dominated by a large swimming pool with a decorative fountain in the middle. Presley remembered when Nora had the fountain installed right before a fancy party with a State Senator.

"Hello, Nora. I thought I'd find you back here."

Nora had been about to take a sip of her wine and she jerked to attention, her eyebrows shooting up and her mouth going slack. She recovered quickly, however, her body relaxing and her expression composed.

"Katie, how lovely to see you. Do please join me. Shall I get another glass? Or do ghosts even drink wine? I don't know. I've never had one in my home before."

Presley remembered what Evan said about staying in sight and not having any weapons outside. She shook her head and took a seat at the table opposite Nora.

"I'll pass. I think I need to stay completely sober around you, sis. You don't seem very surprised to see me."

A smile played around Nora's lips as she swirled the wine in the glass. "I'm not, actually. I never believed you died in the bombing. Officials wouldn't let me see the body. They said you'd been blown into small pieces and burned beyond recognition." Nora sipped her wine. "Something like that would take a great deal of C-4. As for staying sober, do you think it will help? I've been several steps ahead of you your entire life. It must be very tiring for you trying to keep up."

"Not really. I've been pacing myself. You look good. Working out?" It was a running joke. Nora despised sweat in any form. The swimming pool and the indoor gym were purely for show.

"Aren't you a dear? Thank you. It's a new diet. I eat fish every other day." Nora waived her hand at Presley's hair. "I like the red hair. It's much more sophisticated than the blonde."

Presley ran her fingers through the strands. "I had to change my look. It seems I have some enemies trying to kill me."

Nora sipped her wine. "You? Why, everyone loves you, Katie. I can't imagine why anyone would want you dead."

"Someone does. I've been lying low for a while. You, on the other hand, have been a busy bee lately. Selling arms to terrorists and hiring hit men. How did you find me, by the way? I thought I was well hidden in Montana."

"You told me, dear." Nora looked genuinely happy at that moment. "You used your credit card to purchase something online. I had your phone, and the receipt came in your email. A phone call to a police friend was all it took to get the location of the transaction. Another mistake on your part. An almost fatal one."

"You had my phone? That's what I was going back for when the car exploded."

Nora frowned. "Is that how you escaped?" She sighed. "The maître d gave me your phone. He found it on the table. Of course, I held on to it. I knew eventually you'd screw up."

Wow, had she. In her haste to enter Seth's Christmas present into Marion's laptop on Thanksgiving, Presley must have accidentally used her old account name and password. She was a fucking idiot. She might as well have taken out billboards as to her location and posted them on all the highways from here to Montana.

Fuck!

She needed to gather herself. Nora would delight in watching Presley squirm and she wasn't going to do that. Presley blanked her expression and pressed on. She couldn't forget she had a job to do here no matter how much she was perspiring.

"You've always said good help was hard to find. Perhaps you should have taken care of things yourself and not sent a couple of your henchmen. You miscalculated things, sis."

Presley held her breath waiting for Nora's reaction. She was rewarded with anger flaring in her stepsister's eyes. Excellent.

I've got you now. You're going to give me everything I need.

* * * * *

In Seth's entire life he'd never been this nervous or scared. That included when he had to stand up in front of the entire town at a council meeting and give a speech about drinking, driving, and not doing drugs. This was a million times worse. He was terrified something was going to happen to Presley.

He and Evan were in the house next door listening in on the wire Presley was wearing and watching a monitor via the high-powered camera they had trained on the two women. Presley looked surprisingly relaxed but Seth had felt her tension when he'd held her in his arms only minutes before. She was scared and she didn't want to admit it.

Presley had exchanged a few pleasantries with her sister but now she'd gotten down to brass tacks. Getting Nora emotional enough to spill the beans. Despite the fear twisting in his gut, he was proud of how Presley was playing it. Seth watched the monitor intently, looking for any clue they needed to intervene. They could be out the French doors and over to the next house not fifteen feet away in seconds.

Nora slapped her wine glass down on the table, her eyes narrowed. "I don't make mistakes, Katie dear."

Presley leaned back in her chair, taking a challenging stance that made Seth's heart speed up. Damn, he wished he could stand between her and Nora, but this was something she had to do. He understood it but he didn't have to fucking like it.

"I'm alive. That's at least two mistakes." Presley stroked her lips in thought. "Randall's turned state's evidence. That's another."

The shocked expression on Nora's face told Presley her declaration had come as a surprise.

"You didn't know about Randall? I would imagine he has quite a bit to say. About you. You're going to go to Federal prison for the rest of your life. I heard it's not much fun there. Not that that bothered you when your plan was to send me there for life."

Nora's lips twisted into an ugly smile. "Orange is your color, dear."

Presley let the silence stretch and Evan was nodding in approval. Seth had advised her that silence might unnerve Nora. He'd used it on many a suspect during interrogations.

It appeared Nora couldn't take it any longer. "Nothing to say? I'm not surprised. You never had much to say in the past. Nothing worth listening to anyway."

"Is that why? I was boring so you decided to have me killed?"

Nora shook her head. "The original plan was for you to go to prison. Lovely Katie, everyone adored you. A common criminal, betraying her country." Nora tut-tutted. "I used to dream about you being locked up for the rest of your pathetic life. You wouldn't stay pretty for long behind bars."

Nora's expression had turned ugly and Seth could see Presley's fists clenched under the table, but her face gave nothing away.

"But Randall backed out." Presley didn't make it sound like a question. They already knew it was true.

Nora leaned forward, her palms on the table and Seth found himself reaching for his gun. Evan put a hand on his shoulder. "Relax. She's unarmed and we've got men circling the yard. Nothing's going to happen. Presley's doing exactly what we rehearsed."

Presley was doing it and doing it well. Too well. Nora was already angry, her nostrils flaring. "Randall is an idiot. All he had to do was frame you with the paperwork, but could he do that? Hell no. *He liked you.*" Nora practically spat out the last three words. "He couldn't do it, so I knew I had to have another plan. That's when I decided to kill you. The only question was how."

"A car bomb. Very unique." Presley appeared to be holding it together, but Seth could see she was struggling. They needed to end this confessional soon.

Nora nodded. "I did that for you. I didn't want you to suffer. I wanted you dead, but you are my stepsister. I wanted to make your death quick and painless."

Evan pumped his fist in the air. "Yes! She's getting the details we need," he whispered. "Keep going, Presley."

Presley was rubbing one hand with the other on her lap. "That was thoughtful of you. Did you hire someone to plant it?"

"Of course. I don't know anything about bombs. You'd be amazed at what people will do for money."

"Is that why you did it? Selling the arms? Did you do it for the money?"

Whatever tender feelings Nora had been feeling fled. Her face contorted with rage. "Father didn't leave me enough money. He left the best house to you. The others were mortgaged to the hilt. He should have left everything to me. Me! I loved him more than anything, Katie. I worked hard in school to make him proud. I married a rich man and made a good marriage just like he wanted. But did he appreciate it? No. He still loved you. You stole love from me." Nora was shaking a finger at Presley. "I loved Daddy so much. He never loved me the same after you came into my life."

What a maniacal bitch. Love wasn't a zero-sum game, but to her it was.

"You married a rich man. What happened?"

Nora hopped up from the table. "He was an asshole." She whirled and pointed to Presley. "But he liked you. I had to divorce him. Did you fuck him, Katie? Did you fuck my husband?"

He saw Presley swallow hard and then her shoulders straightened up. "I didn't. Taking your things wasn't my style, Nora. That was your game. So when the car bomb didn't work, you sent someone to shoot at me in Montana. They screwed everything up. I bet the FBI are talking to them right now. They'll roll right over on you. You have no friends and no family, Nora, and it's all your doing. You could have had a family but you pushed everyone away."

Nora shoved a finger in Presley's face and Seth went on alert. It was almost time to roll and he didn't like Nora's body language. "I'll keep trying until you're dead. Coming here today was a stupid mistake, Katie, but then you've made so many who's counting? When the authorities find your dead body in my pool, they'll think it was just one more error in judgment on your part. Oh wait, you're already dead. All I have to do is get rid of your body and no one will be the wiser."

Seth didn't anticipate Nora's next move. She launched herself forward, knocking Presley, Presley's chair, and herself into the pool next to the back patio with a splash. Heart in his throat, Seth immediately jumped and was out the double doors and across the lawn in a flash. Adrenaline pumping, he threw off his shoulder holster but didn't stop to take anything else off, jumping into the water with the two women, who were wrestling for their lives. Both women were coughing and choking, and Seth knew they would tire quickly with their clothes weighed down with water.

Nora was thrashing around, trying to push Presley's head under. Presley was obviously the stronger of the sisters but Nora was fueled by rage, making it an even fight. Nora had a handful of Presley's hair and Presley had Nora in a headlock that would have made a professional wrestler proud. It took several attempts on his part to get between the women. Their legs were kicking wildly and the splashing made it hard to see what was happening. He insinuated himself between them, gaining what he knew would be some nasty bruises the next day. He wrapped his arms around Nora, trapping her so she couldn't flail her arms. Two more agents had joined them in the pool, although one seemed occupied holding Presley back. Between Seth and the agent, they quickly had the screaming woman subdued, physically if not mentally. Evan tossed a pair of cuffs down to him and Seth restrained Nora's hands behind her back, marched her up the steps out of the pool, and handed her off to one of the two dozen agents that had descended on the house and grounds.

Nora was screaming as she was led away. Seth waded back in and gave Presley a hand out of the pool, both of them dripping wet. She coughed a few times but other than that she looked uninjured.

"Are you okay? Are you hurt?"

Presley shook her head and pushed a sodden hunk of curls back from her face. "I think I need to start working out." She shoved at his shoulder. "I totally had her. You didn't need to jump in. I could have taken her."

Relief suffused every cell of his body. She was okay and this long nightmare was finally over. "I'm sure you could have, honey. I was simply hurrying things along. You need to stop getting into trouble. You're going to be a full-time job, I can see."

She smiled at him and it took his breath away. "It's a dirty job but somebody's got to do it." She peeked down her blouse with a grin. "Will the water ruin the equipment?"

Evan laughed and handed them a couple of towels the agents had scrounged up. "Probably, but it doesn't matter. We have the recording of what she said. We shouldn't have any trouble holding her. Looks like you're free to pick up your life again, Katie."

Presley shook her head and smiled. "Presley. Katie's dead, may she rest in peace. I'm Presley now." She linked her arm through Seth's and he felt his heart do a flip in his chest. He loved this woman, and he couldn't wait to get her to himself. "We're headed to Montana. First thing tomorrow morning, we're driving back."

"You don't want to stick around and see some sights?" Seth teased. "We could visit Gator Land or Sea World. Maybe Weeki Wachee. Don't they have mermaids?"

"You don't need mermaids, Sheriff. You need snow, am I right?"

Seth looked around the lush greenery. "I don't know. I could get used to the warm weather."

She gave him a disgusted look and threw up her hands. "Men. Give them what they want and they want something else entirely."

"I know exactly what I want. Do you?" Seth challenged.

She pressed her body to his, and he could feel the heat even when both of them were soaked to the bone. "I want to go home, Sheriff."

This time, her home wouldn't be someplace three thousand miles away. This time her home would be with him.

CHAPTER TWENTY-ONE

Presley hummed Christmas carols along with the music drifting from her iPod dock. She wanted to surprise Seth by finishing the decorating of their cozy log home before his shift ended.

Their home.

She liked how it sounded. When they'd arrived back in Montana last week after three days of driving, Seth had stomped up the stairs to her tiny apartment and helped her pack her belongings. She'd moved out and never looked back. She'd thought she might be depressed finding out her sister was a murderer but Seth's family and Eliza were determined to show Presley she belonged in Harper. She hadn't mourned the tragic end to her family long. She would, however, probably have to go back and testify against Nora at some point. It wasn't something Presley relished but at least she wasn't hiding out anymore.

Now she was wearing naughty red silk lingerie and trying to string lights and pine garland on the mantle. Seth had been working so hard this last week, giving his deputies time off since they'd covered for him. He had tonight and tomorrow off and she wanted nothing more than to spend time with him, make love, and watch the Broncos on television.

"Now that's what I like to come home to." Seth's wolf whistle made her whirl around. He was standing in the doorway looking like the God of Sex in his uniform. "A gorgeous woman in lingerie under twinkling Christmas lights. Hell, we even have an angel choir in the background."

Presley let her gaze wander up and down the man she loved. He was hotter than sin and she loved to look at him. His wide shoulders and flat stomach were emphasized by the tailoring of his shirt and his jeans cupped his perfect ass as if they were made especially for him. She had the perfect vantage point to see his ass as he turned to hang his coat by the door. His grin was wicked and his hand went straight to his cowboy hat. He tossed it through the air, across the living room, and it landed perfectly on the back of the sofa. He did that every night, much to Presley's amusement. Her man was really loosening up and having some fun.

"You scared me." Presley put her hands on her hips. "Sneaking up on a poor, defenseless woman like that."

Seth's eyebrows shot up. "Defenseless? Baby, you are about as far from defenseless as you can be. The mightiest of men shake in their boots at the mere mention of your name."

Katie Johnson had been declared dead after the car bombing and Presley didn't want the name back anyway. She was more Presley than Katie. She probably always had been.

"Does that include you, Sheriff?" Presley teased. She draped the strands of lights behind her neck like a feather boa. "Do you shake in your boots?"

Seth glanced down at his black cowboy boots with a mock scowl. "Maybe, if I did something really scary."

"Running from hit men wasn't scary enough for you?"

Seth walked toward her and she felt the rush of love and passion she always did when he was close. He smelled delicious and his clean, masculine scent wrapped around her. It never ceased to make her feel calm and centered. He was her rock and she was his roll, as she liked to tease him.

"I was thinking about doing something far scarier than that, honey." He stopped right in front of her and captured her chin in his fingers, tilting her head so she was looking up into his beautiful blue eyes. They were soft and loving and she felt her entire body fill with warmth at what she saw there.

It was true love.

She placed her hands on his chest and his heart was beating faster than normal. "You seem excited, Sheriff. Are you in the mood for something in particular? Shall we head in to the bedroom?"

He didn't answer. Instead he fell onto one knee, holding her hands in his large ones. She sucked in a breath as she realized what was about to happen. He was either planning to beg for her to fix dinner or propose. Her heart beat wildly at the thought of the latter.

"Seth, what are you doing?" she asked slowly. If he didn't propose now after this big show she was going to be really disappointed.

Seth looked up at her. "Presley Lawson, I know we haven't known each other long, but I think you would agree, the time we have been together has been intense." She couldn't argue there. She nodded in agreement. "I love you and you love me. I figure if I don't get a ring on your finger quick, well, there's no telling what else might happen. You're walking trouble, honey, and I'm just the man to enjoy it."

Presley's eyebrow lifted but joy started to build in her stomach making it flutter and dance. "Enjoy it or tolerate it? You don't like chaos, remember?"

Seth stood up but didn't let go of her hands. "I've been thinking about that. Maybe being in control all the damn time isn't as great as I thought it was. I love you." Seth dug into his pocket with one hand

and pulled out a small velvet box. "Will you marry me? Love me and have a family with me?"

The world tilted and the room spun. Presley threw herself into Seth's arms, laughing and kissing him everywhere she could reach.

"Yes! Yes! I love you so much! Yes!" His arms wrapped around her and she felt safe, warm, and loved. His lips found hers and she was lost to the passion between them, her body responding as it always did to his patient loving. When he lifted his head, she was breathless and he was grinning ear to ear.

"I thought it might take the ring to seal the deal." He pulled away just enough to flip open the top of the box with his thumb. "Let's get this on your finger, honey, so I know it's official." The beauty of the princess-cut solitaire brought tears to her eyes. Seth certainly made her feel like a princess so it was very appropriate. He slid it on her finger, and her hand shook with excitement. He bent to kiss the knuckle. "No changing your mind. This is forever."

She nodded, hardly able to make out his face through the tears. "Forever, Seth. I promise. Not one day less."

"I'll hold you to that." He lifted her up and carried her over by the tree, placing her on her feet. He grabbed some pillows and a blanket from the couch and tossed them on the floor before hitting the power switch on the wall. The room was now bathed in the most romantic glow from the fireplace and the tiny multi-colored bulbs of the Christmas tree. He lifted the light strand from her neck and found the end with the plug. He held it up and she frowned, not sure what he was going to do with it. He knelt under the tree and found the power strip, plugging the strand in so it lit up in his hands. "Lie down, honey. We're going to make love next to this Christmas tree."

She couldn't think of anything she wanted to do more. She settled on the cushions and reached up for him but he laughed and shook his head.

"You touch me and this is going to be all over with too quickly. I want to take my time." He lifted her arms over her head and wrapped the strand of lights around her wrists and then around the leg of a chair, effectively restraining her. If she pulled hard enough, she knew the strand would give way but instead she relaxed, tugging at the bonds slightly. It was secure enough to give her a reminder if she tried to bring her hands down.

His rough hands glided over her flesh, bringing goose bumps to the surface and making her shiver in response. He flicked open the butterfly clip between her breasts and pushed the lace cups away so she was exposed to his gaze. "Beautiful. Just beautiful." His hands slid to her hips and he tugged her panties down her legs, tossing the scrap of lace and silk over his shoulder.

He reached into the box of decorations forgotten at the foot of the tree and pulled out a handful of silver tinsel, dangling it above her breasts. Her teeth sunk into her bottom lip as he swirled the strands around and around the nipples, back and forth between them, until they were hard and tight.

Presley's cunt clenched in anticipation and honey dripped down her thigh as he moved the strands up and down her stomach, then up to her shoulders and neck, and back down to her hips. He leaned forward and pressed a kiss to her quivering abdomen, her breathing shallow as the blood began to burn in her veins.

He dragged the strands down her thighs and then up along the sensitive skin near her pussy. He did it over and over, every time coming closer to her slit but not quite. She was about to scream when he brushed the tinsel over her clit, sending pleasure to every receptor in her shaking body.

Her eyes drifted closed as he tortured the nub, bringing her close to orgasm but never letting her go over. Every muscle was tense and poised for release when instead of the tinsel she felt his mouth close over the swollen button. She arched her back, frozen for a moment. When her climax hit her, she screamed Seth's name, the waves radiating from her center relentlessly until she was limp and drained.

Her eyelids fluttered open and Seth had divested himself of his clothing and was kneeling between her thighs with nothing on but a smile. A condom package dangled from his fingers.

"Is my future wife ready for me? What does she want?"

His voice was deep and it sent tingles up her spine. She couldn't believe she was going to get a lifetime with Seth.

"Fuck me," she hissed. "I need you. Fuck me." Her voice wasn't as smooth as his, but he didn't seem to mind. He tore open the condom with his teeth and rolled it on his cock. She slid her thighs further apart in entreaty. Presley wanted, no, needed, his big cock pounding them both to heaven and beyond. He positioned himself on his elbows, the head of his cock nudging her cunt.

Just as he leaned down to kiss her, he surged forward, thrusting into her waiting and welcoming pussy.

"Yes!" She cried out against his mouth. His tongue traced her lips as his cock pistoned inside of her, each stroke sending her higher and higher until they were floating above the living room and tumbling in the clouds. She wrapped her legs around his waist, pulling him closer and tighter so each time he thrust in, his groin rubbed her already sensitive clit. She was ready to go off like a firecracker again.

Seth's head was thrown back and his jaw was tight as he pumped in and out of her, the pressure growing in her lower abdomen. His mouth dipped down and suckled at a nipple. It sent ripples straight to her cunt and she tightened around him, silently urging him on to completion.

His strokes sped up and the coil wound tightly inside her finally sprung free. Lights danced in front of her eyes and waves of pleasure roared through her from head to toe. Her pussy clamped down on his cock and he groaned as he too fell over the edge. His forehead was covered with beads of sweat as he thrust into her one last time, his face contorted with ecstasy. She loved watching him as he fucked her, the emotions flitting across his handsome features fascinating her. Each time they made love, she fell more deeply under his spell.

As they came slowly down to earth, Presley realized she'd pulled her hands free. She wrapped them around his shoulders when he would have moved away.

"Not yet. One minute more."

He dropped a kiss on her nose. "One minute, then I need to take care of the condom."

"I can't wait to spend my life with you. Thanks for keeping me alive long enough to do it."

His laughter rumbled in his chest. "Thanks for saying yes. Were you surprised or did you know it was coming?"

She giggled and wrapped a leg around one of his, the rough hair scratching against her skin. "Couldn't you tell? I was shocked."

This time he did move away with a sigh. "I'll be right back." He padded into the bathroom and was back in a few moments, cuddling under the blanket with her. "I'd planned to ask you on Christmas actually, but I couldn't wait."

She idly stroked his chest. "I'm glad you didn't. Seth?" Presley levered up on her elbow so she could look into his eyes. "Everything has been pretty exciting up to now. What if you get bored?"

"I doubt that will happen, honey." Seth smiled and shook his head.

"How do you know? It could happen." He thought he knew everything, for heaven's sake. He was smiling like a Cheshire cat.

"I don't think it will. You know when I went into the bathroom to dispose of the condom?" He cupped her jaw in his warm hands. "It was broken, honey. We might be parents in nine months."

She shook her head. "What? Broken? Huh?" She couldn't even string a sentence together. Her brain was buzzing with his words.

Seth laughed. "You wanted a family. Looks like we might get one. I knew you were trouble. Mom and Dad are going to be thrilled."

Presley dug her fingers into his shoulders, her heart starting to swell with love. "Will you be thrilled?"

He got nose to nose with her. "Honey, I can't think of anything that would make me happier. We better get married quick. Lord knows what might happen next. I need to be prepared for anything with you."

Presley grinned. "We can name him Elvis."

"We're not naming him Elvis." Seth shook his head.

"Elvis Aaron Reilly." Presley sighed in contentment. "It has a ring to it."

"We're not naming him Elvis," Seth repeated. He was frowning now.

"If it's a girl we can name her Priscilla." Presley was really starting to enjoy herself. Seth pulled her into his arms.

"Let's keep our options open. I love you but I'm not a pushover."

She giggled and let herself melt in his arms. "No, you're not. I love you, Seth Reilly. I'll name our baby anything you want."

Seth rolled his eyes. "I know you won't stay this cooperative so I'll enjoy it while I can." She snuggled closer to him, the lights of the tree casting multi-colored shadows over the room and Harry Connick, Jr. singing on the iPod about snow.

Life was a funny thing. She'd had to die to be born. She'd lived more in the last few months than all the years before combined. She'd found the love of her life while trying to stay alive. She had everything she'd ever dreamed of, all in a little town in Montana.

EPILOGUE

The next day, Seth strode into the roadhouse. It was Sunday morning and he hadn't wanted to leave the warm bed and Presley's soft body pressed up against his. It was only with supreme will he'd managed to wrench himself from her arms and make the drive to the meeting with his friends.

He sat down at the table, the stench of beer and cigarettes even stronger today than last time. With the falling temperatures, the doors stayed closed more and the smokers stayed inside. Tanner grinned and tossed him a can of soda, the only thing allowed to be served on a Sunday morning when the bar was closed.

"Well, you look in one piece. I've heard the story but most of the other guys haven't. Why don't you fill them in?"

Between sips of Pepsi, Seth reviewed everything that had happened. Reed was laughing when Seth came to the part about Nora and Presley in the pool. "Shit, was it cold?"

Seth shook his head. "Actually, no. Presley said the pool was heated but it was about seventy-five degrees outside to begin with."

Griffin grinned. "Seventy-five in December. I could get used to that."

"Anything new with the drug traffic in the area?" Seth asked. He was ready to change the subject. It felt like all he and Presley did was tell the story over and over to friends and family. The entire town probably knew the tale by now and had changed and embellished on it as well.

"I've had a particular issue in my area," Tanner answered. "Drug-related crime is way up. It used to be my worst problem was with teenagers drinking and driving. Now I have to worry about them getting high on crystal meth."

"I busted a meth lab just last week," Logan declared. "A fucking meth lab in my little town. I never thought I'd see the day."

Jared's expression was dark. "This whole area is getting overrun. I don't like it. I think we may need to call in some federal help."

"At least the vigilante has been quiet in the last month," Griffin offered. "That's something to be grateful for."

Tanner nodded. "Maybe he or she has moved on or worked whatever demons he had out of his system? I'd like to think that, but I doubt it. It's rarely that easy."

The rest of the meeting passed uneventfully and they all stood up to leave. Seth glanced at his watch, happy to see he had plenty of time to get home to watch football with Presley.

"Hot date?" Tanner laughed as they walked out into the cold. Five inches of snow was expected, with more later in the week.

"Presley and football." Seth grinned. He was smiling like a fool all the damn time now but he couldn't seem to help it.

"Sounds good. Hope you both have a good Christmas."

"Thanks. You too, Tanner." Seth gave his best friend a closer look. "You were quieter than usual today. Is everything okay?"

Tanner sighed and stared out at the road and the bleak landscape. "My ex-wife told me yesterday she's getting remarried."

Tanner had been divorced for almost eight years. Seth hadn't realized his friend was still hung up on his ex. He slapped Tanner on the back.

"I'm sorry. That sucks, man."

Tanner frowned and then grinned. "No, it's not like you're thinking. I'm not still in love with Abby. I have love for her. She's the mother of my two children and she's a good person, but I'm not in love with her anymore. She's not breaking my heart or anything. Shit, Seth." Tanner was openly laughing now.

"Then what's the problem?" Seth groused. "You don't know what to get her as a wedding gift? Go with the silver candlesticks."

Tanner sobered. "The guy she's marrying. I don't know. There's something about him that bugs me."

"Did you say anything to her?" Seth shoved his cold hands in his pockets. Fuck, it was freezing out here.

"No. What could I say? My cop radar lights up whenever I'm around this guy? She hated everything to do with my being a cop. She's not going to be welcoming my opinion."

Tanner never spoke of the issues that broke up his marriage. Logan knew what they were but he wasn't talking, and Seth wasn't the nosy type who would keep asking.

"Maybe you'll get lucky and they won't go through with it."

"Maybe. They haven't been dating long. Hopefully, they'll have a long engagement." Tanner looked up at the sky. "We better get going. Snow's on the way. I'll see you next year, buddy."

Seth laughed at their usual December joke. "See you next year, Tan. Have a good Christmas."

Seth hopped into his truck and started the engine, letting the cab warm up. He watched as Tanner backed out and headed down the road to his own town. His friend was rarely wrong about people. If Tanner didn't like the guy his ex was marrying, there was a damn good reason.

Seth gunned the engine and headed down the road in the opposite direction. He had hot wings and an even hotter woman waiting for him. They would do something normal today, maybe watch football, and hang out with friends. But with Presley, it might be normal, but it would never be boring.

THE END

ABOUT THE AUTHOR

Olivia Jaymes is a wife, mother, lover of sexy romance, and caffeine addict. She lives with her husband and son in central Florida and spends her days with handsome alpha males and spunky heroines.

She is currently working on a series of full length novels called The Cowboy Justice Association. It's a contemporary erotic romance series about six lawmen in southern Montana who work to keep the peace but can't seem to find it in their own lives.

Visit Olivia Jaymes at

www.OliviaJaymes.com

6480183R00167

Printed in Great Britain
by Amazon.co.uk, Ltd.,
Marston Gate.